The Fall of '79

a novel

Lee Lewis

The Fall of '79 by Lee Lewis

Published by Livingston Road Press
Casselberry, Florida
http://www.livingstonroadpress.com

http://www.lee-lewis.com

Cover design by Kristen Celey

ISBN-13: 978-1-957871-00-4

For you.

Let your light shine.

1

The Arlington, 1994

Too many of us take for granted a warm bed and a hot shower. I never would again. It was downright luxurious to wake up in my own bed. It was a damn sight better than waking up on a Skee-ball machine. I must admit, though, that they had been surprisingly comfortable. Maybe it was the raised angle of the playing field. I just know that with the sleeping bag laid out on it, it wasn't too bad. But after five months of that, my tiny one-room studio felt like a fucking palace. You couldn't beat a mattress and sheets no matter how thin the mattress might be or how worn the sheets were. And waking up knowing that a hot shower awaited me? Absolute luxury! When I first moved in, I sometimes took three showers a day. You don't realize how important a shower is unless you've actually been homeless and gone without. Oh, sure, I had a friend or two who would let me use their showers, but it's not the same as having your own. The best thing about Phil going to rehab was that I was able to take over this luxury box in the sky. We didn't even discuss it with the building manager. Phil just took his stuff out, gave me the key, and I waltzed in. Nobody seemed to care as long as the rent got paid.

I threw off the blanket, crawled to the end of the loft bed, and grabbed the top of the ladder. My head swam with the remnants of last night's beer, so I slowly turned myself around and put a foot on the top rung. As soon as I felt steady, I swung my other leg out and set my foot on the next rung down. Then I lowered myself the six remaining feet to the floor. I tried to remember how I got home. I remembered being in the bar, then I remembered having last call and talking with Brian. He said he had some weed but needed something to smoke it. So, when the bar closed, we stopped by my place to get my pipe — that same damn pipe I've said I was throwing out so many times — and then we went back to his room. And then....

Here I was. At least I made it to the bed this time. More than one morning I woke up to find myself on the floor. Sometimes the ladder was just too much to deal with.

The whole place was maybe twice the size of a prison cell with a separate bathroom. I had turned the space under the loft into a makeshift kitchen. It wasn't much. A small refrigerator, an old wooden table with a hot plate, some mismatched silverware that Phil had left behind. Probably not the safest idea, a hot plate beneath a wood loft, but I never cooked much more than Ramen on it. I had hung up a tapestry of sorts — a repurposed bedspread of psychedelic purples and paisleys — to create the walls and left an opening near the bathroom door. A couple of pinup lights hanging from the loft gave off just enough light to see the mold starting to grow on the few slices of bread I had left. I knew there was nothing in the fridge but a bottle of mustard, a jar of dill pickles, a few other odds and ends. Nothing that would constitute a healthy breakfast.

The cupboards are bare. Like Old Mother Hubbard. I quickly banished that thought, that *memory*. Didn't need that kind of anger. No Moe of that, I thought with an angry chuckle. Plenty to eat once I headed downstairs. But I wouldn't venture forth without a shower. Yes, a luxurious and long hot shower. I might even decide to jack off. I did that a lot, too, when I first got into the place. Two things you can't do when you're homeless: take showers and jack off. Oh, I may have indulged myself in a public restroom once or twice, but it wasn't something I did in a friend's shower. So, when given the option to shower whenever I wanted, the other just naturally followed.

The hot water flowing over my head and shoulders felt nice, but my hangover precluded me from doing anything but try to get clean. Maybe later, after my shift at the pool hall. That didn't start till three, so I had time. Or did I? I hadn't checked the time yet. I stepped naked into the main room of the apartment, leaving my towel hanging to dry. Who was going to see me? Sure, the window was big, but no one was going to be looking in my third-floor window. Not easy to peep on me. And if they were going to go to that much trouble, then let them have a look. They wouldn't be the first. I don't think I had anything to be ashamed of. Even with all the drinking, I was a pretty svelte twenty-seven-year-old. Maybe not the best-looking guy in the world, and I could probably use a little toning, but who did I have to look good for?

I sat down in the closest of the two chairs in the room. Like everything in the place, they were worn, mismatched, and nothing fancy. But they were functional and didn't break when you sat in them. A coffee table jutted out between them and had my alarm clock on it, crammed in amongst several books, pens and paper, the phone and answering machine. The clock told me I had a couple of hours before my shift. The blinking light on the answering machine told me someone had called and left a message. Must have been after I had left for work and before I got home at whatever time I had gotten back.

I sighed. No doubt the bill collector calling about my student loans. Funny thing about that phone. Even though it was still in Phil's name, the bill collectors had somehow managed to figure out it was my number now.

Fucking loans. College had been my one hope for getting out of this damn town, but even maxing out my borrowing, I couldn't afford both the state college tuition and the rent. Getting a job seemed the answer but working full time didn't leave much time for studying. Then, just as I was pondering quitting, my landlord at the time sold the place where I was living, and I was out on the street. Made going to classes just a bit difficult, so I ended up having to drop out anyway. And those student loan people? They almost immediately put me in default on my loans. Like I had money for them when I couldn't even keep a roof over my head. No money, no home, no shit. Well, fuck 'em. Then almost as soon as I was in the apartment, the phone calls started coming in at the Arlington. No idea how they got that number. So, I just gave up answering the phone. Gary, my boss, gave me the answering machine because he wanted to be able to call me if he needed me. The machine allowed me to screen my calls when I was home.

Not that anyone else ever called. Just Gary and the bill collectors. I'd given everyone my number, but no one in my family had even bothered to see if the number worked. Screw them, too. They hadn't cared enough to help me out when I was homeless, so why would I think anything would change now? Most of the relatives on both sides of my family — grandparents, parents, siblings, aunts, uncles, cousins, you name it — almost all of them lived within a thirty-mile radius of this fucking town, and not one lifted a finger to help when I ended up sleeping on those Skee-ball machines. If I hadn't had my job, I'm not sure what I would have done or where I would have ended up. Gary knew I was sleeping there. And maybe a few of the patrons knew; the rumors buzzed around that place like flies on shit. And I had told a couple of friends. Friends....

You know when you find out who your friends are? Who you can count on? You find out when you're homeless. Gary let me crash on his floor a few times and so did Phil. I had to beg others to let me use their showers once in a while. Yeah, the whole shower thing sticks with me pretty strongly. Like I said, unless you've been there, you can't understand. It's a good thing I'm poor or I might have bought myself a gun and been done with it all. Maybe even taken a few people with me. Not the first time I've had that thought, especially as it concerns family.

Ah, fuck! I needed to get out of my head before the anger took over again. Time to get some breakfast and get on with my day. Another phone message about all the money I owed to some faceless bank could wait till later. I found some clean underwear in the small dresser against the other wall, then picked up my jeans from the floor. It still amazes me some mornings how I manage to put myself to bed in such a drunken stupor. But the jeans looked a little dirty. Had I spilled something on them? Maybe. I grabbed a clean pair. Another bonus of the apartment: the laundry room was literally the next door down the hall. One more convenience you miss when you're homeless. I pulled on some socks, my sneakers, and a t-shirt before I headed out the door and down the three flights of stairs I had somehow managed to navigate the night before.

The sun was warm, and I turned my face up to it as I stepped out of what had once been the lobby of the Arlington Inn. The village of Potsdam had been around since the early 1800s and had at one time been a thriving industrial town known for its sandstone. Stone from the local quarries was in the Parliament buildings in Ottawa. So, when business was booming back in the day, the Arlington Inn had been a first-class hotel. Now, like the village, it was a worn-out relic of its former self, sometimes referred to as Welfare Hotel because so many of the tenants were on the system. At least I had that going for me: I had a job. Not much of one, making little more than minimum wage, but it was enough to keep me in my little room. At least for now.

As much as I despised it, I had to admit that, for the most part, Potsdam was a pretty little village. Most of downtown consisted of the old architecture — built from that same Potsdam sandstone — from the turn of the century or before; the building directly across from the Arlington even had the year it was built carved into the stone: 1888. Market Street was lined with trees, but not big old ones like you might expect in an old town. A beautification project about ten years ago had removed most of the old and dying trees and replaced them with something that was supposed to be hardier to stand up to the harsh, northern New York winters. I don't know if that was true, but I knew I was sweeping up the tiny fruits they dropped on the sidewalk in front of the pool hall all summer long. It was only two doors down from the Arlington, so getting to work required no real effort. Nor did the job itself. Hand out the pool balls, make change for the kids in the arcade, clean the place after closing. An easy enough job so I didn't expect to make six figures, but even in an impoverished town like Potsdam, minimum was not a living wage. Not when the rents were so high. The only thing keeping the town alive were the two colleges, the state college and the private tech school. The landlords all knew they could charge whatever they wanted for rent and the students would pay it. Worked well for the landlords, but it left poor bastards like me sleeping on Skee-ball machines. Christ, I obsess over those Skee-ball machines as much as I do my showers.

The facade of the pool hall was tastefully decorated with wood and stone, keeping with the overall look of the building. The paned glass was clean; I made sure of that as I had made it my task on Sunday mornings to clean the front of both the pool hall and the video arcade. I took a glance through the windows before I went inside. I knew Gary would be there, but I didn't know if he would be alone. Days were usually pretty quiet. I could see him at the table by the counter. He made a shot and as he walked around the pool table, his opponent walked into view.

"Shit," I said, not even realizing I had spoken aloud. Thankfully, the sidewalk was clear and no one heard me.

Leon Booker, or Leon the Fish as he was referred to by most of us, was a tall, lanky, middle-aged asshole. He sold insurance and had a reputation of being more like a used car salesman when it came to the policies he sold. He fancied himself quite a pool player when, really, he was exactly what his nickname implied. He was a fish. Easily hooked, easily landed, easily gutted. He dressed the part of a successful businessman and drove a Lincoln that he replaced every three years like clockwork, but beneath the blood red tie, the crisp white shirt, and the pressed and dry-cleaned slacks, he was white trash through and through. I suppose he'd gotten into the right racket. Everybody needs insurance, whether it's car, life, home, or whatever, so he just sat back and let the cash roll in. He reminded me a lot of Joe, the guy who owned the pool hall. Back in the 80s, Joe had put in the arcade, right at the start of the video arcade craze, and the quarters flowed like water. They still did with all the new tech and game graphics. So, there was no business sense required. But, when he opened the pool hall two years ago, I don't think he gave it much thought. The movie, *The Color of Money*, had started a new craze and Joe thought he would cash in on it. But a pool hall needed more than a soft opening and word-of-mouth. It needed active participation from the owner and some marketing. But Joe figured he'd run it just like his arcade, and that's why the place was losing money. I never saw the books, but in the year or so I'd been working there, I'd only seen it get worse. The billiards fad was fading fast, and Joe didn't seem to have any idea what to do. Sure, the weekends were always busy, but the rest of the week — and especially the days — could see no business at all. And never mind the summers when the students went home. Then the place was nearly dead. At least now that the students were back, things would pick up again. Now that we were into September, the town was starting to show signs of life once more.

I gave the front door a yank and stepped into the small vestibule. I pulled the inner door open and entered the front room. The place was not the stereotypical pool hall with dirty floors and smoky atmosphere. Joe had put some serious money into making it a very classy place. The burgundy carpet matched the walls that were lined with light oak wainscoting. Rather than a dark, seedy look, the large front windows let in plenty of light, and it brightened up the front room. This is where the A. E. Schmidt table was. Joe had put it right up front by the windows so it would be what people saw when they walked by. It was a beautiful table with light oak that matched the wainscoting, leather pockets, and a crisp, like-new felt on the playing surface. Even after a couple of years, the felt looked new. This was because Joe forced us to charge more for people to play on that table. Now, I ask you, where's the sense in that? If you put that table in the front window for people to see, wouldn't it make more sense to charge *less* so that there would always be someone playing there? No, Joe figured that because it was such a nice table, people should have to pay more to play on it. Well, since there was almost always a free table elsewhere in the pool hall, very few were willing to pay the premium for the privilege of advertising for Joe. Besides, the other tables played just as well. We also had very few patrons who could really appreciate a table like the Schmidt. The Brunswicks worked just fine for the average — or in the case of Leon the Fish, below-average — player.

"Indy!" Gary exclaimed. It was a nickname I had gotten because of a leather Fedora I wore in the winter. He said it made me look like Indiana Jones.

"Gary Indiana!" I sang as I stepped up to the counter that separated the front room from the back room. Actually, his full name was Gary Stillwell, but the nicknames were our little inside joke with each other. "What's going on?"

I didn't really have to ask. I could tell who was winning based on the huge disparity in the score recorded on the rack above the table. One side, and I assumed it was Gary's, had significantly more points than the other.

"Kicking ass and taking names," he said. He popped the cue ball and sank the five ball into a corner with a well-executed bank shot.

Gary was an interesting character. He was as different from Leon as you could get. Where Leon was tall and lanky with slicked-back black hair, Gary was short and stout with cropped red hair. Not really fat, but powerful. I'd seen him lift one end of a pool table all by himself to move it back into place after it had been pushed out of place by a couple of brawling students. He had also had no trouble dealing with those brawling students first. And where Leon was dressed like some parody of a businessman, Gary dressed comfortably in his Levi's and t-shirt. Where Leon was a crass blowhard, Gary was easy-going, a guy you felt you could trust when you were talking to him. Did I mention he was one of the few people who let me sleep at his place more than once? Leon never would have offered something like that.

Gary wound up in Potsdam through a strange series of circumstances that ended with him marrying the daughter of a local business owner. She had been going to school in Philadelphia, Pennsylvania, where he lived. I think he had been looking for a way out of that city. And, although he never said it, I got the impression that he *had* to leave, like maybe his life depended on it. From some of the stories he would tell, it seemed like a reasonable possibility. And as far as I knew, he had never gone back. He had followed Melissa back to Potsdam when she finished school and they were married soon after. Their son was born just a few months later. But that was long before I had met him; their son was around eight years old now. He had worked for Melissa's father in his liquor store for a number of years, and in a small town like Potsdam, that makes you well-known in no time. Even my father knew of Gary when I mentioned that I worked with him at the pool hall. Besides, he was a personable guy who made friends easily.

I'll give you an example. Potsdam being a two-college town, there are always plenty of students as clientele for a liquor store. No, I'm not saying Gary sold to minors. What he *would* do was this: Guys would come in on the weekend looking to buy vodka or gin or something and would, of course, want to go for the Stoli or the Absolute or the Beefeater, the expensive stuff. Besides the fact that few of them had a palette to appreciate the good stuff, Gary would convince them to rethink their purchase for other reasons. He related it to me this way.

"Look," he would say, "the good stuff is good, I agree. But what you want to do is buy a small bottle of the good stuff and then buy a big bottle of the cheap stuff. Then, you start with the good stuff. Once it's gone, you aren't going to care what you're drinking after that, right?"

They would, of course, nod in agreement as if to say, "Go on, oh, Enlightened One."

"So, once the good stuff is gone, you break out the cheaper stuff. You won't be able to tell the difference by then, and you get more booze for your money. Stay drunk all night! Am I right?"

He was quite the salesman. It endeared him to the students anyway. He sold a lot of cheap liquor. And as most of the drunks of the town, respectable or otherwise, eventually passed through the doors of Larry's Liquors, Gary ended up being a well-known character and had earned the title of unofficial Mayor. I'd lived in town for twenty-seven years and wasn't nearly as well-known. His reputation might have been the only thing bringing people into the pool hall during the day. Unfortunately, that included people like Leon the Fish.

Gary ran the table for a few more balls before missing a tough bank shot and giving the table over to Leon.

"Your shift doesn't start for a while," Gary said, leaning against the counter. There were no other customers in the place for him to worry about.

"Looking for some breakfast," I replied.

"Breakfast?" Leon interjected. "It's two in the afternoon."

"I work nights," I said, trying to restrain the contempt in my voice. I didn't like Leon Booker, never had. But that's probably pretty obvious.

"Till four in the morning? Damn!" He missed a simple straight shot into a side pocket. He'd only gained two balls to Gary's twelve.

"Melissa made some of her oatmeal cookies," Gary said. "The tin's behind the counter."

"That'll work." Gary's wife made the best cookies.

"If you don't eat them, I will, and God knows I don't need them."

"You didn't offer them to me," Leon said with a sneer.

"That's because I like Indy more than you." He laughed to show Leon he was kidding. But honestly, I don't think he was. I think he tolerated Leon. Everyone did, but Gary *had* to on a different level. Leon was a friend of Joe's. He was also a paying customer and we needed as many of them as we could get to keep coming back.

But, when the back door opened and Jay Stone walked in with a couple of his friends, I reconsidered that idea. There were definitely some customers I'd rather not see coming back. Gary made a move to join me behind the counter where I stood with his wife's cookie tin.

"I got this," I said.

He went back to his game with Leon, and I took a tray of balls from the rack and set it on the counter. Jay and his two friends stepped up to me. Jay was a little taller, the same age as me, and I hated to admit it, but he was a good-looking guy. What was it with God, if he did exist, giving the assholes all the money and the good looks? And then he left nice guys like me broke with a face for radio? Well, maybe not that bad, but still. God was the biggest asshole of all.

"Hey, King," Jay said. "How's it going?"

He always insisted on calling me by my last name, even though he knew I hated it. And he always said it with a little sneer in his voice.

"I'm good," I replied.

"My usual table," he said as he indicated the Brunswick at the back of the room.

Usual table. What an asshole.

"And can I get some new chalk?" he asked. "These are pretty worn."

The chalks in the tray were fine. He just enjoyed being as aggravating as he could. I reached down to the shelf under the counter and took two fresh cubes of chalk and dropped them in the tray, not bothering to remove the old ones that were already there.

"Thanks, pal."

I glared at the back of his head as he and his friends walked to the back table. I flipped the switch for the lights, which also started the timer. Gary stepped over to the counter.

"You okay, Kelly?" He was serious; he called me by my actual name. Gary was a very perceptive guy. Scary sometimes how well he saw through me.

"Yeah," I replied. "He and I just have a history."

And it was history. Fifteen years of it since we first met. It had been Labor Day, right before school started. So, while it wasn't official, I always considered it the Fall of 1979.

2

Labor Day, 1979

Every school year was a new beginning. At least that's how I saw it. Some people saw the fall as the end of summer, but I really wanted it to be a new beginning. This was the year I was going to get everything right. This was the year I would be the popular kid. I would get picked first for the teams in gym class. I'd catch the football and hit the baseball and win the race. This would be the year I would get up the courage to ask Charlotte to go out with me. This year things were going to be different.

But they never were. And I knew that from the first day of the Fall of '79. Okay, technically, it wasn't fall yet. It was still summer till the end of September. But Labor Day always felt like the end of summer. It was the day we moved back from camp, the day before we had to go back to school. My mother's grandfather had bought the cabin on Lake Ozonia, like, a hundred years ago, and we spent every summer up there. From the weekend after school let out in June to Labor Day, we were there. We came back once a week to do laundry and mow the lawn, but other than that, we were at the lake. I didn't mind; the lake was my favorite place in the world to be. It did mean having to spend time with my brother and sister, but when the Brooks girls arrived, I got a break from them. The girls mostly helped to distract my sister and they let her lord over them, which kept her from making my life hell. At least that was something. My brother, Kevin, would usually tag along with whatever they were doing, so I got left alone. Maybe that's why I liked it so much up there: I got to spend a lot of time by myself.

The Brooks' always left a couple weeks before we did. They came up from Rochester. I think maybe school started earlier for them. They went to private school, all four of the girls. Yeah, I figured they must have been loaded. I think their dad was a lawyer or something. So, my last week or two at the lake would become a living hell again once Karen had no other distraction. I still remember before the Brooks' arrived this year how Karen had said she wasn't going to hang out with the girls this summer because she was now fifteen and the girls, who were between eight and twelve, were just too young for someone of her maturity to be hanging around. Well, once the girls arrived, that went right out the window. Karen was the first one over to their cabin to greet them when they showed up. And it was like she made it her mission to turn them against me. She would tell them any mean or hurtful thing she could think of to make them hate me or not want to be around me. Like this year, she told them that I had started to wet my bed over the winter. It wasn't really true. Sure, it happened once when I was really sick, but she didn't tell them that part. She made it sound like I did it all the time, and they bought it. That's her maturity for you. I really hated her. For that and for everything she would do at home. She and her best friend, Mary Chase (yeah, that was really her name) they would whisper and laugh at me whenever they were together. Like this one time when they caught me peeing down by the river and they told everyone that I was playing with myself in the bushes. How do you stand up to something like that when it's her and Mary's word against mine? And it's not like Kevin would stand up for me. He just laughed along with the rest of them. He made comments about it a week later asking me if it had felt good. Bunch of jerks.

I couldn't remember a time when my sister didn't hate me. Did I do something to her once? If I did, I didn't know what it was. Maybe it was because Kevin and I used to get along and hang out and we left her out. But all of that changed a couple of years ago. He and I used to ride the late bus when we were both in elementary school. We used to do stuff together and even talk about Karen. Then he moved on to sixth grade and started riding the early bus with Karen and it was like he turned completely against me. Instead of it being him and me against Karen, it was Karen and him against me. That's when it all really started, and it just got worse ever since.

At least Danny never went along with anything they did. He was about the only friend I had in town. He'd been my best friend since third grade when we first moved to West Stockholm. He and I did just about everything together and that was the one thing that bummed me out when we went to camp. But he and his family usually went to his grandmother's place in Maine, so it's not like I would get to see him over the summer anyway. His dad was a teacher at the tech college in Potsdam, so his dad got the whole summer off to spend with his family. Unlike my father, who worked all summer and only came up to camp on the weekends. So, as soon as we got home, I quickly took my stuff up to the bedroom I shared with Kevin and got ready to go down to Danny's place. Karen had already left for Mary's and Kevin was gone somewhere.

"We're going to be barbecuing soon. Where are you off to?" my mother asked as I headed out the kitchen door. She was turned away, putting groceries in the pantry.

"I'm going down to Danny's."

"He's not there. Your father said he and his family moved over the summer. Back in July, I think he said."

I stopped in my tracks, my hand on the doorknob. "What?"

"His father took a position at another college." She never stopped putting away the groceries as she spoke.

"And Daddy didn't say anything?"

Like I said, my father didn't spend the summer at the lake. So, he had come to camp every weekend for half the summer and had never said a word.

"Well, it's too late to complain about it now," she said as she put a box of cereal into the cupboard.

No, it couldn't be true. I headed out the door, slamming it hard behind me. My bike leaned against the door of the red barn behind our house. I'd left it there after unloading it from the van. I walked it down to the end of the driveway. Our house was on the main drag through town and traffic could sometimes be dangerous. It also didn't help that the driveway sloped down to the road with trees on both sides. It was a family rule that we walked our bikes to the road before we got on them. Of course, I was the only one who followed that rule, but whatever. I didn't really want to get squashed by a car.

West Stockholm is a small town. And when I say small, I mean tiny. Maybe two hundred people in the entire town, spread out over a lot of square miles. The main drag was a county road that cut through the middle of it. The only traffic light was the flasher at the other end where the main drag intersected with a main highway. I think route 11 was a U.S. highway. Anyway, once I was on the main drag, it was easy to fly the half mile or so down to the bridge. The only part of the ride that I didn't like was having to pass by the cemetery. It didn't creep me out so much in the daylight, but it was really creepy at night. The streetlights made weird shadows in the dark. It wasn't that I was scared, really. I knew there were no such things as ghosts. Still, it freaked me out if I had to go by it in the dark.

I came to a stop at the intersection right before the bridge. I could hear the sound of the water over the falls. To the left was Water Street and to the right was the Hatch Road. Danny's house was right on the corner of the main drag and the Hatch Road. It was set back from the road maybe fifty feet or so. It looked the same as it ever did, the gray-blue paint faded just a bit. A small hill rose behind it, which made it look like it sat low to the ground. The yard was freshly mowed. The smell of the fresh cut grass filled my nose. Was that a good sign? I could already see that their Volvo wasn't in the driveway. There was no For Sale sign in the yard and there were no other cars in the driveway. So, maybe Mom was wrong. Maybe they were just out shopping. Yeah, they were just getting school supplies for tomorrow. I walked my bike up the driveway and dropped it in the spot where I always dropped it, right before the cement of the front porch. I walked up to the front door.

I knocked.

No one came to the door.

I knocked again, lightly.

I wanted Danny's mom to open it and have the smell of dinner or cookies or something come drifting as she welcomed me into their home like she always did. I needed it to happen. I was desperate to hear the familiar creak of the hinges, see the clean entry, smell the smells of their home.

I knocked again, harder this time.

Nothing.

No.

I stepped across the porch to a window that looked in on the living room. The light tan curtains weren't hanging inside. The couch wasn't there, and neither was Danny's father's La-Z-Boy, the chair Danny and I had squeezed into to watch *Planet of the Apes* that time it was on TV. The coffee table where I'd spilled my hot chocolate last winter was also gone. I had been so embarrassed when I'd done that and so upset with myself. But Danny's mom had been so forgiving. She told me over and over not to worry about it. She cleaned it up with a dish towel and poured me another cup, all the time smiling down at me. She had such pretty eyes. My mother would have yelled at me for being careless and clumsy, would have fumed about it for days, and I would have been banned from having food or drink in the living room.

Even the living room rug was gone.

They were gone.

My father knew and hadn't told me. He let them leave and never even told me they were going. If I had known, I might have at least been able to be here to say goodbye. I didn't even have Danny's new address. I wanted to smash my fist through the glass in the window. But what would that do other than cut my hand? Danny was gone. His family was gone. I'd never see my best friend again. I felt like crying. I wanted to cry. But I knew if anyone saw me, it would get back to my sister. And then I'd never hear the end of it.

"Look at Kelly, crying like a baby for his little friend. They were probably queer for each other. Miss your boyfriend, you little faggot?"

And Kevin would probably call us butt-buddies. He'd done it before.

I wouldn't give them the satisfaction. I blinked back any tears that might have been in my eyes and walked back to my bike. I picked it up and walked across the road. A path through the tall grass led down to the river's edge. I dropped my bike into the grass and headed down to the water, the sound of the rushing river growing in my ears. The shore was made up of the bedrock that was the foundation of the entire area. At least, I think maybe it was bedrock. Whatever it was, it wasn't a sandy beach like we had at the lake and the water wasn't still and clear. The river was this weird yellowish-brown color. It looked gross, but it was a really nice place to swim when the last of the summer heat returned. The river flowed over a wide but shallow waterfall at the other side of the bridge. It was noisy enough to drown out the thoughts in my head. No, it wasn't. I don't know why I thought it did. The thoughts were still there. The thought of never seeing Danny and his family again, the raw hate I felt for my father for not telling me, even the hate I had for my great-grandfather for buying that stupid camp anyway. If it hadn't been for that, I would have been home to know Danny was leaving. At least I could have said goodbye.

"Hey," a voice said, off to my left.

I looked up to see a kid standing a little further down the riverbank from me. I didn't recognize him. He looked about my age with dark curly hair, dressed in Levi's and a Star Wars t-shirt.

"Hey," I replied.

We were both silent for a long time after that. I stared out at the yellow-brown water as it flowed by, listened to the roar of the falls. I glanced over and saw him pulling at some weeds growing next to the rock shore.

"You live around here?" he finally asked.

"Yeah, up the road." I nodded my head back up the hill.

Silence again for at least a minute, maybe two.

"You're not from around here, are you?" I finally asked.

"We just moved here to a place up there." He indicated the road that went off to the left on the other side of the bridge.

"Livingston Road," I said.

"Yeah, that's it." He took the six or seven steps between us and held out his hand to me. "I'm Jay. Jay Stone."

I shook his hand. "Kelly King," I said.

"King?" he said. "You some kind of royalty?"

"Nah, it's just my name."

He sat down next to me on the rocks. "You go to school in Potsdam?"

"Yeah."

"Me, too. I mean, I will be going. What grade are you going into?"

"Seventh," I replied.

"Me, too!" That seemed to excite him. "Cool, we'll be in the same grade."

I smiled. "Yeah, I guess so. Do you know who you have for homeroom?"

"Mr. Wheaton?" It was a question more than a statement as if he wasn't sure the name was right.

"Oh, man," I said. "I've heard some stories about that guy!"

"Really? Like what?"

"Like that he's really boring. And he has bad breath."

"Really?"

"Yeah," I said. "They say when he leans over your desk to talk to you, it smells like rotten eggs."

"Oh, man, that's gross!"

"Well, I've got Mrs. Crandell. She's supposed to be real mean to her students."

"Aren't there any cool teachers in this school?" he asked.

"Mrs. Burley is pretty hot."

"At least that's something to look forward to!"

We both laughed at that. It was true. I had seen Mrs. Burley a few times in the school year before and had a serious crush on her. I couldn't wait for math class this year.

"You lived here long?" Jay asked.

"Since I was eight." Remembering how young I was, I couldn't help but think again about Danny. He had already been living in West Stockholm when we'd moved. Only four years and he was gone. Dad didn't even get an address for him. I needed to change my mind. "We lived in Potsdam before that. Where did you move from?"

"Utica. My dad works for the phone company and got transferred to the Potsdam garage."

"He fixes phones?" I asked.

"Nah, he's just a mechanic. Keeps the trucks running and stuff."

I nodded. Jay seemed a little put off by my question, like maybe he was ashamed of what his father did. It was probably better than what my father did. I really hoped he wouldn't ask, and I did my best to delay the question.

"What about your mom?" I asked.

"She stayed in Utica."

"Oh," I said, embarrassed. "Sorry."

"It's okay," he said. "They split up a couple of years ago. But it's going to be a real bitch going to visit her on weekends now."

"Yeah, I guess it could be."

"What about your folks?" he asked. "They still together?"

"Yeah." That was something I had never thought about before. What if my parents split up? It seemed like the thing everybody's parents were doing these days. Maybe my parents would get a divorce, too. But I really couldn't imagine it. It's not like they had some kind of lovey-dovey romantic life together. I just couldn't imagine a life where they weren't together.

"So, what does your old man do?" he finally asked.

"He's a…he's one of the managers at the Ames store in town." He was really only the resident assistant manager, but I didn't want to have to explain what that meant. Mostly it meant he was the lowest of the managers and that he didn't face being transferred to another store. That's what made him a resident.

"In town?" Jay asked. "There's an Ames here in West Stockholm?"

"No." I couldn't help but chuckle a little that he didn't know what I meant by that. But then, he was from the city, so why would he know? Utica was a few hours south by car and was a lot bigger than Potsdam. "We say it's in town when we mean it's in Potsdam. There's nothing much here except for the corner store up on the highway."

"Oh, yeah, I've walked up to that store a few times."

"Then you've walked right by my house," I said.

"How come I haven't seen you before now? We've been here, like, three weeks."

"We have a cabin up at Lake Ozonia. It was my great-grandfather's. We stay up there for most of the summer."

"Cool," Jay said.

"Yeah, it's pretty cool."

We sat in silence for a while again, and I just stared out at the falls watching the water.

"You doing anything for Labor Day?" he asked.

"Not really. We just got back from camp. My father's doing hot dogs and hamburgers later, but it's not really a party or anything. What about you?"

"Dad's working overtime today, so I'm pretty much on my own."

I nodded, and we fell silent again. God, had it been this hard when I'd first met Danny? I didn't think so. It seemed like he and I had so much in common that we just started talking like we'd known each other forever.

"We could go hang out at my place," Jay offered.

I looked at my watch and saw that it was nearly four-thirty. Dinner would be at five o'clock. "Maybe for a little while," I said. "But I'll have to get home for dinner pretty soon."

I followed Jay back along the path through the tall grass and picked up my bike from the bushes.

"Aren't you worried somebody might steal your bike?" he asked.

"Nah, nobody would want it." It was probably true. It was an old beat-up bike, handed down to me from my brother when he got a new one for his birthday. As the youngest, I barely got anything new, except maybe my underpants.

We walked across the bridge and took the turn up Livingston Road. He talked about Utica as we passed the post office and a small horse farm. His house was just past the field where the horses were grazing.

"I miss it already," he said. "There was literally nothing to do in this town when I first got here. I'm just glad my friends gave me that going away present before I left."

"What was that?" I asked.

"You'll see," he said with a grin. "Come on."

We reached his driveway and he jogged down to the barn behind the house. It was gray with red trim. I stopped for a moment to look over the front porch. I remembered driving by the place before. It was decorated with what my mother had called gingerbread, intricate woodwork painted white with the same red trim as the barn. I guess it was kinda pretty. But really, the way the gingerbread stuck out over the steps that led up to the porch, and with the carving on the handrails, it looked like the house had teeth. Like it would eat you up if you stepped near it.

"Come on," Jay called from the side of the barn.

I hurried down the driveway, set my bike down by the big garage door in front, then met him at the side. He opened the small side door, and I followed him in. Two windows on each side of the barn let in plenty of light. It was easy to see that it had probably been a horse barn of some kind when it had first been built, but now it was more like a garage, especially with the big garage door at the front. And it smelled of gas and oil.

"Pretty cool, right?" Jay said with a smile.

Sure, if you're from the city and had never seen a barn before. Most of the houses in West Stockholm, at least the old ones, had some kind of barn out back. We had our small red barn where Dad kept his tools and Kevin had taken over the second floor. But I nodded to show I thought it was alright.

"I've already made myself a space upstairs."

The stairs were about halfway down the length of the barn. There was a small room off to the left that looked like it might have been a stable for a horse back in the day. A closed door just beyond it hid whatever might be further back. We took the stairs on the right and headed up to the second floor. There were no rooms or anything up here, so it was as long and as wide as the entire barn. The gambrel roof gave the space a really high ceiling with all the rafters exposed. It was a really big space. At the back of it was a beat-up old couch and armchair as well as a small coffee table set out between them as if Jay had tried to make his own living room in the barn.

Besides that, there were a few cardboard boxes scattered about as well as what looked like some antique wooden boxes.

"Most of this stuff was here when we moved in. I got my Dad to let me have the old coffee table. Not that I drink coffee," he said with a smile.

We walked over to the couch and Jay pointed to the chair, so I took a seat. Before Jay sat down, he picked up one of the couch cushions and pulled out a small, crumbled paper bag. Then he replaced the cushion and sat down.

"You party?" Jay asked.

What did he mean, did I party? Like birthday parties or something? Before I got a chance to answer his question or ask my own, he removed a Baggie from the paper bag. It was filled with what looked like dried and crushed herbs, like what my mother sprinkled in the spaghetti sauce. When he tossed the bag on the coffee table, I could see some sticks and seeds and what looked like a couple of cigarettes in the bag. They were rough like maybe Jay had rolled them himself.

Wait a minute, I suddenly thought. Is that what I think it is?

"That's what my friends gave me as a going-away present," Jay said. "A whole dime bag."

Dime bag? I'd heard that term, though I really didn't know what it meant. I'd never seen pot before, much less a dime bag of it.

Jay took one of the cigarettes out of the bag, then took a Bic lighter from his pocket. He held both of them out to me. So, this was what he meant when he asked if I partied. Did I smoke pot?

"No, thanks," I said. "I don't, you know, party."

"Really?" Jay seemed genuinely surprised. "What else is there to do around here?"

I shrugged my shoulders. I had heard of pot. Or marijuana as it was properly called. And I had heard the stories about it and the pot addicts. I'd seen an after-school special about it on TV as well. Things did not work out well for those kids. So, maybe Jay liked to party, but you'd never catch me getting addicted to that stuff.

"Whatever," Jay said. He stuck the joint in his mouth and lit it. He took a long drag from it and held his breath. It was just like I'd seen in that show. It was so weird to see it happening in person, right in front of me. He blew the smoke directly at me when he finally exhaled. I did my best not to inhale it. You never know how little it might take to get hooked or something. But, when I did breathe again, I found that it didn't smell that bad. Not like the cigarettes my grandfather smoked. Those were awful and made me cough when he smoked around me. This was different. It was a sweeter smell, almost like incense.

Jay held it out to me once more and I shook my head. Then he took another drag and settled back on the couch.

"You don't know what you're missing," he said.

The kids in that show smoked pot because they were alone and unwanted. I wondered if that was the same for Jay. His father was working overtime on a holiday and his mother was all the way down in Utica. He was new in town and didn't seem to have any friends. Maybe he needed a friend and then he wouldn't need the pot.

"You know," I said. "I could call my mother and see if it's alright for you to have dinner at our place tonight. If you want."

Jay took another drag from his pot cigarette before he put it out against the side of the coffee table.

"Sure," he said. "What the hell!"

"I'll give you fair warning, though. My brother and sister can be jerks."

"Fuck 'em," Jay said as he tried to stand up.

I was shocked by his use of *that* word. It's not that I hadn't heard it before; my father swore all the time. But I knew it was a bad word and kids weren't supposed to say it.

"Just point me to the food." He laughed out loud as if it was the funniest thing anyone had ever said. It was weird to see the change that had come over him after smoking the pot.

Jay led the way as best as he could into the house so I could call my mother and ask if it was okay for him to come for dinner. She didn't seem especially interested that I had made a new friend, but she said it was fine if he came over. Jay didn't have a bike. He said his had been stolen just before he moved, and his father hadn't bought him a new one yet. So, I walked mine next to him and we made our way back down Livingston Road and across the bridge.

On the other side of the bridge on the right was Water Street. It was a dead-end street with two houses on the left, two on the right, and a small yellow house at the very end. None of the houses were well-cared for and they had overgrown lawns and hedges. There was even a car up on cinder blocks in front of the closest house on the right. The next house down on that side was the one I wanted to point out to Jay.

"See that house down there?" I asked and pointed down the street.

"That pink one?"

"No, the one past that. They call it the White House. It's supposed to be haunted."

"Really? You ever go inside?" Jay asked.

"No, but Danny and I used to sneak around it and peek in the windows."

"Who's Danny?"

"Oh, he was my friend," I said. "He just moved away. He used to live over there." I pointed to the house to the left on the other corner.

"So, if you never went in, how do you know it's haunted?"

I shrugged my shoulders. "I don't know. That's what they say. And no one ever seems to live there. It's been empty for a long time."

As we were passing by the house on the corner of Water Street, I saw Moe sitting in his usual spot on his porch, a beer in his hand. He stroked his mustache as we came up the road. The house was small, one floor with a garage, and had deep red shingles and a dark roof.

"Who's that?" Jay asked in a whisper as if he didn't want anyone but me to hear his question.

"That's Moe. He's just one of the local guys," I whispered back. I wasn't even sure why I was whispering.

Moe raised his bottle to us, and I waved back.

"Happy Labor Day!" he said.

"You, too," I replied.

"Got big plans?"

"Just a barbecue at home. How about you?"

"Enjoying the fruits of my labors," he returned and took a swig from his beer. "Who's your friend?"

"This is Jay. He's new in town."

"Good to meet you, Jay."

Jay gave him a meager, kind of skittish wave as we kept walking.

"Stop by anytime," Moe called after us.

"Weird," Jay finally said when we were halfway up the hill. He was still whispering, though not as quietly as before.

"What's weird?"

"That guy. Who says 'Hi' like that to a stranger?"

"He was just being friendly."

Jay gave me a look like I was out of my mind.

"You're not in the city, Jay. People here are just, you know, friendly. Moe's cool. He plays Frisbee with us sometimes."

"An old guy like that? That's weird."

He was right that Moe was older than most of us, but it wasn't like he was old like my father. "He's not that old," I said. "Besides, he's got a really cool Firebird. How weird can he be?"

"You think having a Firebird is cool?"

I don't know why, but Jay's question bothered me. Weren't Firebirds cool? Or maybe it was just a city thing. Maybe they had even cooler cars in the city.

"I think it's kinda cool, I guess."

"Sure, if you're the Bandit trying to outrun the Smokey! VROOOOOOM!" Jay made like he was driving a car and jogged up the road a bit, then made a screeching sound and pretended to skid as he turned around and ran back to me, passed me, then did the same screeching skid before coming up next to me again.

Was he making fun of me? I couldn't really tell because he was high. But, if he was, it wasn't very nice. We'd only just met. He did the revving sound a few more times, but when he saw that I wasn't laughing or even smiling, he seemed embarrassed, and he stopped.

"Sorry," he said. "I thought it was funny."

"Whatever."

At the top of the hill, we passed the Methodist Church, which left one more thing before we got to my house: the cemetery. If he was going to make fun of me over a car, I wasn't going to say anything about my feelings toward the cemetery.

"That graveyard freaks me out," Jay said. He moved around to walk on my other side putting me between himself and the cemetery.

"Yeah?" I had to admit that I was glad he thought it was creepy, too, though he hadn't really said it that way.

"Some of those stones must be really old. You ever check them out?"

"Yeah, Danny and I would dare each other to go into the very back."

"Yeah?"

"Yeah, some of the headstones near the back are from, like, the 1800s."

"Wow! You got any relatives in there?"

"Not that I know of," I said. "Maybe. My family's been in the area for a long time."

For someone who was so freaked out by it, Jay couldn't take his eyes off of it. He was still looking back over his shoulder when we reached my driveway.

"Here we are," I said, waking him from his trance.

"Huh? Oh, okay, cool."

My father was standing by the grill cooking the hot dogs and hamburgers, so I introduced Jay to him first. I felt really weird about it. I mean, here was this kid I'd just met, and he was meeting my folks while he was high. It again reminded me of that after-school special where the kid was sitting at the table with his family having dinner while he was stoned. I remember thinking that something like that could never actually happen, but here it was happening in my own house.

"Why do they call him Moe?" Jay asked from out of the blue.

"What?"

"That guy down on the corner. Why do they call him Moe?"

"I don't know. I just thought it was his name."

"Nah, nobody names their kid Moe," Jay said matter-of-factly. "I bet he's hiding his real name. Probably hiding something."

We went inside so he could meet everyone else. I had warned him about my brother and sister, but he and Kevin seemed to hit it off pretty well. Karen was her usual cold self until she saw how much it bothered me that Jay and Kevin seemed to be getting chummy. Then she was all about being interested in Jay and his life in Utica. Mom barely seemed to notice he was there. She just kept working on the salad and the other sides for dinner, her back to us the entire time.

I realized that any friendship with Jay might be over before it started when I was setting the table like Mom had asked me to do. Sure, I invite a friend over, but Karen and Kevin can't be made to set the table even if it was my turn? How was I supposed to be a good host? I looked out the window to see Kevin and Jay heading into the barn. Kevin had pretty much taken over the second floor and made it his own place where he and his friends would hang out. He would chase me out if I even tried to venture up there. But Jay had somehow finagled his way in. And when dinner was over, before I could even offer to walk Jay back to his place, Kevin piped up and said he'd go with him.

That was it. Any idea I might have had that Jay would replace Danny as a friend was really dead. I watched as the two of them walked to the end of the driveway and then turned left down the main drag. If that's what drugs do to you, I wasn't going to have anything to do with them.

3

Hangover, 1994

I'd awakened to a lot of hangovers, but never one that left a ringing in my ears. But, as consciousness began to take hold, I realized that it was not some imagined noise. It was a real ringing. It was the phone. Wow, two calls in as many days. That had to be a record. And that, of course, reminded me of the message on the machine that I had yet to listen to. Well, another bill collector could talk to the same machine and leave another message I wouldn't hear. I rolled back over and tried to pull the blankets over me. But the blanket wasn't there. And neither was the pillow. I was on the floor of my place and not in the loft bed. Apparently, the ladder had presented too much of a challenge. On the plus side, no one was banging on my door telling me to turn down the goddamn stereo. More than one night I had passed out on the floor with some music playing on repeat in the CD player. At least the ringing would stop when the machine picked up. The click of the machine came, the ringing stopped, and my cheesy message played. It had to do with taking any job being offered, not having any money to pay whatever bill they might be trying to collect on, and anyone else could just leave a message.

"Kelly?"

My mother's voice.

"Kelly, if you're there, pick up," she said, and then quieter like she was talking to someone else, "I hate talking to these things."

Fuck, I really didn't feel like dealing with my mother this early in the…. Well, it was probably not morning. I didn't feel like dealing with her this early in my hangover.

"Your sister called you yesterday. Did you get her message?"

Not a bill collector after all. Well, how was I supposed to know? Why would I think it was a message from Karen? She had never called me before. And now, two relatives had called me. Wasn't I special?

"It's about your Uncle Bruce. He's…. There's been an accident."

I sat bolt upright and reached for the phone on the table next to my chair.

"Mom?" I said. My voice was barely there. I hadn't even tried to clear my throat before speaking.

"Oh, you *are* there," she said, the accusation apparent in her voice.

"Yeah, I was in the bathroom," I replied. "What's this about Uncle Bruce?"

"Didn't you get your sister's message? She called you yesterday."

"No," I lied, "I never got it." Well, it wasn't really a lie since I had never listened to the message. "This is an old machine. Not very reliable, I guess. Or maybe she didn't call me." Why not take a jab at her while I had the chance? "What about Uncle Bruce?"

"He's…." She was silent for a long moment. I was pretty sure I knew what she was going to say before she said it. It was as if I'd been expecting this call for fifteen years. "He's gone," she finally said.

Even though I'd expected it, the words hit me like a…well, like nothing I could begin to describe. I got up from the floor and sank into my chair. Numb was the closest description of what I was feeling. A nothingness. Null and void.

"Okay," I finally said.

"There's no need to go into the details. But we're going to get together for dinner at your grandmother's tonight. Do you think you can make it?"

I coughed and cleared my throat. "I don't know. I mean, I'm scheduled to work tonight. And I don't have any way to get out there."

"James and I can pick you up on our way through Potsdam and then drop you off afterwards," she said.

A half-hour car ride with her and her new husband and then another half-hour ride back with them. As if the dinner wouldn't be bad enough.

"Let me go down and talk to Gary," I said, "and I'll let you know."

What the hell was I thinking? All I had to say was that I had to work, and it would all be over. I wouldn't have to spend any time with any of them. But there was something else that played across my mind. It was a memory, a vague one. My head was too fuzzy to recall it exactly, but I felt that this dinner would honor that memory somehow.

"We'll be coming through Potsdam around four-thirty. Why don't we just stop by the pool hall and you can join us if you can make it."

"I guess that can work," I replied. What time was it? How long was it till four-thirty?

"Alright, we'll see you then."

I set the phone back in its cradle. The message light was still blinking on the answering machine. I pushed the Play button and the tape rewound to the beginning of the messages. Then the grainy voice of my sister came through the tinny speaker.

"Kelly, it's Karen," she said. "Pick up if you're there."

My sister, Karen. She had, indeed, called. It must have been late at night, but I had no way to tell; there was no timestamp. There was a silence as she awaited the pickup that wasn't coming. Where had I been? At work or at the bar?

"Okay, fine." I could hear the annoyance in her voice. No surprise there. She was always annoyed by something. Having to call her deadbeat, delinquent brother in the middle of the night probably irritated her no end. Good to know I could annoy by my absence as well as my presence. "Mom called and wanted me to call you. Uncle Bruce died last night."

I had my confirmation. If I thought my mother's call was some kind of hangover hallucination, my sister's message was not. Uncle Bruce was gone.

"I don't have all the details," she continued. "You'll probably want to call Mom in the morning. Anyway, that's it."

The unease in my sister's voice had been pretty clear. I don't imagine it was an easy call for her to make on any level. All these years and she still didn't like me much. Well, she was definitely not my favorite person either. Too much nasty history between us. Same with my brother. Dinner tonight would be sheer joy for all of us.

The machine beeped and started playing the conversation between me and my mother. I had forgotten to hit the Stop button when I answered the phone, so it was all on tape. I pressed Stop to end the playback.

The clock on the table read one-thirty-five, so I had plenty of time to get ready for dinner, if I decided to go. I was pretty sure Gary would have no problem covering for me tonight or at least for the couple of hours it would take. As long as I gave him some notice. I picked myself up from the chair and headed for the bathroom. I'd need to get cleaned up whether I worked my shift or not. And I never missed an opportunity to take a shower. And it was only a shower. I was too distracted by the news for anything else. It wasn't that I was sad, exactly. I needed some time to process all of it. I listened to both my sister's message and the recorded conversation with my mother twice as I got dressed. They were the same messages as they had been the first time I had heard them, but I felt like I needed confirmation that I hadn't imagined it. I did feel a little guilty for not having listened to my sister's message earlier. But how was I supposed to know? How was I supposed to know the message was actually important? The other thought I couldn't chase away was the idea that while I was out getting wasted the night before, my uncle had died.

Get over it. There's nothing to be done about it now. And if I was going to have dinner with the family this evening, that would be enough penance for my misstep. I also needed to get something while I was at the house in Hopkinton. I grabbed my denim jacket from the hook by the door and took it with me. I didn't know if what I was looking for would still be there, but if it was, I wanted to have the jacket. It had the big inside pockets that I knew would come in handy. I headed down the stairs with a small hope that Gary had plans and wouldn't be able to cover my shift. I found him alone in the pool hall today.

"No Fish for lunch?" I asked as I approached the counter.

"No, he was in earlier. A mid-morning snack, said he had a meeting this afternoon." He gave me a quick once-over. "Something wrong?"

Damn, that man was perceptive. I didn't think I was showing anything, and he had picked up on it anyway.

"Well," I said. "I've got a favor to ask. But feel free to say no."

"Let me know what I'm saying no to before I say no," he said with a laugh.

"Can you cover my shift for a few hours?"

"Sure," he replied. "Got a dinner date?"

"Kind of." I felt the words catch in my throat. It was like I couldn't bring myself to say them. "It's just that…." Shit! I hadn't expected it to hit me so hard to say the words myself, but I felt my eyes welling up. I swallowed hard to stop the tears from coming.

"What is it, Kelly?"

"My uncle died the other night," I finally said.

"Oh, man, I'm sorry. Sure, you can take the whole night off if you need to."

I shook my head. "No, that's not necessary. We're having a family dinner this evening, that's all. I'll be back by seven or eight, I expect."

"Don't be silly. Take the night. Hell, I'll probably close early anyway."

"No, really," I said. "I can close when I get back from my grandmother's. And I can work the start of my shift since no one's picking me up till about four-thirty. It'll give you a chance to run home for dinner or something."

"Okay," Gary said. "Let me give Melissa a call and make sure she hasn't planned something I don't know about. Watch the store for a bit, will ya?"

I stepped behind the counter while Gary went into the arcade where the payphone was. I sat down on the stool Gary had vacated. There were no customers in the place, so watching the store was no big deal. I wiped at my eyes. I hadn't expected that reaction to actually speaking about my news. It surprised me. And scared me a little.

"Yeah, Melissa is fine with it," Gary said as he came back into the pool hall. "She told me to give you her condolences. I'll just run next door later and get some spaghetti or pizza."

I nodded, wiping my hands on my jeans. I expected Gary could figure out why.

"You and your uncle. Were you close?"

I looked up at Gary. Close? That was an interesting question.

"Not really," I said. "Well, kind of."

And that was exactly it. We were close and yet we weren't. There was no other way to describe it. As much as it sounded fucked up — and maybe it was — but having not seen him in fifteen years, he was still the relative to whom I felt the closest.

"It's complicated," I said. I got up from the stool to give him back his seat.

"It's family," Gary said as he sat back down. "It's always complicated."

I snorted a bit. "You ain't kidding. I was hoping you had plans tonight just so I would have an excuse to miss dinner."

"You're preaching to the choir, Indy," Gary said with a smile. "There's more than one reason I'm living hundreds of miles from my family."

We both laughed at that. Oh, how I longed to live far away from mine. Not that it made any real difference. No one ever called, no one ever visited, no one cared. I didn't have to move hundreds of miles to be separated from my family.

"Let's shoot some pool," Gary said as he pulled a tray of balls from the shelf behind the counter. I stepped over to the rack of pool cues on the wall and tried to find myself a straight one. Gary grabbed the one he kept behind the counter and then flicked on the lights over the closest table. I chalked up my cue as he racked the balls for a game of Eight-ball.

"You want to hear the funniest part?" I asked. "I'd never even met my Uncle Bruce until my grandfather died. And it was about this same time of year, right when school started."

"Really?" Gary said as he stepped back from the table.

I leaned over the table and gave the cue a few practice strokes.

"I'd heard stories about him, that he'd been in Vietnam and owned a liquor store down in Utica. I might have even met him when I was a baby. But it was the day after my grandfather died that I really met him for the first time."

I drew back and hit the cue ball with as much force as I could muster and sent it flying into the triangle of balls. They split with a satisfying crack. Balls rolled across the felt surface, careened off the rubber banks, and bounced off each other before they all came to a rest around the table.

4

Late Calls and Early Mornings, 1979

I don't know what time it was when I heard the phone ring. It almost seemed like it had been ringing for a while and I was slowly becoming aware of it. The bedroom I shared with Kevin was nearly pitch black. The only light came from his clock radio and it was too far away for me to see what time it was. The phone rang again. The only phone was downstairs in the kitchen. I wondered if anyone was going to get up and answer it. Maybe I should. Then the ringing stopped, and I heard a muffled voice drift up the stairs from the kitchen. It was my mother. I couldn't hear what she was saying, but I could tell that it was her voice. My father's would have been a deep rumble, but what I heard was softer. And my father would've made her get up to answer it, I'm sure.

I started to drift back to sleep. She was talking to someone and sounded upset. Not angry, but the tone of the sound I heard just seemed…upset. As she talked, it was like the sound was fading into the distance. The quality of it changed. It floated right on the edge of my sleep and mingled with a dream as I drifted off again.

It was at breakfast, after we were all gathered around the kitchen table when Mom gave us the news. She stood by the sink washing my father's plate and coffee cup; he had just left for work.

"Grandpa John died last night," she said, her back to us.

My spoon hung in the air between my bowl and my mouth. That's when I remembered waking up. That must have been the phone call she got last night. I looked to both my brother and my sister. Kevin was looking down at his own breakfast, still eating.

Karen, who was sitting across the table from me, was looking out the window. It seemed like she was trying not to cry. That surprised me. Not that she looked like she was about to cry but that I didn't feel like I was going to. I didn't feel like I was going to cry. I didn't feel anything. I stuck the spoon in my mouth and chewed the bite of cereal. Then I set the spoon down on the table.

What was someone supposed to do in a moment like this? Hug each other? That's what they always did on TV. But no one seemed interested in hugging. Should we be bursting into tears? That was also something else they always did on TV. I didn't know what I was supposed to do or even how I was supposed to feel. No one I knew had ever died. No one close, anyway. Sure, Grandpa John and Grandma Ruth weren't really that close to us. Closer than any of my father's family. But he *was* my grandfather. We spent most of the holidays at their house. Christmas and Thanksgiving and Memorial Day. I wondered if we still would.

Did we have to go to school today?

Mom walked toward the living room. Her back was still to us, so I couldn't see if she was crying. "Your lunches are on the sideboard," she said. "You don't want to miss the bus."

I guess that answered the question about going to school. We were going. But there were so many other questions I felt I needed to ask. Except no one seemed like talking.

Our house was one of the first stops on the bus route, so I was able to find an empty seat near the front of the bus. Karen went further back, probably saving a seat for Mary. And Kevin went to the very back like he always did. I would usually save the seat for Danny, but that wasn't going to be necessary anymore. I didn't know who would end up sitting with me. The further the bus went, the more it filled up, and the more worried I got about who would end up sitting next to me. But high school kids didn't want to sit with a middle schooler, and most everyone had their own friends to sit with, so maybe I'd end up with the whole seat to myself.

It gave me time with my thoughts. I still couldn't really understand what Mom had said. I mean, I knew what it meant, I just didn't know what it meant to me, you know? Were things going to change? And what kind of changes would they be? The other thing you always saw in the movies and on TV was the reading of the will. Would Grandpa John leave me something in his will? Geez, that was pretty selfish of me. My grandfather died and I was thinking what I would get out of it. I did my best to push that thought from my head 'cause I knew it wasn't right. The whole thing was already beginning to feel a little like a dream, like a fading memory of something that didn't really happen. The only thing Mom had said was that he had died, and he had died last night. Nothing more. And no one had said anything else. Did I really hear that right? Was it really true? I was having trouble making sense of it.

"Hey." The voice woke me from my thoughts. I looked up to see Jay standing next to the seat. He motioned for me to slide over so he could sit down. I did and looked out the window.

"How's it going?" he asked.

I shrugged my shoulders. Did he really think I'd forgotten how he'd treated me at dinner just the night before?

"Geez, what's your sister's problem?" Jay asked. He was pointing his thumb back over his shoulder. "First day of school sucks, but it's nothing to cry about."

I leaned around to see my sister a few rows back sitting with Mary and crying, then I looked back out the window.

"Our grandfather died last night," I said.

"And your parents made you go to school?"

I looked back at him. It didn't cross my mind at the time that he didn't offer his sympathies. He didn't put an arm around me like Mary was doing for my sister. Maybe guys weren't supposed to feel the same way as girls. Still, it didn't seem right. And he seemed to be completely unaware that I was mad at him for the night before.

"When my grandpa died, I got the whole week off," Jay said.

I didn't know how to respond to that. I didn't know how to respond to any of this. Was I supposed to cry? I felt like I should, but I didn't feel like I could. On all the shows, when somebody died, there was always lots of crying and weeping and hugging and all that. But it wasn't there for me. No tears, not even any real sadness. Just this emptiness. A nothing.

Jay talked for most of the rest of the way through the bus route and on the ride down the main highway to school. The first stop was at the middle school and we headed into the building. I showed Jay to his homeroom and we agreed to meet up for lunch and after school for the bus ride home.

Most of the rest of the day was a dull blur of moving from one room to another. Nothing ever really happened on the first day of school anyway, which was good because my mind wandered all over the place. I remembered birthday parties with Grandpa John and the times he and Grandma Ruth had come up to the lake that summer. We always tried to convince them to stay overnight even though they rarely did. Their house was only a few miles down the road from the lake. All the holidays ran through my head. And hiding his cigarettes on him. What a stupid thing to remember now. But I used to do it all the time. I really wanted him to quit smoking, and I thought maybe hiding his cigarettes or his lighter would help. He'd laugh about it at first, but if we were spending the day at their house and I did it more than a couple of times, he'd start to get mad. So, I'd stop and leave his cigarettes wherever he left them after that. Why was I remembering the times he was angry with me?

We were back on the bus by three o'clock that afternoon and heading home. Jay and I shared a seat on the ride. He talked about the teachers and some of the kids he had met and about the homework he had been given. I had gotten the same homework from most of the same classes, but I really wasn't in the mood to talk. The bus was getting closer to my house and all I really wanted to do was get off, so I gathered up my stuff. We were first on in the morning, which made it an early morning ride, but we were also the first off after school.

"You want to meet up down at the river later?" Jay asked.

I almost couldn't believe he asked. He still hadn't made any mention of what he had done at dinner the day before. But maybe it was the pot. I'd heard it also messes up your memory. Maybe he didn't remember what he did. Should I really hold that against him? Besides, the last thing I wanted to do was sit in the house all afternoon with my sister. Or she and Mary. Or worse, she and Mary and my brother. I needed somewhere to go.

"Sure," I said. "Okay."

"Or you can ride up to my place if you want."

I stood up from the seat. His suggestion surprised me considering how things had gone the last time I was at his place. But even that thought intrigued me. I hadn't wanted to smoke with him. I didn't want to smoke pot. Did I?

"Yeah," I said. "Let's meet at your place."

The bus stopped in front of our house and Karen and Kevin came up from the back.

"Let's go, faggot!" Kevin said.

"If I'm not there yet, just head to the barn," Jay called as I walked up the aisle to the front of the bus and stepped off. Kevin slapped me in the back of the head as he ran up the driveway and into the house.

Yeah, I needed to get out of the house for the afternoon. I had to get out of my head, and maybe hanging out with Jay was the way to do it. Maybe hanging out and maybe something else. Unfortunately, it would be some time before the bus would be swinging by Jay's house and dropping him off. Thankfully, Karen immediately went to her room and closed the door and Kevin grabbed his bike and rode away down the driveway and toward the bridge. I decided to wait on the porch until I figured it was a good time to leave for Jay's.

I heard the roar long before I saw the bike. The sound was so loud and distinct, it could only be a motorcycle. I tried to picture it in my mind. I loved those things and imagined myself riding one every time I rode my bike fast down the hills. The roar lessened as it approached the four corners at the end of the main drag. It was turning at the corners, but which way? The sound revved up after making the turn and then grew louder. It had turned onto the main drag and was coming into West Stockholm. I kept my eyes on the road to watch it go by. But the sound of the engine changed as it grew closer. The motorcycle was slowing. None of the neighbors had motorcycles. Maybe it was someone visiting? Would I get a chance to see the bike in someone's driveway? That would be cool. It was definitely a motorcycle and not Moe's Firebird. His car had a completely different sound.

I caught my first glimpse of it as it pulled into our driveway. I was sitting at the far end of the porch where my bicycle lay. The motorcycle came to a stop on the sidewalk that led to the steps up to our porch. It was a beautiful black machine with black leather saddlebags, what looked like a pack of some kind strapped to the seat behind the rider, and chrome that shone silver in the sun. But who was this guy pulling his bike onto our sidewalk? I couldn't think of a single friend of my parents who rode a motorcycle. The rider's face was hidden behind the dark face shield.

He wore a black leather jacket and blue jeans. His boots were black as well. He sat there letting the bike idle for a bit. While I couldn't see his eyes because of the face shield, I felt like he was looking right at me. He revved the engine once and then killed it, the sound fading into the afternoon. His foot threw out the kickstand and he eased the bike down. That's when he pulled off the helmet and set it on the left mirror of his handlebars. His head cocked a bit to the left, his eyes never leaving me. On some instinct, I rose to my feet. That's when he got off the bike.

He looked to be about as tall as my father who was six feet tall. His long brown hair was pulled back into a ponytail, his face covered with a full beard and mustache. I'd never seen a guy with a ponytail before, at least not in person. Then again, I'd never seen someone on a motorcycle in person either. Who was this guy? His jacket was zipped only part way up, faded Levi's, and boots that clicked and clunked on the concrete as he approached me. A part of me wanted to run from this man. He looked dangerous; the kind of guy I had always been told to stay away from. There was no way he knew my parents or anyone else in my family. Who was this stranger who felt comfortable enough to park his motorcycle on our sidewalk? He stepped up to me and I had to tilt my head up to look him in the eye.

"Who are you?" he asked as he stood over me, his voice deep and gruff. His gaze was hard but not mean. I saw that he had green eyes just like me.

"Kelly," I said. I hoped I sounded tougher than I felt.

"Kelly?" He seemed surprised. A very quiet, "Damn!" escaped him. Then he smiled. "You were about the size of a football the last time I saw you."

Last time he saw me? I couldn't help asking, "You know me?"

"Sure," he said. "Well, not exactly. I remember our last meeting, but I doubt that you do. You were only about a week old, I think."

He held out his hand to me. Without even thinking, I took it in mine. It was the polite thing to do. His hand was big and rough and completely engulfed mine. His grip was tight but it didn't hurt.

"I'm your Uncle Bruce," he said as he pumped my hand up and down.

Uncle Bruce! I'd heard stories of Uncle Bruce, my mother's brother. Some good, some bad. No one really spoke of him too often. The only thing I knew for sure was that he had been in the war. He had been in Vietnam.

"Is your mother home?" he asked as he released my hand.

"No," I replied. "She works till five."

He looked around a bit like he was assessing the situation, nodding his head as he did.

"Okay," he finally said. "Tell her I stopped by. Can you do that?"

I nodded.

"And tell her I'll be staying at the lake."

"At camp?" I asked.

"Yeah, she can call me there if she wants. I'll give her a call once I get settled in. I'll be in town for the funeral or whatever they have planned."

Funeral? Right, he was here because Grandpa John had died. It took me a moment to make the connection that my grandfather was not only my mother's father, but he was Uncle Bruce's father, too.

"I'm sure Mom — Grandma Ruth — is going to do some kind of family get-together. Let Liz — your Mom — know I'll be there."

"Okay," I said.

"Okay," he replied and walked back to his motorcycle. He swung a leg over and sat down. He took the helmet from where he'd placed it on the mirror.

"Question," he said.

I nodded.

"How old are you now?"

"Twelve," I replied.

"Fuck," he said and shook his head. He slipped the helmet back on, hooking the strap under his chin. Then he started the bike with a kick, revved it twice, and steered it around and down the driveway to the road. He took the left turn out of the driveway that would send him off toward the camp at Lake Ozonia.

I picked up my bike from where it lay by the porch and ran down to the end of the driveway with it. I got to the road just in time to see Uncle Bruce's bike flying past the cemetery. I hopped on my bike and started pedaling. I knew I wouldn't catch him or anything, but it was kinda cool to think I was riding with him, my hair flying in the wind. He crested the hill by the church and disappeared down the other side. Even though I couldn't see him anymore, I could still hear that motorcycle, its roar fading the further it went down the road. By the time I reached the top of the hill, I couldn't hear it anymore. He was gone. I coasted down the hill toward the bridge, pretending that I was roaring down the road on a motorcycle instead of my little bicycle. I imagined that black beauty tearing up the Sand Hill Road on its way to the lake. I couldn't help but think of that song by Meat Loaf, "Bat Out of Hell," and the silver black phantom bike. I just hoped that Uncle Bruce's ride wouldn't end the same way. But he'd ridden all the way from Utica, so he knew what he was doing on that machine.

I turned into Jay's driveway just as he was coming out the back door of his house. I skidded to a halt near him by the barn. I leaned the bike against the building and followed him inside.

"You gonna puss out or are you going to party today?" Jay asked.

That was the question. After the way Jay had treated me the day before, I wasn't even sure I wanted to hang out with him. But he'd been alright with me today. And with Grandpa John dying, I was rethinking the idea of smoking the pot. It wasn't that I was feeling sad and wanted to not feel sad. I just didn't feel anything about it. And the excitement of meeting Uncle Bruce had only confused me about how and what I was feeling. Jay had seemed pretty happy after he'd smoked, so maybe it wouldn't be so bad. I just really wanted to feel *something*. And it was only one time, right? Still, I was nervous about the whole idea.

"I was thinking about it," I replied.

"It'll help you deal with your grandfather dying."

So, at least I knew he had been listening when I told him about that, and he'd remembered it long enough to say something. It wasn't an offer of sympathy, but it was something. Maybe he was right that it would help me deal with it all. We climbed the stairs to the second floor and grabbed our same seats as soon as Jay had taken the pot from its hiding place.

"You might want to find a better place to hide it," I said.

"Why?" Jay asked as he took out a pot cigarette and his Bic lighter. "I thought you weren't worried about thieves around here."

"Not thieves, exactly. Mice."

"Mice?"

"Or rats."

"Rats!"

"Yeah," I said. "Barns are known for having mice and rats. Even a stray cat might decide to get into it. You probably want a better container for it, too."

Jay lit the pot cigarette and took a long drag from it. He held it out to me. I hesitated, but then I took the cigarette from him. I held it between my thumb and index finger. Jay exhaled.

"What are you waiting for? It's just a joint," Jay said.

A joint. Yeah, that's what they called it on that afternoon special.

"I've never smoked anything before," I said.

"Not even a cigarette?"

I hadn't smoked one, but I'd watched Grandpa John smoke enough of them to kinda know how to do it. I put the joint between my lips and took a small drag from it. An earthy sweetness filled my mouth.

"You gotta inhale it for it to do any good," Jay said. "Just open your mouth and take a breath."

As I opened my mouth to do that, some of the smoke escaped. But I did feel something get into my lungs. I immediately exhaled to keep myself from coughing.

"That was pretty wimpy," Jay said as he took back the joint I held out to him. He took another puff from it and held it out to me again. In a squeaky voice, he tried to speak without exhaling. "Practice makes perfect."

I took the joint from him and attempted to smoke it again. I don't know that I was getting it yet, but I was able to hold the smoke a little longer the second time. The urge to cough was still too strong for me to hold it in as long as Jay did. By the third time he handed it back to me, I had at least figured out how to take a puff and inhale at the same time. And that time, I was able to hold the smoke longer.

Jay ground out the butt of the joint on the side of the coffee table as he had done before.

"I'll save this roach for later," he said and dropped it into the plastic bag. "Think I'll take this inside, though, to make sure nothing gets into it."

He stretched out on the couch and rested his head on the arm and closed his eyes. "I wish I had my radio," he said. "Tunes always go good with a buzz."

A buzz? I didn't feel anything, really. It certainly didn't feel like I had a buzz or I was stoned or anything like that. Maybe I hadn't smoked enough. Or maybe I didn't hold the smoke long enough. Or maybe pot didn't have any effect on me. Whatever it was, the pot hadn't done anything for my mood. I was still feeling confused and numb. Nothing different than I had felt before I smoked it.

"I gotta remember to bring my radio back with me this weekend," he said.

"What's going on this weekend?" I asked.

Jay sat up quickly and thrummed his hands on the coffee table.

"Going to Utica. Dad's picking me up from school Friday and we're meeting my mother, like, halfway between here and there. I'm staying with her this weekend." He flailed his arms and hands in the air. "And then we do it all in reverse Sunday when Dad comes down to pick me up."

"Oh, right," I said. "I remember you saying something about spending weekends with your Mom."

"Most weekends and holidays and breaks," Jay said. "Gives me a chance to refill my stash once in a while, too! Come on, let's do something!"

"Like what?"

"There's a hoop hanging on the front of the barn. And I got a basketball."

"Sure," I said, even though I was horrible at basketball. I didn't think it was going to matter, though. Jay seemed pretty buzzed, so he'd probably never realize how bad I was. We headed downstairs and out to the driveway. We tried to play one-on-one, but it was too hard to figure out where the lines should be on the black driveway. So, we switched to playing Horse, which worked better until Jay started trying to make weird shots from across the yard and down the driveway, which never went into the basket anyway. His final shot almost broke a window in the front of the barn. So, I took a look at my watch and realized it was nearly dinner time anyway. I still had to tell Mom about Uncle Bruce stopping by.

"I gotta go," I said. "I don't want to be late for dinner."

"That's cool," Jay said. "My Dad's probably on his way home, too. See you on the bus tomorrow?"

"Yeah," I said as I grabbed my bike from the side of the barn.

"Cool, see ya later."

"See ya," I replied, but Jay had already disappeared into the barn to put the basketball away. I swung a leg over my bike and pedaled out of the driveway. If he was going to be gone for the weekend, I guess I'd have to find something else to keep myself occupied.

5

Family Dinner, 1994

I kept one eye on the business and the other on the front window waiting to see James' Chevy Blazer pull up to the curb out front. The closer the clock ticked toward four-thirty, the more anxious I got. I wished I still had my motorcycle, but I'd had to sell it two years ago to pay bills. It had been a piece of crap, nowhere near as nice as the one Uncle Bruce rode back in '79, but I would have been able to ride it out to Grandma's house. I wouldn't be sitting here nervously awaiting my mother's impending arrival. Worse, without my own wheels, I'd be trapped. I wouldn't be able to leave until she decided it was time to go. And knowing how things usually worked out, we would be there until every dish was clean, dry, and put away.

The blue Blazer pulled up out front of the pool hall, and I was up from my stool like a shot. I grabbed my denim jacket from the coat rack by the jukebox.

"I'll see you later," I said to Gary as I headed for the front door. "I'll be back when I get back, I guess."

"No hurry," he called after me. "Try not to kill anyone!"

"No promises!"

I was opening the door of the Blazer and climbing into the back seat before anyone could think to go inside to get me.

"How are you this afternoon?" James asked.

"I'm okay," I said as I closed the door.

"It's been some time since we've seen you," he said.

"Yeah, it's been a while."

My mother didn't even turn around to acknowledge me. All I saw was the back of her head. I wondered if she remembered the last time we'd been in each other's company. Because I did. I remembered it well as it was the only time anyone in the family even came close to helping me out during my homelessness. It had been two months ago when she had invited me to stay the night at their house. It hadn't been an invitation, though, it had been a forced offer. What else could you do when you accidentally run into your homeless child while walking through a parking lot?

I had been heading to the grocery store to grab a snack. It was one of the few days that I wasn't working, but I had still been hanging out at the pool hall. Where else did I have to go? Home? Anyway, she had been coming out of the bank and walking to her car at the same time I was walking through the same parking lot. Talk about your awkward scenes. I'd already been sleeping at the pool hall for nearly three months; she knew this. She couldn't ignore me now, though, and stopped to talk. We basically passed the time of day; she asked how work was going and I replied that it was fine. No acknowledgement or discussion of my situation. She couldn't even look me in the eye. Her eyes fixed on everything else so she wouldn't have to see me. Whether it was some sudden sense of guilt or familial kindness or just having no other idea what to say, she asked if I would be interested in coming over for dinner and to spend the night. As much as I didn't want to, what other options did I have? At least it would be a meal and a shower and, maybe, a restful night. Skee-ball machines were comfortable enough to sleep on, but when I didn't get to sleep until after the pool hall closed and with Gary waking me up before nine in the morning to open the place up, it meant very few hours of good, solid sleep. So, I accepted with the caveat that I bring my own bedding. She said she'd wait, and I walked back to the pool hall to grab my sleeping bag and a change of clothes.

The meal was fine. Better than the pizza slice or fast-food burger that I would have had. Hardly a word was spoken during the meal. Then, James left to see a movie, which left my mother and I alone for the evening. I still wonder if he'd done that on purpose, hoping she and I might work things out, but she kept her nose stuck in a book and I flipped through the channels on their television, neither of us saying much of anything. I finally excused myself, grabbed a nice long, hot shower, then spread out my sleeping bag on the bed in their guest room. I was asleep almost immediately even though it had only been eight o' clock. At least I got a decent night's sleep that night. My mother dropped me off at the pool hall the next morning on her way to work. That had been the last time I'd seen her until now. Two months without even a phone call until the news about Uncle Bruce. That's motherly love for you.

It ended up being a quiet ride out to Hopkinton. No questions about how my day had gone, how the job was going, how I felt about Uncle Bruce's death. The only sound was the folk music coming from the cassette player. It had to be James' music; I couldn't remember my mother ever listening to folk music. There was never any music in our house.

James was alright. He taught at the state college in Canton, about ten miles from Potsdam. You would hope that being related to someone in the state university system, even by marriage, would have gotten me some kind of break to go to school, but the state college system didn't work that way. I found it hard to wrap my head around the fact that he was married to my mother. Even after four years, it was still hard to reconcile the divorce. At least it had been relatively amicable. All of us kids were on our own, such as it was for some of us, so there had been no custody issues. They sold the house in West Stockholm, which didn't hurt my feelings much. I had nothing but bad memories of that place. And yet, I still found myself having dreams about it all the time. How was it that my brain left me haunted by a place I hated so much? Dig that: it was the house that haunted me. Why couldn't I dream about the camp at the lake? That had always been my favorite place. It still was. But, no, my unconscious mind couldn't seem to let go of the one place I despised the most. That was one of the benefits of all the drinking: I didn't dream. The least my parents might have done was share the profits of the sale. It's not like either one of them needed the money, but I sure could have used a couple of bucks.

When we pulled into the driveway at Grandma's house, I wasn't surprised to see that no one else had arrived yet. I'm sure my mother had timed our arrival early so she could help out with preparing dinner. A part of me really wanted to see that big black motorcycle parked up by the barn like it had been so many years ago at another family dinner. Things were different this time and yet so much was still the same.

As expected, Grandma had already started cooking before we arrived. She was stirring a pot on the stove when we walked into the kitchen.

"Mom," my mother said, "I told you we were coming early to help with dinner."

"Don't be silly," Grandma replied. I think she was wearing the same apron she wore for every family dinner. It was pinned to her dress at the shoulders and tied at the waist. The yellow flowers on a field of white were faded from wear and washes. "Hello, James, Kelly."

James walked over to her and gave her a peck on the cheek. "It's good to see you, Ruth," he said. "I just wish it was under better circumstances."

"It is what it is," she replied, never turning her attention from the pot on the stove.

"If you need anything, let me know," he said.

"Of course."

My mother had turned her attention to the sink and started washing the dishes that were already there.

"Come on," James said. "Let's leave the ladies alone."

We walked through the dining room. I felt bad about it. We were leaving them to do all the cooking, all the work. On the other hand, my grandmother always made it a point to chase the men out of the kitchen when there was cooking to be done. It was a matriarchal thing in the family. Even my sister and my brother's girlfriend had been pulled into this almost cultish family tradition. Unless it was a barbecue, the women did the cooking, and the men did…whatever the men were supposed to do. My father and Grandpa John had always disappeared behind a newspaper in the living room, and the kids disappeared into the game room. Honestly, it was incredibly sexist. But it was also "family tradition." My grandmother was adamant about keeping with traditions.

"Shall we try a game of pool?" James asked.

"Why not?" I answered. Even after Grandpa John had died, my grandmother had kept the game room intact. It was, after all, tradition. It was probably the same reason she had kept the house even though she lived alone. It was far too big for one person, but it was the traditional family home and had been in the family for a couple generations, partially built by the same great-grandfather of mine who had bought the cabin. The game room did give us something to do during these awkward family get-togethers. At least now I knew how to play pool.

We were on our second game of Eight-ball when everyone else started to arrive. James and I went back to the kitchen in time to see Kevin and his very pregnant girlfriend arrive. She was about a month away from giving birth to my first niece, so she waddled everywhere she went.

"We would've been here earlier," Kevin said, "but the fat lady here hadn't finished singing."

Patty sat down in the nearest chair and gave my brother a tired look.

"Plus, it takes her forever just to get into the goddamn car."

She lifted her purse from her lap and set it on the table and leaned back in the chair. His jabs were nothing new. Kevin never missed a chance to belittle, in one way or another, the woman he claimed to love. She'd been with him almost a decade, so she was used to his comments. Still, it pissed me off every time he said something like that. Didn't he have any idea how it looked to the rest of us to say nothing of what it must have been doing to Patty? A part of me wanted to say something, to stand up for her, but no matter how old I got, it was like that scared little twelve-year-old was still with me. I convinced myself that I just didn't want to start any shit and turn the evening into a family battle. I didn't know if that would happen, but as much as I hated these people, I just wanted to keep the peace.

My grandmother came over to the table with a plate of celery and a jar of peanut butter and set them next to Patty.

"Now, I don't want you straining yourself," she said. "But could you help out with this?"

Because of her condition, Patty was relegated to the easy tasks like filling celery sticks with peanut butter or Cheez Whiz. Kevin already had his head stuck in the refrigerator. Grandma had anticipated him and stocked the fridge with Coors Light. That was Kevin's beer. He grabbed one from the shelf and handed it to me. I didn't ask for one, didn't really like Coors Light, but I wasn't driving, so I took it. It might help me make the best of a bad situation. Just as I was about to suggest we retire to the game room, I heard another car pull into the driveway.

"That'll be Karen," my mother said as she looked out the window. Without even turning to me, she said, "Kelly, go help her? It doesn't look like Peter came."

Of course, he didn't. Her husband of just over one year rarely came to family get-togethers. He always found a reason like picking up a shift or having tickets to some game. Football, baseball, hockey. It depended on the season. Anything to avoid being around us. I couldn't blame him; I did my best to avoid these people, too. I wondered which reason he'd given this time.

I went out to Karen's car as she was getting Zachary, my nephew, out of his car seat.

"The diaper bag on the other side needs to come in," she said. She hoisted the seven month old boy into her arms and headed up the porch steps and went into the house.

Not even a hello. No "thank you." I wasn't even sure if she knew it was me helping out. She just assumed someone would be there. Why not? Her husband couldn't be there, so someone else would be. It made me wonder if he had been around to conceive the kid. I smiled to myself at that thought as I grabbed the bag, slammed the car door, and went back into the kitchen. I set the bag down by the door.

"Shall we finish our game?" James asked.

"Lay on, MacDuff," I said, happy I could recall some piece of my stunted education.

Kevin followed us back to the game room.

"What are you playing?" he asked.

"Eight-ball," James said. "But I'm only trying. Kelly is the only one really playing."

"I got winner," Kevin said and sat down to drink his beer.

I finished the game quickly when I sank the eight ball in a side pocket.

"My turn," Kevin said as he took the cue from James and chalked it. "My break."

I racked the balls for play, then stepped back. Kevin hit the cue ball hard and knocked the balls all over the table. The two ball dropped into a corner pocket.

"I've got solids," he said.

Of course, the rules of Eight-ball dictated that he didn't have to take solids. That was a barroom rule more than anything. I wasn't going to argue since he had no decent shots anyway. He tried for a ridiculously complex bank shot and missed.

"I got stripes," I said and proceeded to sink four balls before missing a bank shot to a corner.

Kevin took over and dropped a couple of balls before I was able to play again and I ran the rest of the table, finishing by sinking the eight ball in a corner pocket.

"Another one." It wasn't a question. Kevin hated to lose at anything, especially to me. He started re-racking the balls even before I had a chance to say anything. I punched the cue ball just as Kevin was lifting the rack from the balls. They danced all around the table. I saw the look Kevin gave me. He was saying "Asshole" with his eyes, and I couldn't help but smile to myself.

Patty came into the room just as I was making my first shot after the break. She was carrying a beer for Kevin.

"About time," he said. He took the bottle from her and shoved his empty into her waiting hand. He gave her a contemptuous look when he saw that the bottle wasn't open. He twisted the cap off, then held the cap between his thumb and middle finger. He held his hand up to his ear and I froze for just a moment as he snapped his fingers and sent the cap sailing across the room. A tiny shiver ran down my spine when he did it. I remembered another bastard doing something similar and I did not want to think about that.

"Who's winning?" Patty asked as she put her arm around Kevin's shoulders.

I kept my mouth shut figuring I'd let Kevin answer if he felt like it. He didn't say a word as Patty looked from one of us to the other. James cleared his throat uncomfortably.

"I'm going to grab something to drink," James said. "Kevin's got a fresh beer. Would you like something, Kelly?"

"Cutty Sark," I replied as I reached over the table to take a shot.

"Oh." James was surprised by my request.

"Grandpa John used to keep a bottle in the corner cabinet of the dining room."

"You think there's still one there?"

"Might be. If not, I'll take a beer."

"On the rocks?" James asked. "If there's Cutty Sark."

I banked the nine ball into a side pocket. "No, neat is fine."

He left the game room to fill my order, and I continued to sink the striped balls on the table. I had to give James credit for trying to be "pals" with all of us. He and my father even feigned getting along. I know the old man had a lot of anger toward him; he'd let me know that one night when I ran into him in the bar in West Stockholm. That's one fucked-up way to come upon your father. He'd been there for a while because he was definitely drunk. And as James McMurtry sang, "whisky don't make liars, it just makes fools." And his tongue was foolishly loose that night. But anger was the wrong word. He was bitter about the divorce. It had been four years, maybe a little more than that now, since they had separated. My mother had certainly moved on while my father wallowed in the past. He couldn't seem to get over her, which was odd considering how awful their marriage had been. Of course, I had seen evidence that Mom and James had been seeing each other well before my parents separated. I had stumbled upon it by accident, but the evidence was pretty conclusive.

I couldn't help but wonder if Dad knew and if that's where some of his bitterness came from.

About a year ago, Mom and James had taken a two-week cruise and James had suggested she let me use her car while they were gone. This was before my bout of homelessness. Anyway, the first day I had the car, I figured I'd take a ride up to the lake as it had been months since I had been there. So, I hopped in the car and looked through the cassettes in a case on the hump in the front seat. I wasn't sure if there would be anything I wanted to listen to, but I took a look. Among the cassettes was a mix tape James had made for her; I recognized the handwriting on the insert. And written in his hand was a title of the mix tape which read, "For my love, Christmas, 1989." Now, some might have seen that and just brushed it off as a nice gesture on his part. The problem was this: my parents didn't separate until June of 1990. So, the tape had been created and given to my mother many months before the separation. What would anyone make of something like that? It didn't really make any difference now. My mother and father got their divorce and James and my mother had been married for two years now. In the words of my grandmother, "It is what it is." Still, it made me wonder about all those nights and weekends my parents went out separately. As I got older, I had heard the rumors. Small towns were full of them. And those rumors had included talk of my mother and more than just one other man. I hadn't wanted to believe them at the time. Or maybe I hadn't cared enough to think about it. But looking back on it now, it made me wonder who she had been with all those nights so many years ago.

James came back into the game room just as I was about to sink the eight ball.

"I found the Cutty Sark," he said as he handed me a whisky tumbler only about a quarter full of amber liquid.

"Thanks very much." I took a drink; the whisky was smooth and warmed me as it went down. I set the glass down on the rail of the table, then sank the eight ball once more. Kevin started racking the balls again. He hadn't said a word this time.

"You two can play," I said. I handed my cue to James. "I see pool balls in my dreams these days."

"Probably not the only balls you dream about," Kevin said.

I really wanted to respond with a "Fuck you" or at least a "Grow up" but in deference to James' presence and the fact that we were in our grandparents' house, I just shook my head and left the room, choosing once again to keep the peace rather than let him know what I truly thought. Patty followed me out of the room.

I did wonder when Kevin would grow up. At least I was trying. I marked down holding my own tongue as a step in that direction. I felt sorry for Patty and put my arm around her shoulders as we walked through to the dining room.

I liked Patty – just don't you dare call her Patricia! I couldn't for the life of me figure out how a nice girl like her ended up with a douchebag like my brother. Or worse, why she stayed with him. They'd been dating for so long, he had gotten her pregnant, and he still showed no signs of asking her to marry him. He had even cheated on her at least one time that I knew of – did infidelity run in the family? – and he treated her like shit! And still she stayed with him. It made no sense to me; but then, very little about their relationship did. After everything he had done, she would still marry him in a heartbeat if he would ask. Was that love or just stupidity?

"Still pregnant, I see."

"Still pregnant," she said with a laugh. "I'm hoping this will end in another couple of weeks."

"It can't go on forever, can it?"

"You shut your mouth!" She playfully swatted at my arm. "Don't even joke about that!"

"Well, at least Kevin is good practice for dealing with a child. Soon, you'll have two."

"Oh, leave your brother alone."

"Maybe you should have done that," I said and laughed. "You wouldn't be in this situation if you had."

She swiped at me once more as we came into the kitchen. That's where I found my sister sitting at the kitchen table with the baby on her lap. At least now Karen had an excuse to not help with dinner.

"Peter couldn't make it?" I asked.

"He and Scott had tickets to a game," she said without looking up from the toy keychain she held out for Zachary.

Just as I had thought. I was beginning to think I should have just worked instead of coming all the way out here. But then, I had my own thing to do. I picked up my denim jacket and headed for the back door.

"Where are you going?" Mom asked without lifting her head from the pot she was stirring.

"Just outside for some fresh air," I replied.

"Well, we're just about to eat."

"I know. I won't be long."

I stepped out the back door, closing it behind me, and then stepped down to the driveway. I headed straight for the big red barn behind the house. If I had said where I was truly going, I'm sure my grandmother would have piped up and asked what I thought I needed to do in the barn. It's not that the barn was off-limits to us kids any longer, but I didn't feel like talking about my reasons for going out there. It was personal and nothing I wanted to share with any of them. I walked up the small ramp that led to the big barn door. It was unlocked, as I figured it would be, so I grabbed the rusting handle and gave the great door a heave. The door itself was about seven feet tall and twelve feet wide so it did not move easily on its track. It creaked and the rusty wheels squealed their protest, but the door slowly slid to the left revealing the dark interior. One small and very dirty window on the back wall let in a dim yellow light. That and the light now coming in through the three or four feet of space I'd created by opening the door was the only light that illuminated the interior. It was enough for me to find my way to the small closed door in the middle of the left wall. Its hinges creaked as I pushed the door open.

The small side room behind the door was a little brighter as there was a window at both the front and back of the room. It ran the depth of the barn, about fifteen feet or so, and was only about six feet wide. A dust-covered wooden bench lined the wall just inside the door, and there was an old metal stool sitting right where I remembered seeing it all those years ago. But Uncle Bruce wasn't sitting on it this time. That had been the first time he really let me get to know him, even if it was only briefly. And I remembered the one thing he had shown me while I was there with him. I didn't know if it would still be there, but I took the folding knife out of my pocket and walked to the back corner of the room. It was easy to find the right board even after all this time because it was the one that had a few small slivers missing from having been pried off a few times. My own knife took another sliver as I pried the narrow board from the wall one more time to reveal the space behind.

"I'll call you," my mother said as I got out of the Blazer.

I closed the door and walked away without another word. She wouldn't call. Why would she? I turned back to say something, at least acknowledge her statement, but the truck was already pulling away. So, I turned back to the door of the pool hall and stepped inside.

"Hey," Gary said as I walked up to the counter. "I said you could have the whole night off."

"I know," I replied. "I need the hours. I can close."

"Up to you. You feel like working?"

I stepped behind the counter. "Yeah, I don't feel like going back to my place just yet." And it was still a little early to be heading to the bar. I checked my watch so I could fill in my timecard. Only eight o'clock. It felt so much later. Einstein was right: time was relative. And time *with* relatives was even worse.

The pool hall was crowded for a Thursday night. Only one table was dark, the Schmidt in the front room. We might actually make some money tonight.

"How was dinner?" Gary asked. He pulled a stool up to the counter and took a seat. I guess he had decided he wasn't going anywhere just yet.

"Alright, I guess, if you enjoy an entrée of dysfunction with a little maladjustment for dessert."

Gary laughed his deep, throaty laugh. "Yeah, family can be that way."

The players at the table to the left signaled that they were done, so I turned off the lights. They brought the tray of balls to the counter and paid their tab. Rather than put the tray back, I dumped the balls into the polishing machine next to the rack.

"You don't have to do that," Gary said. "I'll polish them in the morning."

I shrugged my shoulders as I applied a drop of polish to each ball and turned the machine on. It hummed to life and the balls spun in their little holes. I sat back down to let the polisher do its job.

"So, dinner was good?" Gary asked.

"Yeah, the food was great. My grandmother's a great cook. It's just the company I could do without."

Gary nodded but didn't say anything. I knew he was waiting to see if I'd continue. It was his little trick to get you to talk. Don't say a word and the other person would fill the silence. I'd heard therapists did it all the time, too. I didn't mind; I wanted to talk about it with someone who would actually listen, and Gary was a good listener.

"I mean, we got together because my uncle died. And no one said a word about him all evening. What was the point of us all getting together if no one was going to talk about the guy who was the reason we were getting together? I realize that we kids didn't know him as well as my mother and grandmother but come on! Someone dies and you don't even mention his name? They did the same thing at a dinner we had when my grandfather died. Which is funny because my Uncle Bruce was the only one who said anything about the man and that was only after he'd had a few drinks and he and I were alone."

"So, the two of you were close?" Gary asked.

I turned to look at Gary. I still wasn't exactly sure how to answer. It required some consideration. But I think Gary took my silence for something else.

"You don't have to tell me," he said. "I don't mean to bring up any painful memories or anything."

"No," I said, "it's nothing like that. I'm just trying to figure out what the question really means."

"What do you mean?"

"Well, it's like I said before. I hadn't heard from him in a long time. I wrote to him and he never wrote back. So, you might think we weren't close. And I guess maybe we weren't. I know my brother and sister weren't close to him. They didn't feel about him the way I did, but they didn't know him like I did, either."

The truth was that I loved the man more than anyone else in my family even though I had barely known him. That seemed like a strange idea, but Uncle Bruce really had meant so much more to me than anyone else. We had shared something, something that didn't require us to see each other or for him to write back, because I know he had felt it, too. I just think that he didn't know how to feel what he felt. How could I express that in words without sounding like a complete idiot? It's not like I was going to tell Gary *why* I felt that way. That was none of his business. But, if I could, I wanted to make him understand.

"You ever have that friend — or relative — that one guy who you could tell anything to?" I finally said. "You know, someone you feel like you can tell him anything and he won't get mad. He won't judge you for that. He just listens and makes you feel better just because he was there."

"Yeah," Gary said. "Maybe once or twice."

"That was Uncle Bruce. That's the way he made me feel. No judgment, no criticism, no blame. He just listened." It was more than that, so much more, but I couldn't bring myself to include Gary. Not in the way I had included Uncle Bruce. Sure, I liked Gary and considered him a friend, but he and I weren't *that* close. There were some things I simply couldn't tell him. And I certainly wasn't going to spill my guts in a public place like the pool hall.

"I get it," he replied. "It's good to have people like that in your life. Well, I mean, it's good that you had that kind of a relationship with him."

Gary actually blushed a little. He must have seen it as a faux pas. Yes, it was past tense now. I had *had* that in my life, but he was gone now.

"He was the coolest," I said. "Just a nice guy." I looked again at Gary. He was a nice guy, too. In some ways, he reminded me of Uncle Bruce, which was funny. I probably knew Gary much better than I had ever really known Uncle Bruce. Yet, I couldn't bring myself to tell Gary the whole story. Not yet anyway. Maybe someday.

"How's your Mom taking it?" he asked. "He was younger than her, right?"

"Yeah, he was seven or eight years younger. How's she taking it? Beats me. I don't think I've ever seen that woman express an emotion. You know, when my grandfather — her father — died, I never saw her shed a tear."

"Everyone grieves in their own way."

"I guess so."

The four players from the back table came up to the counter with their tray of balls and I cashed them out. I turned off the ball polishing machine and switched out the polished balls for the ones that had been turned in.

"Certainly not like I imagined it should be," I said. "Not a tear to be found in the house tonight."

But something about what I said stopped me. It was true that I had never seen my mother shed a tear for her father nor had I seen her shed a tear for her baby brother. There was something in my head, some dusty memory that I couldn't quite touch. Was it just that they were showing strength rather than vulnerability, stoicism versus emotion? If that were the case, it actually pissed me off even more than if they had openly wept in each other's arms. No wonder I had such issues with my own emotions. That's probably what kept Uncle Bruce so distant as well. No one in this family was willing to show any vulnerability, any chink in their armor. I know I never dared. Any time I had, I was ridiculed and belittled. No one dared to show that they cared. Or maybe they didn't care. No, Uncle Bruce had done it. That cool, strong, stoic, and tough man had been vulnerable. He had let me see it. More than that, he had let me show it without fear. Did all the others have feelings that they were afraid to show? Were they so afraid that they couldn't shed a single tear for those they claimed to love? And worse was the thought that followed: was I destined to be just like them?

Another table finished their play and I cashed them out. I was about to sit back down when the back door opened. I looked up to see who had entered and my breath caught in my throat.

The man who walked in was about forty with cropped hair and clean-shaven face, accompanied by a young kid. With the button-down shirt and pressed slacks, he looked completely respectable. He looked at me. He recognized me and even with the short hair and no mustache, I recognized him. And that's when time seemed to stop. All the sound around me reduced to just the clink of the billiard balls and the sound of my own heartbeat. I couldn't hear my breathing because it had stopped. Then there was nothing in my ears but the thump, thump, ba-thump of my heart. I heard the creak of the hinges as the door closed behind him. When it thudded closed, it was like everything opened up and I was hit by a wall of sound, everything flooding into my ears even louder than before. As silent as it had been a moment before, it was now a cacophony. The loud mumble of voices, the colliding balls, the electronic noise from the video games, the calliope that was the song on the jukebox. It melded back into the regular noise of the pool hall and the arcade next door. I was still acutely aware of it all, but at least it returned to normal. And in all that…sonicity, I clearly heard the man say, "Come on, let's go somewhere else."

"I wanna play some pool," his companion said. He was a young kid, probably not yet fifteen.

"So, let's go play in the bar." The man said, his eyes never leaving mine.

"I ain't old enough to get in the bars."

"Don't worry about it. Anybody can get into Backstreets."

I heard a final "Those tables suck" from his companion as the two turned around and left the pool hall, the door closing quietly behind them.

"Hey, Kelly," I heard Gary say, "you alright?"

I lowered myself slowly to the stool where I had been sitting. "Yeah, it's cool."

"You sure? You looked like you were about to pass out there for a second."

I gave him a smile. At least, that's what I tried to do. It might have come across as less than that.

"Just…just the whole day finally hit me, I guess."

"I told Melissa I was working all night, so if you need to go, you can."

"Nah, I'm good. Just need to catch my breath."

"You're sure?" I could hear real concern in Gary's voice and see it on his face. He showed me more emotion in that one moment than my entire family had shown all night.

"I'm sure." I gave Gary another smile, and I felt like this one actually looked like a smile. "Really, you can go if you want."

He slapped me on the shoulder. "Go home and miss all of this?"

I returned his smile with a bigger one of my own, then opened the cash drawer. We always kept a few bills marked for the jukebox. "Well, then, play some better music," I said and handed him two marked one-dollar bills.

He went to the jukebox to pick out a few good songs and my smile faded as soon as his back was turned. Jesus, it's amazing how the sight of one fucking asshole could make my whole night worse than it already was. More disturbing memories were the last things I really needed.

6

Moe, 1979

It was my first Friday night home without Danny being around. More than likely I would have been spending the night at his place if he hadn't moved away. Now I was stuck trying to find something to do all by myself. Even Jay was gone to his mother's for the weekend. Mom and Dad were out doing whatever they did on a Friday night, and Kevin had left soon after dinner to spend the night out with his friends. That left me alone at home with Karen. I grabbed my bike and walked it down to the road just as the sun was setting. I didn't know where I was going or what I was going to do, but I knew I needed to find somewhere to go before she realized she and I were alone and she made my night hell.

The cemetery was already looking pretty creepy in the fading light, but I pedaled past it as fast as I could. Then I was coasting down the hill toward the bridge. Moe gave me a wave from his porch, and I waved back as I flew past and continued across the bridge. Just for the heck of it, I turned up Livingston Road and headed toward Jay's house. I knew he wasn't there, but I couldn't think of anywhere else to go. I figured I could ride past, then turn around and head back to the bridge. I'd probably just end up going home after that, but at least I was out of the house for a while.

Jay's house was dark except for the light shining from the porch. There was no car in the driveway, so I figured Jay's dad was out. He might have been at the same bar as my father, wherever he was. I didn't know where he and Mom went on Friday nights, but I knew they didn't go out together; they took separate cars. Did they go to bars or someone else's house? They spent so much time somewhere else, but I never knew where or what they did.

I dropped my bike on the front sidewalk and walked up the front porch steps and approached the door. I don't know why. No one was home. And it's not like I was going to break in. Still, I peeked in the front window. The porch light gave off too much light for me to see anything. I came down the porch steps and was about to head down the driveway and around the side of the house when I heard a car approaching. I crouched down in the dark next to the house. What did I think I was doing? If it was Jay's father, he would pull in the driveway and the headlights would shine on me no matter where I tried to hide. The shadows would be gone. But the car kept going past the house and up the road. As soon as the taillights disappeared, I bolted for my bike and set off back down Livingston Road toward the bridge. I wasn't really doing anything bad but coming that close to getting caught scared the life out of me. My heart was still pounding in my chest when I got to the bridge and it wasn't from pedaling the bike. I had coasted all the way down the hill from Jay's place.

I stopped my bike on the walkway of the bridge and leaned it against the railing. The moon was coming up and looked like it was full. It shone a lot of light onto the falls as they roared below me. The water was a silvery foam as it came rushing over the rocks and collided with the big cement pier in the middle of the bridge. They called the churning water the Whirlpool and said it could drown you if you got caught in it. The pier was where some kids jumped into the river. I never could bring myself to do it. It was, like, twenty feet to the water, and there was no way to tell where the rocks were down there or if you'd hit a more shallow part of the river. I didn't want to get hurt. But it was fun to watch the others do it. Even my sister had finally decided to jump last year. We hadn't been down swimming yet this fall, but I figured she'd go for it again if she got the chance. I spit over the railing and watched my tiny drop disappear in the churning water below.

I pulled my bike from the railing and got back on. I rode down to the corner where the streetlight lit up the intersection. I saw that Moe was still sitting on his porch. I rode my bike along the edge of the circle of light thrown onto the pavement. Doing so drew my bike closer to Moe's house. I could see he had a bottle of Michelob on the table next to him.

"Hey," he said as I rolled past.

I steered my bike around the rest of the circle and started back again.

"Hey," I said as I rolled past him.

I started around again and as I passed Moe's porch, he called out once more. I stopped this time to talk with him. His face was hidden by the darkness, but his mustache and chin lit up red when he took a drag from his cigarette. Then the light from the cigarette faded and left his eyes in darkness. He became a shadow again when he finished and blew smoke into the night.

"Where's your partner in crime?" he asked.

"He's at his mother's for the weekend."

Moe picked up his beer and took a swig, then held it in his lap. "Nobody else to hang with?"

I shrugged my shoulders.

"Well, you're free to hang out here with me," he said. He motioned to the empty chair on the porch.

I couldn't help but feel a little excitement at the offer. A grownup was asking me to hang out with him. And Moe was alright. He mostly kept to himself, but he was usually on his porch in the evening with his beer and waving to everybody that drove by. Once in a while he would even play Frisbee with the kids when they hung out at the bridge. He would be lifeguard and watch us when we were swimming. And I didn't care what Jay thought about Firebirds. I thought it was a great car and I thought Moe was pretty cool for having one. When he took it out, the whole town knew it because he roared up the main drag as he headed into Potsdam. It was definitely awesome to be invited onto his porch. Still, I did my best to play it cool as I set my bike down in the yard and stepped up and took the seat next to him.

For a while, we just sat there as the night brightened with the rising moon, not saying anything. He sipped his beer, and I caught him looking my way, at which point I looked away fast. God, he must have thought I was just a stupid little kid sitting there with nothing to say. I had a couple of thoughts in my head, but they all seemed dumb, so I kept my mouth shut.

"How was your summer?" he finally asked.

"Pretty good," I said, surprised by how loud my voice sounded in the silence.

"I don't think I saw you around much."

"We were at our camp at Lake Ozonia."

"That would explain your absence," Moe said matter-of-factly and sipped his beer again.

"We came down once a week to do stuff like mow the lawn and wash our clothes, but that was about it."

"Yup."

"It's nice up there. I get to go swimming and skateboarding down the hills. I go hiking in the woods."

"Sounds like fun."

"Yeah, it is," I said. I leaned back in my chair and tried to tip back on the back legs like Moe was doing. I looked over at Moe again and saw he was looking at me. I think my sudden silence was making him uncomfortable. Then he said something I didn't expect.

"You want a beer?" he asked.

"What? No. I mean, I'm not old enough to drink."

Moe snorted and smiled. "How old are you?"

"Twelve," I replied.

"Hell, that's old enough in my book." He got up from his chair and reached for the handle of the screen door. "But you can't drink it out here on the porch," he said as he disappeared into the house.

I wasn't sure what to do. No one had ever offered me a beer before. I knew it was wrong. But, really, it was just a beer. My father drank them, even my Grandpa John had drank them. And I'd already smoked pot with Jay. So, was this really so bad? Besides, if I got caught, it would be Moe who would get in trouble, not me. Right?

"You comin'?"

I looked up and saw Moe standing inside the screen door. What kind of a kid would I look like if I didn't do it? I pulled myself up from the chair. He held the screen door for me as I stepped into the living room and then he closed the main door behind me.

"I'm cool with it, but I don't need nosy neighbors turning me in. Hope you don't mind."

"No, that's cool," I said as I looked around the living room. It was small and, I guess, a bit shabby. I didn't know what Moe did for a living, but it could not have paid well. The couch was old and dirty and torn. The coffee table held a huge ashtray that looked like it was made from a hubcap or something and there were a few car magazines and empty cigarette packs lying around. I saw what looked like the edge of a Hustler magazine buried under some of the other books; the last two letters — ER — and what looked like a boob and a nipple were visible. The whole place smelled of cigarettes. And something else. Something like dirt but not dirt. I wasn't sure what it was. But that was okay with me. Not only had a grownup invited me to hang out with him on his porch, but he had also invited me inside, too. For a beer.

"Come on into the kitchen," Moe said as he stepped through a door at the back of the living room. He flipped a light switch that bathed the room in a dull yellow light from a fixture in the middle of the ceiling. I glanced up to see that the globe surrounding the single bulb was stained and yellow and filled with dead bugs. It didn't offer a lot of light for the room. There was a door on the back wall that I assumed led out to the backyard or at least what there was of a backyard. It was mostly weeds and overgrown shrubs out back. I remembered a cement patio out there, too. The two windows — one over the sink and one next to the back door — were both covered with heavy curtains. I guess Moe liked his privacy.

"Here you go," he said as he held out a Michelob he had retrieved from the fridge. He twisted the cap off before he gave it to me.

I have to admit that I'd only had one other beer in my entire life and, really, that was just a sip my grandfather had let me sneak when Grandma wasn't looking. I think I had been about ten at the time. I remembered I didn't like it much. So, I was slow to raise the bottle to my mouth. I could see that Moe was watching me pretty closely and I didn't want to seem like some kind of baby about it. I pressed the bottle to my lips and took a big gulp.

"There you go," he said.

It's hard to describe what it tasted like. It was harsh and stale and nothing I really wanted to drink. But I swallowed the mouthful of liquid and took another, smaller sip. The first one landed hard in my stomach, but at least I was going to keep it down and keep drinking so Moe would hopefully think I was cool.

"Nothing wrong with a cold beer on a warm night," he said as he took a seat at the table in the middle of the kitchen. There was another chair on the other side of the table, so I took it.

"It's what weekends were made for," I said, feeling stupid as soon as I said it. But Moe seemed to like it. He smiled and held his bottle up to me. I held mine up and he clinked his bottle against mine. He took a swig and I did, too. It was awesome! I felt so cool, drinking a beer with a guy who drove a Firebird. How much cooler could it get?

"You smoke?" Moe asked.

"Cigarettes? No."

"Good," he said as he pulled a cigarette from the pack on the table. "These things'll kill you." He lit the cigarette and took a deep drag from it. "But I wasn't talkin' about cigarettes." He leaned in over the table and looked me in the eye. "I mean, do you, you know, smoke?"

I wasn't sure what he meant. I told him I didn't smoke cigarettes. What else was there to smoke?

Oh! Did he mean…?

"You mean?" I asked, more sheepishly than I had planned and my voice kind of tapered off.

"Yeah," he said and leaned back in his chair, a broad grin on his face. "You know what I'm talkin' about, right?"

"I think so. I mean, yeah. Yeah, I smoke." And then I thought to use that term Jay had used. "I party."

"I thought so. You looked like a cool kid to me."

Did I? Did I look cool to him? No one had ever said I looked cool. I took another drink from my beer and swallowed it down.

"Then, you're in luck, my friend." Moe got up from the table. "I just got in some really excellent California Sense. Wait right here."

He stepped out of the room, leaving me alone with my thoughts and my beer. How amazing was this? Not only had I been invited onto the porch and then into his house, but he had given me a beer and now we were going to smoke pot. Maybe it had been a good thing that Jay was gone for the weekend. Of course, considering that I hadn't really felt much of anything when I had smoked with Jay, Moe was probably wasting good pot on me. But it might be fun to watch him get stoned. It was fun watching Jay. At least, I assumed he was talking about pot. I didn't know what he meant by California Sense.

Moe came back with a small tray that had a plastic bag filled with what I guessed was the California Sense as well as a Bic lighter and a small glass pipe. The pipe was mostly blue, but it had strings of other colors weaved into it. He sat back down, setting the tray down in front of him. He took a small pinch of the weed from the bag and stuffed it into the bowl of the glass pipe. Another little pinch and it was full.

"This is some really good shit," he said and held the pipe and Bic out to me.

My father sometimes smoked a tobacco pipe, so I had some idea of what I was supposed to do, but when I held the flame to the bowl and sucked, nothing seemed to happen. The flame barely touched the pot, and it wouldn't burn.

"You ever smoke a pipe with a carb?" Moe asked.

"A what?" I asked stupidly. "No, I've only ever smoked joints." And really, it had been only one joint.

"A carburetor. Let me show you." Moe took the pipe and lighter. "There's a little hole on the side here to let in air." As soon as he pointed it out, I saw it, and he put his index finger over the hole. "Then, when the bowl is lit, you release the carb."

Moe then demonstrated how the "carb" worked by putting his finger over the hole, lighting the bowl, then lifting his finger, and taking a long drag from the pipe. He sucked in one more time and handed the pipe and lighter over to me. The weed was still burning well enough, so all I had to do was put my finger over the carb and suck. I let my finger off the carb and my lungs immediately filled with smoke. Try as I might, I couldn't help but cough. The first hack was more of a spit as I tried to keep from coughing, but then it became a full-blown fit.

I'll give Moe credit for not laughing at me. I was so embarrassed that I couldn't hold my smoke. But it was only the second time I had ever smoked, and it was the first time on a pipe, so I hadn't known what to expect. I coughed some more. It felt like it would never stop.

"Take a drink of your beer," Moe advised. "That can help."

I did as I was told, and the beer did cool my throat and calm the cough. I handed the pipe and lighter back to Moe.

"That one'll hit you," he said.

I didn't know what he meant by that, but I gave him a smile to show I was cool. At least I hoped he still thought I was cool. He took his own pull from the pipe and handed it back to me. I was much more careful when I took my next drag. It was smaller and I didn't inhale so deeply. I was able to hold it without a single cough.

"Trooper!" Moe said, congratulating me. "Let's do something."

At the moment, I didn't want to do anything but sit at the table and recover. I took another sip of my beer after I exhaled.

"Like what?" I asked.

Moe answered quickly. "How about some cards? Got a deck right here." He picked up the deck that was on the table and set it in front of me. The top card was a five of hearts and it had a nude lady on it. I picked up the deck and leafed through the other cards. They all had pictures of naked women. I'd seen boobs before, but there were so many women, a different one for each card. It made me feel a little funny to be looking at them.

"Spades?" I said absently as I looked through the deck.

"Nah, something more interesting. You know how to play poker?"

I knew of poker and knew some of the combinations, like a pair or a full house, I just wasn't sure what beat what in the game.

"Yeah, we can play poker," I said.

Moe looked around the kitchen. "Damn!" he said. "We got nothing to use for chips." He got up from the table and started looking through the cupboards. "Maybe I've got some crackers or something." He opened one door after another without finding anything. "The cupboards are bare," he said as he looked.

"Like Old Mother Hubbard," I said and giggled. Wow, what was this that I was feeling? I was lightheaded. When I turned my head, it felt like my brain was a second behind my body. I turned my head again and waited for my brain to catch up.

"Old Mother Hubbard went to the cupboard to get her poor dog a bone," Moe said, then turned toward me, crouching forward like some kind of monster. "But, when she bent over, old Rover drove her, and she found he had a bone of his own!"

I burst out laughing as if I'd never heard anything so funny. I was lightheaded, giddy (was that even a word?), and just felt…funny. But I liked it. A lot. Wow, was this what it was like to be stoned? The first time I had smoked with Jay, I hadn't felt anything. But this…. This was fucking wild!

"So, no chips?" I asked when I got myself back under control.

Moe sat back down at the table, took a drink from his beer. "No chips. Need another beer?"

I lifted the bottle and realized it was nearly empty. At some point, I had finished most of my beer. Either I had been thirstier than I thought or time had played a trick on me. "Yeah, I guess I do."

Moe got back up from the table, opened the fridge, and took out two more beers. He sat back down and put one of them in front of me. He hadn't opened this one for me. He twisted the top off his beer, then put the cap between his thumb and middle finger. He held his hand up near his ear, then seemed to snap his fingers, and the bottle cap flew across the room like a tiny Frisbee, bounced off the wall, and landed somewhere on the kitchen floor. He looked at me, challenging me to try. I twisted the cap off and tried to do the same as he had done but only managed to throw the cap onto the table. Still, I couldn't help but laugh at my feeble attempt. It probably wasn't cool, but I didn't care. And Moe laughed with me, so it must have been cool enough.

"I got it!" Moe said suddenly.

"What?"

"We can play strip poker!"

"What's that?" I asked. "How do you play?"

"It's just like regular poker, but instead of chips and an ante, the one who loses the hand has to remove a piece of clothing."

"Like if you lose, you have to take off your shirt?"

"Or pants or whatever you have left."

What a crazy idea! But why not? We were just a couple of guys hanging out in a kitchen on a Friday night getting drunk and stoned. Seemed reasonable, I guess.

Moe grabbed the deck, shuffled the cards, and started dealing. "You in?" he asked.

I sat up in my chair, took a swig of my beer, and said, "Sure."

I don't know how long we'd played or even how well I was doing. For some rounds, I had to trust that Moe was being truthful about who won. Did a four-of-a-kind beat a full house? I didn't know. And I really didn't care. I was having so much fun. I was on my third beer and Moe had lit the pipe again while I was dealing a hand of what I think was Seven Card Stud. But even the names of the different games escaped me. At the end of the last hand, I was down to my underpants and that was all. It looked like Moe was in his underwear (he wore boxers, which I thought was cool) and his socks. I didn't even know or care what time it was.

Moe sat back in his chair, the deck of cards in his hands, and looked over at me. I sat back in my own chair, took a swig of my beer, and smiled.

Moe smiled back. "You're stoned."

"Yeah," I said, "I think I am."

We both laughed.

"One more hand?" he asked.

I looked down at my underpants, then looked up again. "That might be all I've got left!"

We both laughed again. Moe leaned forward to shuffle the cards. He shuffled once, then went to shuffle again and the cards flew from his hands. Naked women went flying across the room, over the table, and onto the floor.

"Oopsie!" he said and laughed. "Lemme get those."

He swept up the cards on the table in front of him, picked up some of the cards near him on the floor.

"Going down!" he cried, and then he disappeared under the table.

I let out a laugh and leaned my head back and closed my eyes, reveling in the great time I was having tonight. I was drunk or I was stoned or I was both. I didn't care. It felt good, and it was nice to feel good for a change.

I didn't really notice it at first. I thought maybe it was something from the high, but something was pressing against my crotch. Just a light touch, really, but I felt it. Was there a card there that Moe was grabbing? Whatever it was, there was nothing I could do to stop my…reaction to it. My eyes flew open, but I didn't move. In another moment, I knew what it was, I just didn't know what to do. My head was too foggy, and I didn't want to piss off Moe. And it did feel good. Like everything else this night, it felt good. Maybe he *was* just grabbing for a card that had landed in my lap. But, when I felt the elastic band of my briefs being pulled, I knew that wasn't true. He tucked the band below my balls. I was exposed, completely. And I was frozen in my seat. I didn't even dare raise my head from its position on the back of the chair. When I felt myself engulfed in a warm wetness, I knew only one thing could be happening. I squeezed my eyes shut, felt the waves wash over me.

When it was done, he pulled himself back up into his chair, crawling out from underneath the table. I still hadn't moved from my original position. My head still lay back against the chair, and I stared at that dirty yellow light fixture, my breathing was fast and shallow. I reached under the table and pulled my underpants back over myself. When I finally sat back up in the chair, I couldn't bring myself to look at him. I looked at my beer bottle. I would've taken a drink, but it was empty.

A plastic bag landed on the table in front of me. It was the pot.

"You can have it," he said as he pulled on his pants. "You earned it." He picked up the rest of his clothes and started out of the kitchen. "You can stay if you want. My bedroom is the second door. But if you wanna leave, turn off the lights and lock the front door before you go."

And he was gone. I heard a door close. I assumed it was his bedroom door.

My socks were lying next to the chair and I put them on, left sock first, then the right one. As I reached for my jeans, I stepped in something on the floor, something wet, a wet spot. I picked up my foot and looked to see if I had spilled beer on the floor. Whatever it was wasn't yellow like beer; it looked like milk or something. I picked up my jeans from where they were crumpled in a pile next to my chair. I pulled them on one leg at a time. The sound of the zipper was hard in my ears. I sat down again to slip my sneakers on my feet. I pulled my t-shirt over my head and stuck my small arms through the holes.

The pot was there in its plastic bag, wrapped up and ready to go. It was mine for the taking. He said so. He said I had earned it. It was mine. I could take it. It was a lot of pot. It would get me stoned a lot. But I would need papers or something. I had no way of smoking it. I looked across the table to where he had been sitting. The pipe was still there. The lighter, too. I stood up. I stuffed the bag in the left front pocket of my jeans, walked over to the tray on his side of the table. I put the pipe and lighter in my right front pocket.

The light switch was right by the door as I left the kitchen, so I switched it off. I couldn't find a switch for the light in the living room. Maybe it was on the ugly lamp in the corner by the couch. I didn't look. I turned the lock in the doorknob and closed the door behind me as I stepped out onto the porch. I made sure not to slam the screen door.

My bike was laying where I had left it in front of the house. I could see it clearly in the light from the moon and the streetlight. The moon looked like it was all the way across the sky from where it had been earlier. What time was it? Did it really matter? I walked my bike across the intersection and back to the bridge. I stopped before I got to the pier in the middle of the bridge and leaned the bike against the railing. I stepped around the bike to lean over and looked down at the dark water below. It was shallow here. The sound of the falls roared in my ears.

It was my own fault. I was the one who went up on his porch, drank his beer, smoked his pot. Besides, it's not like I stopped him from doing it.

I could just see bubbles floating by in the water as it flowed under the bridge. I watched them as long as I could, leaning over the railing a little to see them disappear past my view.

I didn't want to do it. I didn't want to like it. But I didn't stop it. And, it had felt good. Did that make me gay?

My face was hot. My clothes didn't feel right on my body. I tugged at my t-shirt to try to make it sit right. There was a wet spot on the bottom of my left sock. I didn't know what to make of the night. Worse, what if Moe told someone? But who would he tell? Karen or Kevin for a start. He knew everybody in town. He could tell anybody he wanted to. What if he was to tell them?

I looked down at the water again. This part of the river, so close to the rocky bank, was only about a foot or so deep. Nobody jumped from here. I wondered if it would hurt if I did.

Maybe it was my buzz wearing off, but I was suddenly tired. Really tired. I needed to go home. I wanted to go to bed. I pulled my bike up, turned it around, and rode down to the intersection again. Out of the corner of my eye, I saw the light still burning in the living room window of his house as I sped by and pedaled up the hill. By the time I made it to the top, my legs were so tired I could barely keep up my speed as I passed the church and the cemetery. But I was turning into the driveway soon enough, dropping my bike back by the barn. I stepped to the side of the barn to take a leak so I wouldn't have to worry about using the bathroom when I got inside.

Only my mother's car was in the driveway, so Dad was still out. I couldn't be sure that Mom was even in bed to say nothing of whether or not she was asleep. The house was dark; she was probably in bed at the very least. Had she even noticed I hadn't been home? Hadn't been in my bed? She never checked on us. That was just something TV moms did. I crept up the steps to the porch, trying my best not to make any of the boards creak. I opened the door as slowly as I could, again trying to avoid any noise at all. I was creeping through the house just as slowly when I saw the lights of my father's van coming up the driveway. Not only did I need to get upstairs and into my room fast now, but the noise of his entry would mask any noises I might make. So, while I still took the stairs slower than usual, I didn't worry so much about the noise as Dad came into the house.

The bedroom was dark with only a sliver of light from the moon coming in the window; it was hidden by the trees outside. I undressed quickly and quietly, climbed up into my bunk and pulled the blankets up to my chin. I turned onto my side, faced the wall, and curled up into a tight ball, closed my eyes, and hoped for sleep to come quickly. I just wanted to sleep. Sleep forever and never wake up.

7

Bali Hai, 1994

Eleven o'clock was the usual closing time on a Thursday night, but since both the pool hall and the arcade were dead at ten-thirty, Gary decided we could close a little early. He'd hung around all night to keep me company, helping me clean up and cash out the pool hall receipts before he bid me good-night and hopped into his little white Honda Accord and headed home. I checked the contents of the inner pocket of my denim jacket and thought about heading upstairs to my apartment, but it was still early. I had a few hours before the bars would close.

My current favorite hangout was the Bali Hai. Being a college town, I had several bars I could choose from. Each one had their own drink specials to lure the students in. I knew I didn't want to go to Backstreets and chance running into Moe. Besides, I had my own drink special waiting for me at the Bali. You see, the bartender — they called him Tigger — he worked Thursday nights and he was a big fan of this football video game we had in the arcade. So, when he came in, I made sure he didn't pay for his games and, in turn, when I came into the bar, he made sure I didn't pay for my beer. Oh, I'd make every effort to pay by laying my five-dollar bill on the bar. He would take it and return with my change: five one-dollar bills. It was a great arrangement because the only people getting screwed were the owners. Tigger and I made out alright.

As expected, being a weeknight, the bar was nearly empty when I stepped inside. It was called the Bali Hai because it had, at one time, tried hard for a tropical theme. But that theme had been new decades ago and now just looked like a sad tourist trap you might find on a backstreet of Freeport. The fake grass-thatched roofing over the bar was thinning like male pattern baldness, the huts that formed seating areas on one side of the bar were leaning in an invisible hurricane wind, and the grassy carpet was, in many places, worn down to the hardwood floor beneath. But it was a college bar. No one came for the ambience; they came for the cheap alcohol, the dark corners, and the lighted dance floor. The owner knew this, which is why she didn't waste any time or money fixing up the aging and dilapidated fixtures and furniture.

"Hey," said a high-pitched voice from the corner of the bar.

I turned toward the sound and saw Mary Ellen getting up from her stool. She came over and gave me a hug before dragging me back to the bar to sit next to her. She and Tigger and a couple of students were the only ones in the place.

In any other situation, Mary Ellen would have been an incredibly attractive young woman. She was still good-looking, but her twenty-four years had been hard on her. She was small, only about five feet tall, and thin as a rail, dirty blonde hair flowing down past her shoulders. I think she tried hard to maintain that tiny waist, which made me wonder how she was able to do it when it seemed like she drank her weight in beer every time I saw her. She was a student at the state college with a double-major in biology and art. Something about becoming a science illustrator or some such thing. She was pretty intelligent when she was sober. We'd had our share of intense conversations while slowly getting plowed. But, once she had a few drinks, she became trashy and belligerent. And that was too bad. Like I said, she was a nice girl. The worst part was that she was also a single mother. I'd never met her daughter, but she would talk about her on occasion. I could only assume Mary Ellen had a babysitter for the girl while she was at the bar, which seemed to be every night. How she could afford it all, I'd never know.

I almost had a chance to find out about the babysitter once. It had been a Thursday night as well, about a month ago. Mary Ellen was a little more loaded than usual and some townie had been hitting on her most of the night. I wasn't too far gone and could see that she wasn't enjoying the guy's advances, so I sidled up next to her and struck up a conversation. The guy took the hint after a few minutes and wandered off. But, as drunk as she was, I didn't trust her going home alone. She agreed to let me walk her there. She lived a few blocks away, off Market Street in an apartment on Walnut Street. When we got to her front door, she took me in her arms and flattened her lips against mine. It was a very hot, very passionate kiss. Her hands were all over me. And then she asked me if I wanted to come inside. Oh my God, I remember thinking, this girl wants me. But then my rational mind kicked in and realized that she was very, very drunk. If I were to go inside, I'd be taking advantage of her in that state. She wasn't sober enough to consent to anything. And as much as my dick protested by standing up for itself, I told her no. I held the door for her and watched her step into the front hallway and then disappear through a door on the right that led to her apartment.

I argued with myself for the entire walk home over whether I should have gone in, but in the end, I knew I had done the right thing. The next time I saw her, it was like she didn't have any memory of what had happened. From that night on, I decided to keep an eye on her and try to keep her out of trouble. Sometimes she didn't make it easy.

"Haven't seen you in a while," she said as we sat down.

"I've been around," I said. "But I'm working a lot of hours and had some family stuff to take care of."

"Right, right," she said distractedly. I could tell she'd already had a few.

Tigger brought me my usual beer, Molson Golden, and we went through the Dance of the Five-Dollar Bill. She held her own bottle up to me as I was raising mine. We clinked the bottles together and each took a drink.

"How's your life?" I asked.

"Ugh, school, kid, school, kid, and school," she replied. "It feels like it's never going to end."

"I remember that feeling. At least the school part. But I had work instead of a kid."

"And now that it's over?"

"Well." I took another drink of my beer. "It didn't end the way I wanted it to. Now it's just work."

"That's something," she said.

I chuckled. "It ain't much." I took another swig of my beer, a long one.

"Tigger," she said to the bartender. "We need something more."

Tigger was also a student at Potsdam. He had come up from Rochester to study anthropology. I always wondered what made these kids choose Potsdam for their education. Was the school really that good? I'd had no choice as I couldn't afford to go anywhere else. And, as it turned out, I couldn't afford Potsdam, either. Tigger was a big fellow, a little on the heavy side, and a bit of a strange dude. Friendly enough, but very quiet. Not what you'd expect in a bartender. Take the deal we had to trade video games for beer. We'd never spoken about it. It was just a thing we did. I'm not sure he and I had ever had a conversation that lasted longer than five minutes.

"What are you thinking?" he asked Mary Ellen.

"Some better music for a start!" she replied.

"I'll see what I can do," Tigger said with a smile. He was both bartender and DJ for the rest of the night and had access to the DJ booth above the dance floor.

"And then we need shots!"

"Of what?" he asked.

Mary Ellen turned to me. "Of what?" she asked me.

I shifted the contents of my inner pocket a little. "I don't need a shot," I replied.

"Well, sure, no one *needs* a shot, except maybe for the flu." She laughed at her own joke. "But what do we *want*?"

"Something cheap," I said. "I don't get paid till tomorrow."

"Bah." She pulled a twenty from the small pile of bills in front of her. "No problem. I'm buying. Tigger, what do you suggest?"

"Depends on what you're in the mood for." Tigger dealt with the drunks with a calm that would impress a priest.

"Nothing too harsh," Mary Ellen said. She waved her hand like a Southern belle with a fan. "I have a sensitive palette."

She looked at me again, then cast her gaze at Tigger, then looked off to her right at nothing. I looked to Tigger and he returned my smile.

"Something smooth?" Tigger asked.

"Yes!" she responded and looked back at him. "Smooth. Like my friend here." She put her arm around my shoulder then and pulled me toward her.

"I got just the thing." Tigger disappeared around the other side of the bar.

Mary Ellen rocked me back and forth, her arm still around me. I got the feeling I would be walking her home again tonight.

"Don't you have class in the morning?" I asked.

"Yeah, but not till later."

"What about your daughter?"

"She's got school earlier than me."

"I know. Shouldn't you get home to her so you can get her off to school on time?"

"She'll be fine. My…Margaret will see that she gets to school."

I must have said something to upset her because Mary Ellen took her arm from around my shoulders. She picked up her beer and took a drink as she sank into her stool. She looked away again to nothing off to her right.

"Here we go," Tigger said as he came back around the bar with three full shot glasses. He set one down in front of me and one in front of Mary Ellen. He kept the third for himself.

"What's this?" Mary Ellen asked.

"Something smooth," Tigger replied. "On the house."

She and I picked up our shot glasses and the three of us clinked the glasses together. And as if on cue, all three of us slammed back our shots at the same time.

Yup, it was smooth. I'd had it before. And peach schnapps had to be one of the smoothest shots out there.

"Oh, Tigger," Mary Ellen said. "That was perfect. Just what I was wanting. Now, about that music."

"Can I get another beer before you play DJ?" I asked.

"Me, too, please," Mary Ellen said.

Tigger brought us each a beer. He took Mary Ellen's money, pretended to take mine, then went to change the music.

"Sorry if I upset you," I said.

"About what?" she asked.

I couldn't tell if she had truly forgotten or if she was just being polite and moving on. I guess it didn't matter. We both took long drinks from our beers.

I was on my third beer when I heard the front door open, and I turned to watch Moe and his young friend walk into the bar. Jesus, there was no escaping my past tonight. Looking at Moe's companion again, I knew there was no way the kid was old enough to be in a bar. Maybe they had gotten away with it down at Backstreets, but I knew Tigger would not let them stay.

"You gotta be kidding," I heard Tigger say before he walked over to where they stood at the bar.

Mary Ellen grabbed me by the arm and rocked me back and forth to the music. She was saying something to me about the song that was playing, but I didn't pay her too much attention. My eyes were glued on the confrontation taking place at the other end of the bar. I couldn't hear what was being said, but I could see Moe waving his arms around as if trying to justify why they should be allowed to stay.

"You can leave," I heard Tigger say, "or I can call the cops and have them escort you out."

"Yeah," Moe said, probably thinking he'd call the barman's bluff. "You call the cops."

I pulled my arm from Mary Ellen's grip and pushed back my barstool noisily as I stood up. Moe must not have seen me when he first entered the place, but he looked up and saw me now. I might have been intimidated in the pool hall, but it was amazing how much courage and resolve a little alcohol can give you. There was no trepidation, no panic or anxiety now. I had never been much of a fighter, but I was ready and willing to defend Tigger and my bar if that was what was required.

"Fine," Moe said to Tigger while never taking his eyes off me. "Whatever."

Moe and his companion walked from the bar to the door. They had to pass me to get there, and I just stared Moe down as he shuffled by. He paused at the door after his companion was already out on the sidewalk. I don't know what he was thinking. I'm not sure what I was thinking. But I took a step toward him at that moment, and he made a quick exit to the street.

"You know that guy?" Mary Ellen asked when I sat back down next to her.

"Somebody from my past," I said. "Nobody, really."

"You sure? I've never seen you look so serious."

Tigger set another beer down in front of me. "On the house for backing me up."

I finished what little was left in my third beer and picked up the new one. "Cheers!" I said and took a drink.

We still had another hour till last call, but Mary Ellen said she was getting tired and needed to go. I insisted on walking her home. It's not that the streets of Potsdam were dangerous, I just didn't feel comfortable letting her stumble home on her own. I had a good buzz going for myself and considering how drunk she had been when I came in, I wasn't sure she'd be able to see straight enough to read the street signs.

"You're a good guy," she told me as we stood on the sidewalk outside the house on Walnut Street.

"That's what I've heard," I replied with a smile.

"No, I mean it!"

I smiled still and said, "I know."

"Are you alright to get home?"

"No problem. It's a nice night for a walk."

She gave me a hug and a kiss on the cheek before making her way up the porch steps and into the house. I waited there on the sidewalk until I saw the light of the front room come on. I saw her small silhouette and then the shadow of another person. That must have been Margaret, whoever she was. I had enough issues of my own that I didn't even want to think about worrying about hers. I headed back up Walnut Street and took a right when I reached the intersection with Market Street.

I wasn't lying about it being a nice night for a walk. It was just chilly enough to make the denim jacket worth wearing. Of course, I couldn't button it up due to the contents of the inside pocket, but that was okay. I stopped for a moment and looked up and down the empty street. No one was around, so no one would see. I pulled the bottle of Cutty Sark out of my inside pocket, twisted the cap off, and took a swig. Who needed a jacket when you had that to warm you up? I replaced the top and stuck the bottle back in the pocket.

I'd been waiting all night to take a drink from that bottle. I had pulled it from Uncle Bruce's hiding place in Grandma's barn. I'd thought about having a drink with Gary while we were closing up the pool hall, but it didn't seem right. Then I'd thought of suggesting it when Mary Ellen wanted to do shots. But that would have required me explaining why I had a bottle of Cutty Sark in my jacket. Besides, she'd wanted something smoother than whisky. And it just seemed right, somehow, that I would drink from the bottle alone. The only other person I really wanted to share it with was Uncle Bruce and that would never happen now.

What a fucking night! Between the family dinner, seeing Moe again after all this time, and then getting drunk with Mary Ellen, it turned into something else. I stopped again, checked the street, and then snuck another swig from the Cutty Sark before continuing on again. Was this my life? I wondered. Was I destined to be this person, this useless drunk stumbling home to his one-room apartment for the rest of my life? Where was the bright future? Where was the hope? Where were all those dreams I had once? Then again, had I ever had any dreams? I suppose everyone had them at one time or another. I could remember watching *Emergency!* on television when I was a kid and dreaming about being a paramedic 'cause Johnny Gage was so cool. I didn't even know what a paramedic was, but I wanted to be one. And an architect. I remember having dreams of being an architect and drawing designs on graph paper. They all ended up looking like the *Brady Bunch* house, but at least it was something. But all of that cost money. That was one thing they never told you: dreams cost money. Instead, they'd tell you that you could be anything you wanted to be.

Bullshit. That's what it was. You want to be an architect? Well, it's going to cost money to go to school for that. You want to be a doctor? Good luck with that. But, even more than money, it required someone believing in your dream. No matter what they said, no one achieved their dreams on their own. Even without direct help, you needed moral and emotional support. You had to have that. How else were you supposed to believe in your dreams — in yourself — if no one else did? I still remembered my grandmother's exact words when I informed her I was going back to college that first time. She had said, "It'll be good to have a couple of years of college under your belt." What the hell kind of support is that? She basically told me in that one sentence that she didn't believe I would finish. And, hey! Look at that! I didn't! I guess she was right all along.

About a block from the Arlington, still on Market Street, I stepped into the alleyway between the furniture store and the Town House restaurant. It was dark enough that no one would see me there unless they were really looking. I sat down and leaned against the wall. I pulled the bottle of Cutty Sark from my pocket and took several swigs from the bottle before I put it back in my jacket. There's a dream I had never had: being a bum sitting in the alley drinking from a bottle in his pocket. Truth be told, I hadn't sunk that low if I was drinking Cutty Sark. It wasn't a single malt, but it was better than the cheapest stuff. Now, if it had been a bottle of MadDog or something, *that* would be a real low. Or maybe some Boone's Farm Strawberry Hill. I laughed at the thought of that stuff. It had been fifteen years since I'd had a taste of that. And something sweeter than wine that night, too.

I held the bottle out so I could see it in the dim light. This was the legacy. This is what I had left of Uncle Bruce. I took another long drink from the bottle. It was still more than the rest of the family had ever given me.

8

Family Dinner, 1979

I didn't want to get out of bed. I had a headache and just felt kind of blah. But that wasn't even the reason. I couldn't get what had happened out of my head. I wanted to forget it, but I couldn't. I'd roll over in bed and try to go back to sleep, but it didn't help. To top it off, I felt so dirty, like I needed to get up and take a shower. So, I did. But it didn't help. I still felt like I wasn't clean, like no matter how much soap I used, I couldn't get it off of me. I took another shower about an hour later and it still didn't help. It was like there was nothing I could do to get the dirt off, to get clean again. After that, I went back to my room. I wanted to stay there, stay in my bed. Really, I just wanted to be left alone. But there was the dinner we had to go to at Grandma's.

I hated it when we all had to pile in the car because I always got stuck in the middle with Kevin on one side and Karen on the other. Even though I was smaller than both of them, I still felt squished. And the seat beneath me was lumpy. I had to try to keep my feet on the hump. If a foot slipped off either side, I was kicked by whichever sibling I offended. I didn't want to be around anyone anyway. I didn't want my shoulder touching Kevin's or my leg touching Karen's. I didn't want anyone touching me. I'd tried to act like I was sick when Mom called us to get in the car, hoping she'd let me stay home instead. But she wasn't buying it and pulled me off the bed. As I sat there between my siblings, I looked up to see the back of her head. She'd hardly said a word for the entire trip.

It was about a half-hour ride to Grandpa's. Well, I guess now it was just Grandma's house. This would be the first time seeing her since Grandpa died. I still hadn't cried, and I still didn't feel like I wanted to. Or needed to. I felt sad because I was going to miss seeing Grandpa John, but I wasn't so sad that I was going to cry. What was wrong with me?

Or maybe it wasn't me. Kevin hadn't cried. And Karen had only cried that morning on the bus. Mom hadn't cried, not that I'd seen anyway. And it was her father. Shouldn't she be even sadder than me? But then, how would I feel if it were my father?

My eyes moved to the back of my father's head. He was going bald and there were flecks of gray in the black hair that remained. He was getting old, and he would die someday. I wondered if I would cry when it happened. I closed my eyes and tried to imagine that it had been my father who had died instead of my grandfather. I tried to picture him in a coffin, although the only time I'd seen something like that was on TV. But I still tried, imagined him lying there in his dark suit, his hands crossed on his chest, eyes closed. I could see it in my head, but I still didn't feel the sadness that I thought I was supposed to feel. What did that mean? Was there something wrong with me that I couldn't cry for my grandfather or my father? Was I just dead inside? Did I just not care?

Dad turned the car into the driveway at Grandma's. The great red-and-white farmhouse dominated the left side of the driveway while the big red barn stood behind at the end. On the right side of the barn was a small carport and Grandpa's   or I guess, Grandma's — car was parked there. And just before the end of the driveway in front of the barn was a motorcycle. It was the same black bike that had pulled into our driveway a couple days earlier. I'd forgotten that he had gone up to the lake after he stopped at our house, and it hadn't even crossed my mind that he would be here. But it was a family dinner, and he was family. Of course he would be here. I found the thought of actually meeting him again both exciting and terrifying. He'd seemed kinda scary when he stopped by the house, but I still wanted to see him again.

We piled out of the back seat with Kevin nearly slamming the door on me. "I thought you were going out the other side," he said. He was up the steps of the porch and into the house before I could say anything. He knew I was coming out his door. He was just being mean, as usual. Karen was next into the house, followed by my mother and father. I was the last into the kitchen. Grandma was there standing by the stove, an apron of white with yellow flowers pinned to the dress she wore. It was deep blue with white polka dots. She wore it to many of the family get-togethers.

"Mom," my mother said, "I told you we were coming early to help with dinner."

"I know," Grandma replied, though she never looked up from the pot she was stirring. "But I needed something to do."

My mother went over to help her. "Is that Bruce's bike in the driveway?"

"Yes, he's around here somewhere," Grandma said.

Kevin and Karen went through the dining room and into the game room beyond. That's where the pool table was. I would have followed, but I was no good at playing pool and they just made fun of me when I tried. I followed Dad into the living room. He picked up the newspaper and sat down in Grandma's chair to read. I was about to take a seat on the couch when I saw him through the open front door. The porch wrapped around the front and one side of the house, and Grandpa had made screens so that when the weather was nice like it was today, they could leave the doors wide open "to catch a summer breeze," as he had once said. I stepped to the door and peered out. Uncle Bruce was sitting in Grandpa's porch chair smoking a cigarette, looking at the road. A car was cruising by, so he probably didn't hear me when I stepped out from the living room. My heart was pounding in my chest. He was dressed much the same as when he had pulled into our driveway, but without the leather jacket. Now he was just wearing his Levi's and a light blue button-down shirt. The beard and long hair made me think he was a hippie. Grandpa had always said hippies were long-hairs who never shaved. But I'd also heard that hippies wore weird clothes, and his clothes were regular like anyone would wear.

"Your grandmother won't let me smoke in the house," he said. He turned to look at me. It felt like his eyes looked right into me. "I probably shouldn't be smoking around you kids, either." He dropped the remainder of his cigarette into the beer bottle he was holding. I couldn't help but notice it was a Michelob, and my stomach tightened. He got up from the chair and brushed past me as he went back into the house.

"Charles," he said to my father as he passed through the living room. He took the left at the stairs and disappeared. I stepped over to my grandmother's porch chair and sat down. I scooched back; my feet wouldn't even touch the floor unless I stretched my legs out. It was uncomfortable to put my arms on the arms of the chair, so I just let my hands rest in my lap. I turned to stare out at the road like Uncle Bruce had been doing, unable to find what he had been looking at. I wondered how long it would be till dinner and then how long we would be staying after that. Not that it really mattered. Jay was still at his mother's, so I couldn't hang out with him. But there was a good chance everyone would be going out for the night. Karen would end up going to Mary's and Kevin would head off to wherever it was he went. Mom and Dad would go out to do their separate things. I could have the whole house all to myself. And I still had that pot. It made me uncomfortable to think about how I had gotten it, but I did have it. I could get high. Maybe. I wondered if smoking it the next time would be as good as the last time. Or, you know, if I would get high. I hadn't gotten high when I first smoked with Jay. Maybe it was the beer that had done it, and I didn't have any beer. Would I still be able to get high? Should I smoke it by myself? I guess I'd find out if I got the chance.

I pulled myself out of Grandma's porch chair and went back into the living room. Dad was still lost behind the newspaper, so I sat down on Grandpa's side of the couch. To the right was a tall shelf that held the family photo albums. I liked looking through them, especially the older ones with pictures of people I didn't know. The first few albums were dated long before I was born and were filled with black-and-white pictures of great aunts and uncles, great-grandparents, people who were related to me, family that I would never know. Most were labeled in my grandmother's precise handwriting. Names like Aunt Alice and Uncle Augustus, dates from the early 1900's in some of the older albums. It wasn't as much fun looking at them on my own without Grandpa or Grandma telling me about the people in the pictures. I liked it better when someone could tell me who these strangers were and how we were related. Maybe Grandma would go through some of them with me after dinner.

"Would you get me a beer?" my father asked from behind the newspaper. I didn't even realize he knew I was there in the living room.

I got up from the couch and headed into the kitchen. I could hear Grandma and my mother talking as I came in. I'm not sure they'd heard me enter. They were both facing the stove. Every now and then one of them would walk over to the window on the other side of the stove and look out.

"That's at least his fourth beer," Grandma said.

"It's just how he deals with things," Mom returned.

"By not dealing with them? That's what the drinking does. Keeps you from dealing with things."

I assumed they were talking about how Uncle Bruce was dealing with Grandpa's death. But then, I had no way to know how anyone was dealing with it. No one showed much sadness. No one was crying. I felt bad that I didn't feel worse about Grandpa's death, but it didn't seem like anyone in the family cared. Not enough to cry.

"How long has it been since he's been here?" Grandma asked. "Cards for Christmas and birthdays. And then we don't hear from him for months."

"I know."

"Does he talk to you?"

"No, not really. I try calling him every month or two, but it usually ends up with me talking more than him."

"Well, I think it's ridiculous, not talking to your family, not talking to your own parents."

"He's here for the funeral," Mom said.

"And then he'll be gone again." Grandma stirred the pot in front of her. "Probably the last time I'll see him. The next time he comes up will be for my funeral."

"Mom, stop it! He's here. Let's just have a nice meal."

I stepped to the refrigerator and pulled the door open. Grandma looked over at me, but my mother kept her gaze out the window.

"Dad wants a beer," I said. I was ashamed for my eavesdropping. Grandma always said it was wrong, and her gaze let me know that she did not approve of me sneaking into the kitchen like I had. I took a Michelob from the bottom shelf and got out of the kitchen and from beneath her gaze as quickly as I could.

It was another hour before dinner was ready. I heard Mom call from the dining room to wash up. Karen and Kevin were together washing their hands in the downstairs bathroom, so I headed upstairs to use the other bathroom. It was at the end of the hall on the right. But, when I reached the top of the stairs, I stopped cold. Was someone crying?

My grandparents' bedroom was the first door on the left at the top of the stairs. It sounded like the crying was coming from that room. I tiptoed up to the door and peeked around the jamb.

She was sitting on the other side of the bed, turned away from me, facing the windows on the far wall. It was my grandmother. The apron was gone, but she was still wearing the same dark blue dress with white polka dots. Her head was down, her hands up to her face. She was crying. It wasn't loud; I wouldn't have heard it if I hadn't come up the stairs. I'd never seen her cry before. I hadn't expected her to cry. She was always so strong and proud and…. I didn't know what the word was. She never showed emotion. It scared me a little to see her crying now. She was the only one besides Karen who I'd seen cry. I didn't know what to do. I wanted to go into the room, maybe give her a hug. But then she'd know I was there and would probably be mad that I was spying on her. Or that's what she would think, anyway.

"Mom!" I heard my mother call from the bottom of the stairs. "Everything's on the table."

She sat up straight then. She had a handkerchief in her hand, and she wiped it across her eyes.

"I'll be right down," she called back. There was no sign of her tears in her voice when she answered.

I quickly scooted down the hall and into the bathroom. When I was finished and headed back down the stairs, she was gone from the bedroom. She was in the kitchen when I reached the bottom, so I was off the stairs before she came back into the dining room. She probably never realized that I had been up there.

Dinner was roast beef, something we only ever had at Grandma's house and only on special occasions. She and Mom had also made the roasted potatoes I liked. And there were beans and pickles and more food than all of us could eat. But that's how Grandma prepared family dinners. You never walked away hungry from her table. Uncle Bruce finished at least two beers during the course of the meal. The alcohol seemed to relax him, and he actually started speaking to us as we worked our way through dinner.

What was strange is that no one talked about Grandpa. No one even mentioned him, except when the story someone was telling included him. And then whoever was telling the story would kind of trail off as if Grandpa was a forbidden topic. Uncle Bruce started telling a story about Grandpa's fear of dogs, but Grandma gave him a look that shut him up. I didn't understand it. I wanted to hear the story. I thought that's why we were here. I thought we were getting together for him.

After dinner, my mother insisted on doing the dishes. She told Grandma to relax; she and Uncle Bruce would take care of the clean-up. I'm not sure Uncle Bruce had agreed to that as he seemed awfully surprised when she made the announcement. Karen and Kevin went back into the game room to play pool, and Dad wandered back into the living room. I convinced Grandma to go through some of the old photo albums with me to tell me about those relatives I didn't know. To make it easier, we sat at the dining room table with the books. I could see my mother and Uncle Bruce standing by the sink in the kitchen. She washed and he dried. Grandma was pointing out a picture of two of her cousins and explaining their relationship, but I was more interested in the conversation going on in the kitchen. Sure, it was rude, and it was eavesdropping, but they were talking so loud that it was hard *not* to hear them. Uncle Bruce walked to the fridge and took out another beer.

"How many does that make?" my mother asked, her back to me, but her voice loud enough to hear clearly.

"Don't start," Uncle Bruce said, his voice deep and gravelly.

"An alcoholic who owns a liquor store."

"I said, don't start."

"Or what?" she asked. "You'll go away for another five or six years?"

"Or nothing." He leaned against the counter, took a long drink from the beer before he picked up the dish towel and started drying the plates my mother was setting in the dish rack. "What difference does it make to you anyway?"

Uncle Bruce looked into the dining room, and I quickly looked away, turning my attention back to the album on the table. I snuck a peek up and through the doorway but quickly looked away again when I saw that Uncle Bruce was still looking at me.

"We'd like to see you more often," my mother said to him.

"Why?"

Dishes clattered together in the sink.

"What do you mean why?" She was angry. I could tell.

"I mean what's the point?"

"We're family. That's the point."

Uncle Bruce laughed, but not loud. "Sure, okay."

"What do you mean by that?"

"I mean it's not like you and I were ever close. Hard to be brother and sister when you were gone by the time I was ten. And her?"

I glanced up long enough to see Uncle Bruce nod his head in my direction. My mother whispered angrily at him, too low for me to hear what she said. Uncle Bruce spoke back to her in the same way. I could see he was getting angry.

"Just drop it!" he finally said. It was loud enough for my grandmother to look up from the photo album and look in their direction. The two of them washed the dishes in silence for a few minutes.

"I'm going back next Saturday. I've got a business to run."

My mother handed him a freshly washed plate.

"You could run a business up here. Open a store in Potsdam. God knows you'd get the customers."

Uncle Bruce chuckled a little. He dried the plate, put it away, and then took another drink from his beer. "No, that would definitely not work."

"Well, why not?"

"Because I can't move back here," he said. He seemed to be getting angry again. Then he calmed a bit, took another drink from his beer, his eyes down. "The best thing I did was get away." He seemed to say this last to himself more than to my mother.

"Why not?" she asked.

"Why not?" Uncle Bruce swirled the bottle in his hand, then took another swig. "Because after I got back, everything was different."

"What do you mean?"

"I was different," he said, still looking down at the bottle in his hand.

"Different how?"

He chuckled again. "In ways you couldn't possibly understand."

Uncle Bruce looked up then and caught my eyes as he looked through the doorway at me. Something caught me then, too, and I found I couldn't turn away. We just looked at each other for what seemed like a long time.

"It might be too dangerous," he finally said.

"For who?" My mother's voice carried that tone she sometimes got when she didn't believe what you were saying but she went along with you anyway. Like when she caught you lying about eating the last cookie.

"For me," Uncle Bruce replied. He was still looking directly at me when he said, "Maybe for you." He took another drink from his beer, still staring right at me. And then something changed. He stood up straight, shook his head like he was trying to clear it, and set the beer on the counter. "Look," he said, "can we just drop it? I'm going back to Utica next Saturday and that will be that."

"Why not just go now?" she asked. "I mean, if we mean so little to you, why not just leave now?"

"I wanted to spend some time at the lake. I've also got a few things to take care of, and then I'll no longer be your problem."

"You're not a problem," my mother said as she put another plate in the dish rack. "At least think about coming back more often. It doesn't only have to be when someone dies."

"I'll think about it," he said and turned to put the plate he held into the cabinet.

"Kelly!" Grandma said. "Are you listening to me?"

Her voice startled me, and I quickly turned my attention back to the photo album. "Yes, Grandma, that's great-uncle Malcolm," I said. I took another glance into the kitchen and saw Uncle Bruce smiling at me.

"I need a smoke," he said. He set the dish towel on the counter next to the dish rack and headed out the back door.

"What about the rest of these dishes?" my mother called after him.

He answered her, but I couldn't hear what he said. She went back to finishing the dishes by herself, and I turned my full attention to the photo album as Grandma pointed out some of Grandpa's cousins from years ago.

When she found that Uncle Bruce had left the dishes for my mother, Grandma excused herself from the table and took up the dish towel that Uncle Bruce had abandoned. I got up from the table and walked into the kitchen.

"Can I go play in the barn?" I asked.

"There's nothing in that barn for you," Grandma said.

"Why don't you go play pool with your brother and sister?" my mother asked.

"Nah," I said, "I'm just going to go outside."

"Well, don't go far," my mother said. "We'll be leaving soon."

"And put the photo albums back, if you're done with them," Grandma said.

I did as I was told and put the albums back on the shelf next to the couch. It was strange when I walked into the living room this time. I really expected to see Grandpa John sitting in his spot on the couch next to those shelves. And I felt the shock this time to come into the room and not see him there. It was the first time I think I actually understood what it all meant. I was never going to see him again. He was gone. He wasn't coming back. And those tears I hadn't cried started piling up behind my eyes. I blinked fast, trying to hold them back. I swallowed hard. As soon as the albums were back on their shelves, I went as quickly as I could out the open front door, onto the porch, then out the screen door, and down the steps. I stopped when I knew I was out of sight of everyone, then sat down, my back against the porch. It was only then that I let the tears spill from my eyes. I didn't sob or anything like that; I didn't want anyone to hear me. But the tears rolled down my cheeks with a force I hadn't expected. I wiped my nose with the back of my hand and wiped my hand on my Wranglers. I must have sat there for a good five minutes or more trying to get control over those tears. I couldn't let anyone see me like this. No one else was crying like a baby. Karen and Kevin would only make fun of me if they saw me. Like everyone else, I had to be strong, had to hide this sadness that had finally found its way down to my heart. When I felt like I'd gained some control, I wiped my eyes with my t-shirt before getting up from the ground. I walked around to the side of the house and headed up the driveway.

I expected to see Uncle Bruce since he had headed out the back door to have a cigarette. But all I found was our car and his motorcycle. At least I'd get a chance to take a closer look at his ride. I didn't know much about motorcycles, but I was fascinated by them, and it was cool that I could get a closer look at one. It was flat black with no markings to tell me what make it was. It might have been a Harley or a Honda. I didn't know. I wanted to climb onto it and take a seat, but I was afraid I'd do something wrong and tip it over or break it or mess it up somehow. So, I admired its shiny chrome from a foot away, scared to even put a hand on it. And then it struck me again: where was Uncle Bruce? I looked around and saw that the barn door was open a bit. It hadn't been when we had pulled into the driveway.

I walked over to the big red door and peeked inside. The only other light came through a small window at the back of the barn. The window was caked with dirt and dust, so what little light it let in was yellow and dull. It reminded me of that kitchen light at Moe's. I pushed that from my mind and stepped into the barn. It smelled musty. As my eyes adjusted to the darkness, I heard a noise off to the left. I could just make out a closed door, the door framed with slivers of light around the edges. I knew there was a little workshop or something through that door, but I'd never been in it. Grandma had said there was nothing out here for me, so I had never been allowed to explore. But knowing Uncle Bruce might be in there made me curious. And scared. He had been looking right at me when he said he could be dangerous. What had he meant by that?

My curiosity got the better of me and I walked over to the closed door. As soon as I reached it, all the sound inside the room stopped. I froze and even held my breath. The hinges creaked painfully as the door slowly opened and light poured over me. All I saw of him was his shadow; the light came from somewhere behind him.

"What do you want?" he snapped.

"Nothing," I replied. "I'm sorry." I started backing up toward the barn entrance, turning around as soon as I could to make my escape.

"Wait," Uncle Bruce called. "Kelly…."

No, I wasn't going to wait. He *was* dangerous and I needed to get away from him. I was doing what I should have done the night before. Getting away.

"Please," he said. "You don't have to go."

I stopped just before I reached the open front door. This wasn't like the night before. This was my Uncle Bruce. There was a difference, right? I turned around to see him standing in the doorway.

"Come on in," he said. "I'll show you my lair."

He disappeared into the workshop. I heard him moving around inside the little room, and I stepped toward the light. When I reached the door, I peeked around the corner and saw him sitting by what looked like a workbench. There was an old floor lamp in the corner that gave off most of the light. Along with the stool he sat on by the bench, there was also a beat-up armchair and a small table with an ashtray and his bottle of beer.

"Welcome to my version of the Bat Cave," he said. "Or my Fortress of Solitude. Whichever. It's not much, but it was mine."

I stepped down into the room. It ran the depth of the barn, about fifteen feet, and was only about five or six feet wide. Everything was covered in a layer of dust as if no one had been inside the room in a long time.

"You're the first person to step inside besides myself. Well, maybe," he said. "I expect Mom or Dad — that is, your Grandma or Grandpa — have probably been in here since the good old days."

A shelf above the bench had some knick-knacks like an old bottle and a cigar box as well as a bunch of old paperbacks with some titles I didn't recognize and some that I did like *Moby Dick* and *Lord of the Flies*.

"My treasures," he said when he saw me looking over the shelf. "Things that I thought mattered back when I was about your age. Go ahead, take a look."

I stayed where I was.

"This was my refuge," he said. "I spent a lot of time here." He pointed to a box on a shelf below the bench. "In there are my comic books. Might be worth something these days. Just fun reading back then."

Then something set a spark in his eye. "Wait a minute!"

Uncle Bruce got up from his stool, took a knife from his pocket, unfolded it, and walked to the back wall of the room. He started fumbling with a couple of the boards on the wall and pried one off with the knife. He was able to pull a second board off after that, revealing a small space behind.

"Haha!" he exclaimed. "If they'd been out here, they never found this."

From the little cubby hole in the wall, he extracted a couple of magazines and tossed them on the workbench. Both of them had the word *Playboy* emblazoned across the top. I wasn't sure what to make of that; it made me a little uncomfortable to see the women on the covers. But Uncle Bruce was still interested in the cubby hole. Then he pulled out a tall green bottle.

"I'll be damned!" he said. "It's still here."

He held in his hands a liquor bottle. I didn't know much about booze, but I could see a ship below the words "Cutty Sark" on the bottle's label. I assumed that was the name of the stuff.

Uncle Bruce held up the bottle as if it were a trophy. The floor lamp cast weird shadows and highlights on the wall as the light passed through the colored glass.

"I stole this bottle from your grandfather's liquor cabinet back in '67. He wasn't much of a drinker, so he never realized it was missing." He held the bottle up to the light. "Still about half-full. Or half-empty, depending on your point of view." Uncle Bruce smiled at me then, spun the top off the bottle, and took a drink. He swallowed and gave me another smile. "Still as drinkable as it was twelve years ago."

Twelve years. He had stolen that bottle the year I was born.

He put the top back on the bottle and stuck it back into the cubby hole. It was only then that he noticed the magazines he had tossed onto the workbench.

"Shit," he said. "You don't need to see those."

He picked them up and stuffed them back into the hole as well, then replaced the boards he had pried off.

"This is our secret, right?" he asked.

I nodded.

Uncle Bruce gave me a wink. "Our secret," he said again. He bent down to pull a box out from a shelf under the workbench, leaned a little too far, and fell to the floor. I stepped toward him, thinking I could help him up.

"No!" he snapped. "I'm fine."

His gruff voice sounded so angry that I took a step back toward the door. He looked up at me as he was pulling himself to his feet.

"Sorry, I didn't mean to yell." He sat back down on the stool. "I'm not mad at you."

I nodded even though I didn't really know what he meant. I could tell he was drunk. Even if he hadn't fallen down, his words were slurred. That was a little scary. I didn't know him well to begin with, so I didn't know what he might be like drunk. My dad could be mean and yell when he had too much gin. Uncle Bruce leaned on the workbench, his head in his left hand.

"Fuck," he said, but then looked up at me as soon as he said it. "Sorry. I shouldn't be using that kind of language." He took a cigarette from a pack in his shirt pocket and stuck it between his lips, then took it out again. "Nope, shouldn't be doing that either. Damn! There's not much I can do with you around."

I turned and took another step toward the door to leave. Even Uncle Bruce didn't want me around.

"Wait, that doesn't mean you have to go. It's probably better if you stay. You'll keep me out of trouble."

I turned back to look at him but remained near the door. He threw his head back and took a deep breath before blowing it out toward the ceiling. Then he looked back at me.

"You don't say much," he said.

I shrugged my shoulders.

"That's okay. I get it. I don't usually say much myself. But it looks like I'm going to have to carry this conversation."

He chuckled at his own joke. I couldn't help but smile.

"Ah," he said, "a reaction. So, there is something going on behind those eyes." He looked a little closer. "Green eyes, too, I see. Well, that's the color all of us good guys have."

His eyes were more red than anything else, but I remembered his green eyes from the day he stopped at the house. We had that in common, he and I.

"So, how you doing with all this?" he asked. "Miss your grandfather?"

I shrugged my shoulders again. I still felt the sting of the tears I had cried earlier, but I wasn't going tell him about it.

"I get that, too. Your grandfather, my father. You and I are both pretty stoic about it. Everyone in this family is stoic about it."

Stoic? What was that? Did it mean we didn't feel things?

"But the old man was pretty stoic as well. Rarely said a word to me growing up. Didn't say a word before I left or after I got back. You know I was in the war? In Vietnam?"

I nodded again.

"Jesus, Kelly, I'm not gonna bite. You can say something if you want."

I looked down at the old wood of the barn floor. It kinda felt like he had bitten me with his anger. "Yeah," I said quietly.

"Hey, he speaks. Albeit, shyly, but he speaks."

I felt the heat in my cheeks and could only guess that I was blushing. I don't know if Uncle Bruce could see it in the dim light of the room, but I sure felt it. I hated being noticed like that. It didn't matter if it was Uncle Bruce or being called on in school. I was always embarrassed when I had to speak up.

"Don't worry about it. I never said much when I was your age either. You and I, we're like two peas in a pod, I think. Let's just hope nobody drafts you into doing something you don't want to do. Yeah, that's right. I was drafted into an army I didn't want to join to fight a war I didn't want to fight. You're too young to really know anything about it, I suppose, and that's probably a good thing. It's nothing you should have to know about. Not yet. It'll be in the history books, and you'll hear a lot about it over the years, I'm sure. Just know that the whole thing was bullshit."

Uncle Bruce picked up the bottle of Michelob that was still sitting on the small table by the armchair and took a drink.

"You know, they say that time heals all wounds. But they're wrong. It just leaves scar tissue."

I wanted to ask him what he meant by that, but that was the moment Karen's voice ripped through the evening air calling my name.

"Sounds to me like your presence is requested elsewhere," he said. He set the bottle down on the workbench and twirled it in his fingers.

I took a step toward the door. He looked so sad, so…alone. Was that what it meant to be stoic? To be alone? If it was, then I guess I was stoic, too. Is that what Uncle Bruce felt? I didn't want him to feel alone. I wanted him to know that I cared. Even though I didn't really know him, he seemed so much like me. But what could I say? I couldn't tell him how I felt about Grandpa John dying. What could I tell him to make him know that he wasn't alone?

"Uncle Bruce," I finally said.

He looked up from the bottle, his eyes finding mine.

"You're not going to ride up to the lake, are you? I mean, not right now, are you?"

I saw a brief flash of that anger in his eyes, the same anger I had seen when I took a step to help him up from the floor. Oh, God, I said exactly the wrong thing. I'd pissed him off. But almost as soon as the anger flashed, it was gone, replaced by something else. His gaze softened then, and a small smile crossed his lips.

"Nah," he said. "I'll probably crash on your grandmother's couch for a while."

"Good," I replied. "I wouldn't want you to get hurt."

I turned to head out to the driveway. I expected Karen's yell was to indicate we were going.

"Hey, Kelly."

I took the step up into the main room of the barn, then turned around to look back at him sitting by the workbench.

"Thanks for listening to the rants of your crazy Uncle Bruce." He smiled then and I couldn't help but return it.

I walked over to the main door, then stepped out into the evening light. My parents were already in the front seat, Kevin was on his side of the back seat, and Karen stood next to the car waiting for me to take my place in the middle. I slid in and Karen got in next to me.

"Call me if you need anything," my mother said as my father started backing out. I caught sight of Uncle Bruce standing in the barn doorway watching us pull away. He was a strange, scary, maybe even dangerous guy. But I decided I liked him for what that was worth. He had invited me into his den, his fortress of solitude. And that was cool.

9

Son of a Bitch, 1994

The best thing about waking at the lake was the cool breeze that would blow lightly through the cabin in the morning. With all the windows open, a crosswind moved from one end of the place to the other. It rustled the old curtains. They were white — or at least they had been at one time — with about a one-inch border of color. Each window had their own color, a different color for each room. Orange, green, maroon, and blue. On my side of the floor where Kevin and I slept, the curtains were bordered in baby blue. Like the sky only darker, softer. The breeze carried on it the smell of the forest, deep and green. It blew gently across the sheets and blankets, and I would open my eyes to greet the new day with a smile.

My smile quickly faded when I looked up and saw the high ceiling of my studio apartment and not the open rafters of the cabin roof. I wasn't at the camp and what I felt wasn't the cool summer breeze off the lake but was, in fact, the cold autumn wind off the river that carried with it the smell of diesel and gasoline exhaust from the traffic below. To drive home this reality, a diesel engine roared. I gathered it was a big truck taking off from the corner as the light turned green.

"Fuck." I rolled over onto my side. At least the carpet was clean and shaggy enough to be comfortable. But even I had to admit that waking up on the floor two days in a row was a bit much even for me. On the other hand, the news of the last few days was enough to justify a couple of benders. Seeing Moe after so long hadn't helped.

So, I could forgive myself for staying almost until the bar closed. And then I did something after that. What was it?

Wait, why was I feeling a breeze? I rolled over onto my back and sat up. The window that looked down on the street was wide open. The breeze was coming from the open window. But why was it open? With no screen, I never left it open. There were enough bugs in the place without inviting more in.

My memories of the previous night were fuzzy after a point. It was intermittent, like flashes of events and action in a weird movie trailer. Some things, like watching that asshole Moe leaving the Bali Hai with his companion, were clear as day. I remembered walking Mary Ellen home. And the Cutty Sark! I looked over to the coffee table between my chairs and saw the bottle there. It was empty. I remembered finishing it in that alley down the street. I recalled stopping in front of the pool hall and peering inside and how ghostly it looked in the faint light from the street. My memory of climbing the three flights of stairs to my room was missing completely. Still, I had not only made it up the stairs but also into the apartment. The ladder, though, had apparently been too much. But when did I open the window? I closed my eyes and thought hard, trying to will the memory back into my mind. I opened my eyes slowly as something came to me. I didn't remember opening the window, but I remembered. I remembered sitting on the windowsill and looking down at the street with a single thought in my head.

I wondered if it would hurt.

I laid back down on the floor.

Would she weep for her boy? That was a thought that had followed the first one.

I closed my eyes and laid my arm across my head. I just wanted to fall back to sleep, dream a little more about the lake and the cool summer breezes. If I only had a car. I could at least ride up there, maybe spend a day off just hanging in the cabin and taking a swim even though the water would probably be cold by now. A ride up to the lake would do me good, maybe even stay a few days and enjoy the quiet and the solitude. But, with no wheels, that wasn't going to happen. And I had Uncle Bruce's funeral tomorrow, Saturday. As much as I didn't want to attend, I needed to be there for him. Strange thought for me, a guy who doesn't believe in an afterlife. I mean, it's not like Uncle Bruce was going to know if I was there or not. In the end, a funeral is for the family more than it is for the deceased. As much as I despised them, as much as I wanted to deny being part of this family, I was going to show up. For him.

And I had to work my regular three o'clock shift today. Joy. Gary had let me know I could take more time if I wanted it, but Joe didn't offer any bereavement pay and I still had to make the rent. I picked myself up from the floor and headed into the bathroom. The alarm clock read two o'clock, so I had no time to goof off if I was going to get something to eat before my shift.

I ended up getting a sandwich to-go at the sub shop down the street and taking it into the pool hall so I could eat it before I started. As expected, Leon the Fish was there. At least Gary was cool with me eating on the job. But let's face it: working in a pool hall and video arcade wasn't tough. Hand out the balls, make change for the kids. Not rocket science.

"How you doing today?" Gary asked as he leaned against the counter. He and the Fish were deep into a game of straight pool.

After the way I had awoken and after my thoughts of the night before, it was a bit of a loaded question. But I wasn't going to burden Gary with my issues. Besides, the last person who needed to hear my business was Leon.

"I'm doing alright," I replied as I finished up the sub that would pass for my breakfast, lunch, and dinner, and then crumpled up the paper and bag it had come in. I tossed it all in the trash can by the counter.

"You don't look alright," he said.

"What do you mean," I asked.

"I don't know," he said as he approached the pool table to take a shot. "You seem a bit out of it."

"It was a late night."

"Again?" Leon asked.

I wanted to tell Leon about the stories I'd heard of his binges at some of the so-called classy bars in town, like Uncle Max's or

Maxfield's, but I never knew how far I could take it. Leon and Joe were rather close, so I didn't dare say much. Gary had the virtue of being the boss and being closer to the same age as Leon. Maybe it was a generational thing. Or maybe I was still stuck with the old adage of respecting your elders. That had certainly been beaten into my head as a child. It was hard to get over that kind of trauma even when those elders were more ignorant than you.

"Dinner with the family will do that to you," Gary said. "Why do you think sales at the liquor store always went up around the holidays?"

"What's the holiday that brings your family together?" Leon asked as he bent over the table to take a shot.

I knew I had to answer the question or Leon would never let it go. "My uncle died," I said.

"Nothing like death to bring a family together," he said as he missed one more shot.

I looked up at him in disbelief. Screw respecting your elders. Maybe I should just punch this guy in the mouth.

"Jesus, Leon," Gary interjected. "His uncle just died."

Leon put his hands up in a defensive position. "Sorry."

"You really can be a crass bastard," Gary finished. Only Gary could get away with saying that. And it saved me from an assault charge. I'm not a big guy, but even I could take down a douchebag like Leon. I think any of the kids who hung out in the arcade could. He only acted tough. Everyone knew him for the weasel that he was. But I needed this job too badly to make any real trouble.

"The offer still stands," Gary said as he took another shot at the table. "I already talked to Melissa about taking your shift."

"I'm actually okay with working," I replied. "Better than sitting up in my room."

"Or hanging out in the bar," Leon said.

Gary stood straight up then and threw his pool cue onto the table, knocking a few balls from their place.

"Hey," Leon said.

"I'm done," Gary said. He walked behind the counter and turned off the lights for the table bringing their session to an abrupt end.

"We haven't reached a hundred yet," Leon protested.

"I'm done," Gary repeated. "You wanna keep going, you can play with yourself."

Leon started to break down his pool cue so he could put it into its case. "I've got to get back to the office anyway," he said. "Your forfeit means I win."

"Yeah," Gary said as he rested his cue back in the corner where he kept it behind the counter. "You win."

Leon took out his wallet.

"It's all good," Gary said.

"Someone's got to pay for the time," Leon said.

"I'll take care of it."

Leon shrugged, got his suit coat from the coat rack, and put it on.

"I'll be in Monday," he said as he headed toward the front door. Gary didn't answer him, but Leon gave a final wave without looking back before he walked out.

Gary gathered up the balls from the table, put them into the tray, and handed the tray to me. I put it in the rack with the other balls. I grabbed the brush from a shelf underneath the counter so I could brush down the table. Gary took it from me.

"I got this," he said.

I wasn't going to argue with him and not because I wanted him to do my work for me. No, it was because I don't think I'd ever seen Gary so…tense. He was always such an easy-going guy. This was a side of him I'd never seen. He was genuinely pissed over what Leon had said. He didn't take out his anger on the pool table; he swept it calmly from one end to the other, taking care to go in a single direction and not stretch the felt. When he was done, he handed the brush back to me so I could put it back under the counter. Then he grabbed a stool, set it next to the counter, and sat down. In all this time, he never looked at me.

"Thanks," I finally said.

Gary turned to look at me then. "For what?"

Honestly, I wasn't sure what I wanted to thank him for. For being a friend? For standing up to a guy I couldn't bring myself to confront? For understanding, in his own way, what I was dealing with?

"I don't know," I replied. "For frying the Fish?" I smiled and he returned it with his own broad grin.

"He is a Fish, isn't he?"

We both laughed then. They didn't come any fishier than Leon.

"We need some music," Gary said. He went over to the jukebox, opened it with his key, and rang up several credits. He pushed a few buttons and Bob Seger's "Main Street" came from the speakers. It was a good song, especially that one line that both he and I spoke in unison when it came up.

"In the pool halls, the hustlers…and the losers, used to watch them through the glass…."

Gary was the hustler. He'd hustled his way out of Philly and hustled his way into this job. He hustled everyone he met if he wanted or needed to. So, what did that make me? The loser. Had been all my life. And it continued to this day. Being homeless, college dropout, living in the Arlington. All because whatever it took to make it in the world had been denied me. Be it family, money, luck, whatever, I had none of it. Loser at school, loser at love, loser at work, loser at life. I was destined to live out my years as some minimum wage worker. That was my lot in life. So, better to suck up and accept what was to be. What did I possibly have in my arsenal to fight my fate? As I had confronted it last night, without even realizing it, there was only one other path it seemed I could take. In the end, what difference was it really going to make? Really? What difference would it make? Sure, Gary would have to find a new worker, but any slug could do this job. Who else would care? Family? I seriously doubted it. Uncle Bruce might have cared, I think. Maybe. Hard to tell now that he was gone. What did I have to keep me from finding out if it would hurt?

The back door of the pool hall opened, and four kids walked in. School had let out about an hour earlier, so it was time for the townie kids to start filling the place. Potsdam had few other places for them to hang out and even with the overall declining interest in video games and pool halls, we still got their quarters and dollars. But this group was a little different. I recognized the boy leading them in. He stepped up to the counter.

"Can we get the back table?" he asked.

He wasn't a tall kid; he was about the same height as me, with dark hair, a slim build. He was one of the few kids I knew by name because he was the son of my sister's best friend. His name was Michael Chase. Legally, I wasn't allowed to let him play. The laws of New York State required customers to be at least sixteen years old and I knew for a fact that Michael was only fourteen. But I handed him a tray of balls just the same. He took it and met up with his friends at the table farthest from the counter. I flipped the switch for the lights but set the rate to two players rather than four. Gary looked over at the computer after I sat back down.

"You entered the wrong number, Indy," he said.

"I know," I said. "I like to give this kid a break."

"You? I've never seen you give anyone a break. Hell, I've seen you charge someone double just for giving you the stink eye! What's so special about him?"

"Long story," I said with a smile.

Gary shook his head. "It's your shift. Do what you want." He stood up from his stool. "I gotta get going. You sure you're alright to close tonight?"

I couldn't take my eyes off the kid playing at the back table. But I did look up at Gary. "Yeah, I'm good."

"And you're good to work tomorrow, too?" he asked.

"Yeah. Uncle Bruce's funeral is in the morning. I can make my shift."

"Alright," Gary said. "I'll see you tomorrow." He gave me a little wave and headed toward the back door. He gave a final glance at the kids at the back table before leaving.

I got up from my chair and walked to the jukebox. I was going to play something good. I wasn't going to let these kids waste those credits Gary had put on it. I punched in the numbers for a couple of songs that I wanted to hear but also a couple songs that I thought they might actually know. I sat back down behind the counter just as "I'd Do Anything for Love" by Meat Loaf started playing. It seemed apropos considering the first album had been so popular back when I'd known his mother, back in the 70s. And that one night.

10

Mary Chase, 1979

We got back home from Grandma's around eight o'clock. Kevin immediately grabbed his bike and disappeared down the road. The rest of us headed inside, but as soon as my mother and father had changed, they headed out again. I was a little surprised to see them leave together; they took off in the same car. I settled down on the couch in the living room thinking I might find something good to watch on the TV. I'd have to wait for Karen to go out before I could even think about taking out my pot. She was already on the phone, so I expected her to leave for Mary's house any time. But, when she hung up the phone, she came into the living room and sat down in the armchair across the room from me.

"Aren't you going out?" I asked.

"No," she replied. "Mary's not home. Her mother said she went out."

I could tell Karen was upset by that. The two of them were inseparable, so the thought that Mary might have gone somewhere or done something without her was probably killing her. I couldn't help but enjoy the moment. It was pretty rare that Karen got screwed over. She was always the one screwing over somebody else. Usually, it was me. But then I realized Mary had actually screwed me over as well. If Karen wasn't going out, then it was she and I alone in the same house for the whole night.

I got up from the couch and headed upstairs to my room. I wasn't going to hang out in the house all night with Karen there. And there was definitely no way I could smoke the pot. I didn't have anywhere to go, really, but the thought of being alone with her did not appeal to me at all. I opened my underwear drawer and took out the plastic bag of pot and quickly stuffed it into my pocket. The Bic lighter and the pipe were next. I headed down the stairs and out the door before Karen could even say a word.

It wasn't that late, but it was dark. I picked up my bike from where it lay next to the driveway and walked it down to the road before I got on. Then I headed off toward the bridge. I pedaled past the graveyard as fast as I could. It wasn't that I was scared, exactly, it just gave me the creeps when I was by myself, especially in the dark. Besides, where I was planning to go would prove to me my own bravery. I was heading for the scariest place I knew of down on Water Street.

The White House was supposed to be haunted. And maybe it was. No one ever seemed to rent it or live there. If someone did move in, they usually moved out soon after. Maybe it was like that Amityville Horror house and those who moved in got scared away. I'd read that book over the summer and it had scared me near to death! Or maybe it was just a big old empty dark house. The stories about it being haunted were probably just stories to keep kids from hanging out there. Or just to keep the little kids away 'cause the bigger kids hung out there a lot. I hoped no one was hanging out there tonight. I wanted to get high, and I didn't want anyone around to see.

I was coming up on the corner fast. A quick glance at Moe's and I saw his house was dark. Good. I didn't want to have to deal with him. Water Street had only two streetlights. One was on the corner by the bridge. The other was at the other end of the street, which was maybe a few hundred feet away. Or maybe it was further. I don't know. But the middle of the street was dark. So, I quickly guided my bike into the darkness and swung down the driveway on the far side of the White House. This allowed me to walk the bike behind the house and over to the window at the back, the one that was supposed to be unlocked. The river flowed by off to my left, the sounds muffled a little by the trees that lined the riverbank. I laid my bike down and hopped up onto the porch by that window. It looked closed. I didn't see any handle on the outside of it, so how was it people got it open? But looking closer, I saw that it wasn't completely closed. It was open about an inch. That must be it; they just didn't close it all the way. I slipped my fingers into the opening and pushed the window up far enough for me to climb in. Then I pushed it back down, leaving about the same one-inch gap.

The place was creepy. Barely any light came in from the streetlights and the little that did threw weird shadows on the walls. It took a few minutes for my eyes to adjust to the dark. It looked like I was in the living room; it was hard to tell with no furniture. There was a fireplace set in the far wall and a large mattress sat in the very middle of the bare wood floor. It was twice the size of my bed. The floorboards creaked as I walked over to it. I sat down and was just about to take the pot out of my pocket when I heard it.

I wasn't sure what it was. All the ghost stories and movies say that ghosts rattle chains, but it wasn't that. It wasn't a whispered voice telling me to get out. It was a creaking sound, just like the sound I had made walking to the mattress. It was like someone or something was tiptoeing around somewhere else in the house.

Do ghosts walk? I suddenly wondered. Or was there someone else here with me? And if so, who? Which would be worse? I could imagine my brother or some of his dirtbag friends hanging out drinking beer or something. Or maybe it was some murderer on the run. Well, unlike those morons in the movies, I wasn't about stay and find out what it was. I got up from the mattress and slowly started making my way toward the window, trying not to make a sound. I glanced over my shoulder, and that's when I saw the light. It was faint and it flickered a bit.

I froze where I was. I couldn't see the source, but the light started to get brighter like it was coming closer. And even if there were no chains rattling, the light was ghostly. As I stood there frozen, unable to make a move for the window, the source of the light came around the corner, and I felt the goosebumps and the hair on the back of my neck stand up as I saw the candle floating in midair as if some invisible entity held it up.

"Who's there?" a voice whispered.

I couldn't speak. My voice was as frozen as the rest of me.

"Come on, I see you over there by the window."

It was a girl's voice, a familiar voice. And when I realized whose voice it was, I wasn't sure if I should be more afraid.

"Mary?" I asked.

It took her a moment before she replied.

"Yeah," she said. "Who's there?"

I pulled the Bic lighter from my pocket and flicked it. The flame blinded me as it flickered. I held it up to get the glare out of my eyes. It lit up my face.

"Kelly? What the hell are you doing here?"

The lighter was getting hot, so I let go of the lever and the flame went out.

"Nothing," I said. "What are you doing here?"

The floating light moved closer, and I was finally able to see the person holding the candle. It was Mary, and she held the candle in one hand and a bottle of something in the other.

"Karen was looking for you," I said.

"So what? I can't just be alone for a night?"

Her voice sounded strange and she stumbled a little as she came into the room.

"I guess that's okay," I said.

"Oh," she said in her snide way. "Thank you very much for your approval!"

She sat down on the mattress and set the candle on the floor. I could see now that it was in some kind of holder, so it stood up there on the floor.

"That's not what I meant," I said. I knew it was pointless to try to make any sense out of a conversation with Mary. She was as stubborn as my sister.

"Well, what *did* you mean?" she asked angrily.

"Nothing!" It was the only defense I could think of.

She put the bottle to her lips and took a drink before she set it down next to the candle. In the light, I could just read the label: Boone's Farm Strawberry Hill. She looked into the flame of her candle, the light dancing across her face, and passed her hand over it. It was a slow pass.

"Don't burn yourself," I said.

A strange smile crossed her lips. It wasn't the kind of smile you make when you're happy or about to laugh. She actually looked kind of sad. She looked up at me then and started to pass her hand over the flame again, even slower this time, back and forth, slower and slower until her hand hardly moved.

"Stop it!" I cried. I couldn't help myself. I flopped down on the mattress and pulled her hand away from the flame. She laughed then, and I could smell something strange on her breath. Of course, it was the Boone's Farm. I picked up the bottle and saw that it was half-empty.

"Hey," she said as she took the bottle from me, "that's mine, you little thief." Then she held the bottle out to me. "I'm just kidding. You can have some if you want. I already drank one."

"One what?" I asked.

"One bottle." She set the bottle back down on the floor and lifted her hand back toward the flame.

"Don't!" I said and pulled her hand away again.

"Oh, what do you care?" She pulled her hand from my grip.

"I don't," I said. "But you're going to burn yourself."

She laughed a little. "Oh, I've already been burned."

I didn't know what she meant, and I wasn't going to ask. She probably wouldn't have told me anyway. She and Karen were always doing things behind my back, never letting me in on their secrets. This would probably be no different. What was I even doing here? Mary didn't like me any more than Karen did. I started to get up from the mattress.

"Where're you going?" Mary asked, slurring her r's.

"Somewhere else," I said.

"Don't go." She grabbed my wrist. "You don't have to go, I mean. Do you?"

I looked down at her in the flickering light. She almost seemed desperate for me to stay. Now I was confused. When she and Karen were together, they couldn't stand to have me around. They couldn't get rid of me fast enough. Did she really want me to stay? Or was this whole thing some prank she and my sister had dreamed up to get me? I wouldn't have put it past either one of them.

"You said you wanted to be alone," I finally said.

She let go of my wrist, her gaze going back to the flame. "I know what I said. But…."

But what? I wondered. Why were girls so confusing? I wished she would just tell me what she wanted. Maybe I needed to be the one to ask.

"Do you want me to stay?"

She didn't look up from the candle's flame, but I saw her head nod. So, I stopped moving toward the window and just stood where I was. What did she want from me?

"You can sit down," she said. Again, she never looked up from the flame. It was almost like she didn't really see me there. But I did as she said and sat down next to her on the mattress. Neither one of us said anything for the longest time. She just stared at the candle flame. I picked at a hangnail. She picked up the bottle and took a drink. Then she looked at me as she held out the bottle.

"You can have some if you want."

I shrugged my shoulders.

"It's strawberry," she said, stretching the first syllable out as she said it.

I took the bottle and gave the opening a sniff. It definitely smelled like strawberry, which was something I liked. I took a drink from the bottle. It burned my tongue a little, but it had a nice strawberry taste, so I took another drink before handing it back to Mary. She took a drink and then set the bottle down again.

"So, what are *you* doing here?" she finally asked.

"Nothing. I just wanted to be alone, too."

Her eyes left the candle flame and she looked over at me.

"Bullshit," she said with a grin. "You're too scared of this place to just walk in here for no reason."

There was the bitch that I knew she was.

"I'm not scared!" I replied. "I just never had a reason to come in before."

"Oh, but you have a reason now?"

Darn it, she caught me there. I had my reasons, but she didn't need to know about it.

"Come on, Kelly. You came here for a reason. What is it?"

"What was your reason?" I asked.

"I told you: I wanted to be alone."

"Yeah, but you said you wanted me to stay," I shot back. I took another drink from the bottle. "Kind of a strange request for someone who wants to be alone."

She had been playful in the conversation, but she shut down again, jerked the bottle from my hand and took another drink. She turned her attention back to the candle flame. It was my fault; I could sense that. She had tried to change the subject to something else, but I had brought it back to her wanting to be alone. She obviously didn't want to talk about it. So, it was up to me to make things better. What else could I do but tell her the truth about my reason for being there? If she and Karen had planned some kind of trap, I figured they would have sprung it by now. I dug into my pocket and took out my bag of pot. I dropped it on the floor. Her eyes picked up on the movement and saw the bag.

"Oh, my God," she said slowly. "Karen's little brother is a doper?"

Oh no! That was a mistake. Now she was going to go back to Karen and tell her what I had, tell her that I smoked pot. My life was over as of this very moment. Even if Mary and Karen had not laid a trap for me, I had tripped one myself. I reached for the bag so I could stuff it back in my pocket, but Mary grabbed it before I could.

"Hold on there," she said as she picked it up. She opened the bag and put her nose into it. She sniffed the contents and her eyes got big. "Holy shit, Kelly! Where did you get this?"

I shrugged my shoulders. I wasn't about to tell her.

"And you've smoked this?"

I took the pipe out of my pocket and held it close to the flame of the candle so she could see it.

"Holy shit...."

I shrugged again and couldn't help but smile. I think she was actually impressed. I was able to impress my sister's best friend. I handed her the pipe.

"Wow," she said as she took the pipe. I handed her the Bic, too. I didn't know if Mary smoked, but I knew Karen did not. She was adamantly opposed to smoking anything. But Mary took a pinch from the bag, put it into the pipe, then lit it like a pro. She even knew how to work the carb. She inhaled deeply and handed everything to me. She didn't exhale for the longest time. She just watched me as I fumbled with everything to light the bowl and take a hit. She smiled as I coughed, but she never made fun of me for it. She blew the smoke in my face when she finally exhaled.

"Little Kelly," she whispered. She took the pipe and Bic and took another hit. After she handed everything back to me, she took another drink from the bottle, and then turned her attention back to the candle. I decided to wait before I took another hit. Instead, I just watched her watching the flame. Her hand danced over the candle's flame again, but she didn't hold it in the fire like she had before, and it created weird, creepy dancing shadows on the walls and ceiling. We were both quiet for a while and I felt my head getting fuzzy from the pot.

"What do you think of me?" she finally asked.

I wasn't sure how to answer her question. I'd come to the conclusion that this wasn't some kind of trap laid by her and Karen; Mary really was here all by herself. But what did she want me to say? That she was a bitch like my sister? She wasn't being that way to me now.

"You probably think I'm a bitch," she said.

Oh, wow, does pot make you able to read minds? Because it was like she had just read my thoughts. My very thought about her being a bitch and how she and Karen treated me like shit.

"No," I said, hoping to hide any more thoughts from her.

"Yeah, you do. Your sister and I treat you like shit."

Get out of my head! How was she doing that? But I just shrugged my shoulders. I don't know why I kept doing that. She wasn't looking at me and probably couldn't see me shrugging.

"I'm sorry," she said without looking up. "You're okay. But, you know, when Karen and I are together…."

She didn't finish her thought, but I think I understood. It was kind of like me and Jay. When we were together alone, we got along fine. But, when we were around others, like Kevin, it was like he was a different person. It was weird, I guess, but that's just the way it was.

"You probably think I'm a slut, too," she said.

"No," I said. It was true. I'd never thought of her that way. I guess I'd never thought of anyone that way. Oh, I'd heard the word and I knew what it meant, kinda, but were people really having that much sex? I didn't think so. I mean I had my…experience. I still wasn't sure what to make of that. It had left me scared and confused. But I couldn't believe my sister was having sex. Or my brother. That was something married people did. Still, after last night….

She looked up from the candle and looked me in the eye. "Really?" she asked. "You don't think I'm a slut?"

"Yeah," I said. "Don't you have to have sex with lots of people to be a slut?"

Something in her eyes changed then. I'm not sure what it was. There had been this distant, glassy look before, like she didn't really see me there. But that changed. She saw me. I could feel that. Something was different and she really saw me for, like, the first time in my life. The next thing I knew, she wrapped her arms around me and hugged me tight to her.

"You are the sweetest boy ever," she said.

Unsure of what to do, I hugged her back. I didn't know how to feel about all of this. She'd always been such a bitch to me. But she seemed so sad tonight, like she needed someone to listen to her. Or maybe she needed someone to give her a hug. I guess I had finally said the right thing.

When she finally let go of the hug, she kept her hands on my shoulders and held me at arm's length. She looked me right in the eye. I have to admit that it was a little uncomfortable, but I didn't look away. Then she pulled me toward her, and we kissed.

Well, really, she kissed me. It was so unexpected. I didn't know how to react. Her arms wrapped around me again, so I wrapped my arms around her. And then I felt her tongue pushing against my lips. I opened my mouth a little and her tongue darted into my mouth. It was weird but at the same time, it was incredible! I really liked it! Our tongues met somewhere in the middle. She tasted like strawberries. As we kissed, she pushed me down on the mattress. I couldn't even believe that I was making out with my sister's best friend. The high from the pot helped me along as I rolled with everything that was happening. And all I could smell was Love's Baby Soft.

She pulled away from me then and I thought maybe it was all over. She must have realized what she was doing and decided it wasn't right. But I could see in the flickering light that she was still looking right at me. Her eyes were locked onto mine. I didn't know what it meant, didn't know what to do. I laid back on the mattress, her body hovering over me. She smiled again and not just with her mouth. She was smiling with her eyes, too. Then she lowered herself down and kissed me again. I didn't wait to let her tongue dart into my mouth this time. God, she was so hot. I wrapped my arms around her again, but she pulled my left arm from around her and held my hand. Her thumb rubbed along the back of my hand. It was soft and gentle. I never thought Mary could be so gentle, but she was. Then she put my hand on her boob. No, that's not right. She put my hand on her breast. She had breasts. I didn't know what she wanted me to do, so I just squeezed it a little. She moaned against my lips, so I guess it was the right thing to do. It was at that point that I realized she was unbuttoning her top. And even though her shirt now hung open, I didn't move my hand from where it was.

"Go for it," she whispered between kisses.

I didn't know what she meant. And I didn't dare move. I couldn't bring myself to say anything to her. I just kept kissing her. But, when I felt her hand on my, you know, down there, I started to understand what she meant. She took no time at all to undo my Wranglers and put her hand inside my underpants. I slid my hand inside her bra and ran my fingers along the soft skin of her breast.

"Oh," she said, "my little man."

She pulled back once more and looked me in the eye again, my hand on her breast and her hand inside my pants. She kissed me again, and the rest was paradise by the dashboard light.

It was still dark when I woke up, but I could see a little bit of light coming in the window. I wasn't sure if it was the streetlights or maybe the sun coming up. I had no idea what time it was. But the flame had gone out. The last bit of wax from the candle clung to the holder. And I knew Mary was gone. I was alone. My bag of pot was still there and the pipe, so she hadn't thought to steal my stuff. She had taken the bottle of Boone's Farm. I was naked from the waist down except for my socks and covered in a dirty blanket we had found lying on the floor. The rest of my clothes and my sneakers were in a pile next to the bag of pot.

I rolled onto my back, put my hands behind my head. Even with the buzz fading, I couldn't help but smile. I had fucked a girl that night. And even better, I fucked my sister's best friend. A fifteen-year-old. What would Karen have to say about that?

But then it hit me. What *would* she say? What would Mary say? Would she even tell anybody? Of course, she would. Girls probably talked about that stuff, right? And she had called me her "little man."

Little.

That word stuck in my head. What did she mean by that? Maybe nothing. But maybe something. It didn't change anything, really. We still had sex. It had moved from kissing and all that to actual sex. Sure, she had helped me, but it was still sex. I had been on top of her, and then she had been on top of me, which really freaked me out. I didn't know people could have sex like that. But it was amazing.

The sky outside the house did seem to be getting lighter. Was it morning? Had I — or we together — spent all night in the White House? I remembered holding her when we were done. She kept telling me what a great guy I was and how much she had needed me. I wasn't sure what she was talking about, but I just laid there and let her talk. It seemed to be the thing she wanted to do. She kept her arms wrapped around me and held me close to her, the scent of Love's Baby Soft surrounding us. I would tighten my own hold on her every once in a while, when it seemed like she wanted it. I must have fallen asleep to the sound of her voice without realizing it. It was soft and reassuring. To awake alone in the cold of the morning was kind of a bummer.

I grabbed my underpants from the floor and slipped into them while I was still under the blanket. Then I got my jeans and pulled them on, followed by my sneakers. I stuffed the pot, the pipe, and the Bic back in my pockets and made my way out the window that had been my way in the night before. The way out was the way in. My bike was still where I had left it, leaning against the house. Only a few hours had passed, but it felt like so much longer. The warmth of her body against me, her lips on mine, the whole night seemed like some distant dream already. But I knew it wasn't. Sure, I had gotten stoned and maybe a little drunk on the Boone's Farm, but it had still been real. I couldn't help but smile. I had sex!

I jumped on my bike and started pedaling up Water Street toward the main drag. All the houses were dark, including Moe's, but the sky was definitely getting lighter. I wondered if I would be in trouble when I got home. Did anyone even notice I had been gone all night? If anyone knew or noticed, it would be Kevin since we shared the bedroom. Or maybe Karen. She was nosy enough to have noticed. Well, wouldn't I have a story to tell her if she asked? And wouldn't she be surprised when I told her what had happened?

The house was dark as I walked my bike up the driveway. No one was stirring. Maybe that was best. I laid my bike down next to the porch and opened the door as slowly as I could. Two nights in a row. This was two nights in a row I'd been out so late that almost everyone else was in bed. If I could be as quiet as possible again, maybe no one would know. I stepped inside and quietly closed the door behind me. The clock on the wall let me know it was four-thirty. Wow, I don't think I'd ever been awake at four-thirty in the morning before. I did my best to tiptoe through the house, up the stairs, and into my bedroom. Kevin was fast asleep in the lower bunk. He probably hadn't even noticed I was gone when he got in the night before.

Good. As much as I wanted to scream it to the world that I had sex, I still wanted to keep it my secret. I bet he's never had sex, I thought, as I climbed into bed. That made me smile even more. I had sex before my older brother and maybe even before my older sister. I doubted she had had sex yet, either. I fell asleep that early morning assured of the fact that I was the only one of the three of us who had been laid.

11

Mary Chase, 1994

Christ, I needed a beer. Maybe I should have let Gary cover my shift. Being a Friday night, we were open until two in the morning, which meant there was no going down to the bar after work this time. If I'd given it some thought, I could have picked up a six pack or a bottle of something, but by the time two o'clock finally rolled around, I doubted I'd be in any mood to drink. Besides, the funeral was in the morning, and it would probably be better if I didn't show up hungover. After my most recent morning experience, maybe a night off from it wasn't such a bad idea anyway.

I looked back at the far table to watch Michael Chase and his friends playing pool. Or trying to play. They were just kids, so they had no real idea about the game. Hell, not one of them could even make a decent bridge with their hand. If they had been playing at the table by the counter, I might have offered them a few pointers. I was no Minnesota Fats or Earl Strickland, but I still could have taught them a few things. But I wasn't about to approach them uninvited at the far table. That would just seem…creepy. Still, they were currently the only players in the place. The bell at the door to the arcade rang, and I got up to make change for one of the kids over there. As I sat back down behind the counter, I heard the front door open. Turning on my stool, I saw Mary Chase walk in. She stepped up to the counter.

I'd seen her around town on occasion, usually walking through a parking lot or turning the corner in a supermarket aisle. After my sister finished high school and went off for her stint at college, Mary stopped coming around. She worked as a clerk and cashier at Ames, so I saw her there once in a while, but I always tried to avoid her if I could. I'm not sure why. I guess it was just one of those things. We both knew what had happened and we both knew what the outcome had been and we'd both silently decided it wasn't something we were going to talk about. She had never come into the pool hall before. Her look of surprise told me she hadn't known I was working here. Some instinct told me to stand, so I was on my feet when she reached the counter.

"Hey, Kelly!" she said. "I didn't know you were working here."

I couldn't help but smile. There she goes reading my mind again.

"Hey, Mary."

I tried to look her in the eye, but she looked away as soon as I tried. To be fair, I did the same thing when she finally looked back at me. I looked toward the back table instead to see if Michael had noticed his mother come in. It was apparent that he had but he was trying to make it look like he hadn't so he could keep playing.

"So, how are you doing?" she asked, her voice a little too eager; it couldn't hide her apprehension.

"I'm good," I replied. "How are you? I see you up at Ames every now and then."

"Yeah, I'm full-time now. And I finally got the day shift. You should stop by and say hello when you're there."

"You're usually on the register or busy. I wouldn't want to get you in trouble."

I sat back down on my stool and gestured to the stool Gary had left next to the counter.

"I can't stay long," she said.

"Here to pick up Michael?" I asked.

She sat down and leaned an arm on the counter next to me. "Yes, I didn't know if you knew who he was."

"I get to know most of the regular kids who come in."

"I hope he's not giving you any trouble. You'd tell me if he did, right?"

I smiled. "No, he's one of the good kids," I said. "Doesn't cause any trouble. Doesn't spit on the floor."

"Ewww!" she said. "Do some of the kids do that?"

"Mostly in the arcade. The ones who chew tobacco. They spit in between the machines."

"That's disgusting!" She shook her head as she said it. "Well, if you ever catch Michael chewing or smoking or anything like that, you let me know."

We sat silent for a while. At one point, Michael looked up from his game and his mother waved to him. There was no denying her presence for him now.

"So, where are you living these days?" she finally asked without taking her eyes off her boy. He was bent over the pool table trying to take a shot.

"Right here," I said.

"In the pool hall?"

I wanted to say, "Not anymore," but that would require a long explanation of its own. "No, I'm upstairs. Got a room in the Arlington."

She looked at me then with something approaching pity. That's how most people felt when I told them where I was living. It was as if the Arlington just wasn't fit for human occupation. And that was something else: how many of these judgmental people had ever actually set foot inside the Arlington or any of its rooms or apartments? They judged based on what they had heard. On rumors. I had to admit that when I first met Phil and found out he was living there, I had the same judgmental attitude. But, when I finally went up to the place a few months before he went into rehab, I found it was nowhere near as bad as the rumors had made me think it would be. Sure, the paint was faded, and the carpets were threadbare. But Phil kept his room clean and I did as well. It was as good as any other place I'd lived, just much smaller. And, more importantly, much cheaper.

"It's cool," I said. "I got a nice cheap room that's convenient to work. And the bars."

She smiled at that last. "No DWI's?"

"Nope. But then, you gotta have a car to get one of those."

That might have been more than she wanted to know as she turned her attention back to her son and his friends. I guess no one likes to hear about someone else's hard times. I didn't see it like that. As bad as it might look to an outside observer, it was still better than it had been a few months earlier. I saw my position as moving in the right direction. Or maybe it was just rationalizing my shitty situation.

"Where are you at these days?" I asked.

"Oh, I'm still in West Stockholm."

"Livingston Road?"

She took a beat before she answered as if she were ashamed. "Yeah, I'm at my dad's place."

I nodded, though I doubt she saw it as her gaze never left the back table. So, she lived with her father. So what? I would have been happy if my old man had even offered his place to me when I was homeless. To be able to get a full-time job in this town was something all by itself even if it didn't pay a living wage. Top it off with trying to raise a child on her own and I didn't think she had anything to be ashamed about. But I couldn't bring myself to say it. It seemed no matter how much older and wiser I might get, being around my sister's friend turned me back into that awkward twelve-year-old, the boy who had no idea what he was doing.

"How's Karen?" she asked.

"Alright, I guess. Same as she always was."

"Do you see her much?"

"Not much, but we did have a family dinner last night."

"Oh? What was the occasion?"

"Our uncle died," I said.

Mary turned to me then and she took my hand in hers. It surprised me so much that I looked down at our hands together.

"Oh, my God, Kelly, I am so sorry!" she said. "I thought maybe it was someone's birthday or something."

"It's okay," I said, looking back up and catching her deep dark eyes again. I put my hand on hers.

"I should call Karen," she said. "Or send a card." She let go of my hand and turned back to look at her boy. "It's just been so long since we talked."

"I think she'd like that."

She sat thinking for a minute before she suddenly stood up from the stool. "I'm going to run across the street to the drug store and see if they have any cards. Would you give it to her for me?"

"Of course."

"I'll be right back," she said to me, then looked to the back table. "Michael, I'll be right back. Finish up your game. We're going home as soon as I return."

She rushed out the front door. The boys at the back table looked at each other as if they had no idea what was going on. Oh, to be that young and clueless again. They wrapped up their last game and started to collect the balls as I turned off their light. Michael and his friends exchanged money and then his friends left through the back door as he brought the tray of balls up to the counter to settle the bill.

"Where'd she go?" Michael asked.

"Across the street to the drug store," I said. "Have a seat if you want." I pointed to the stool his mother had vacated and he sat down.

"You know my mom?" he asked.

Jesus, that was a loaded question.

"Yeah, we went to school together. She and my sister were best friends back then."

"You grew up in West Stockholm?"

"I did," I said proudly. "About halfway between the corner of Route 11 and the cemetery."

"Cool."

I think this had been the longest conversation I'd ever had with the boy, and it seemed to be over already. He looked around uncomfortably, probably wishing his mother would come back.

"Your mother tells me you're living up at the end of Livingston Road."

"Yeah, we take care of my grandfather," he said.

"That's cool. You ever go swimming down at the river?"

"Yeah," he said. The topic seemed to excite him. "We go down there to swim all summer long. You ever get caught in the Whirlpool?"

Ah, the infamous Whirlpool. It wasn't really a whirlpool. As the water came over the falls, at one particular point, it ran up against the big thick concrete pier. The swirling water was caused by the unstoppable force of the river's current colliding with the immovable object of the bridge support. If you found yourself caught in that swirl, it pulled you underwater by one force and churned you back up by another.

"I have had that unfortunate experience," I said.

It was not an experience one soon forgets. I never saw my life flash before my eyes, but it was probably the closest I'd ever come to drowning. We had been swimming one fall afternoon. I was fourteen at the time. This was after school started up again, but the day had been hot enough to need to cool off at the river after we got home. I was standing on the rocks just below the falls when I was suddenly sucked into the Whirlpool. Before I could even think to try to get away, it pulled me in and shoved me underwater. I felt my knees scrape against the rocks on the bottom. I had barely caught a breath before it had happened, so I fought as hard as I could to get back to the surface. I came up long enough to take a big gulp of air and to see the other kids standing nearby trying to reach out to me before the force of the water pulled me back under again. My eyes open, all I saw were the yellow-white bubbles of the churning water all around me. It seemed like an eternity before the current forced me back to the surface where I was able to get another breath of air before being violently pulled back to the bottom of the river once more. I was too busy struggling for my own survival to count how many times this repeated, but each time my feet touched bottom, I tried my best to push myself out and away from the falls. I'd like to say I was thinking how to get myself out of it, but there was no conscious thought. It was pure instinct that put my feet to the river bottom, and I was finally able to push myself away from the falls. It was only when I found myself resting against the other side of the bridge support that

I realized I was out. It was a long time before I swam out to the falls again.

"I got caught in the Whirlpool this summer!" Michael exclaimed.

"But you got yourself out," I stated.

"Yeah! But what a ride!" he said.

I had to admit that it was a badge of honor to have survived the Whirlpool even though I'd never heard of a single person drowning in that river. Getting out by yourself was the only way to survive. No one could jump in to help you. At least, no one ever did as far as I knew. You risked getting yourself caught up in that same vortex if you did.

"It's scary," I admitted. "But pretty exhilarating. Not that I ever want to do it again."

"Yeah, me either."

We both smiled at that thought.

"Okay, let's go." Mary was back. She walked up to where her son sat at the counter. She had a strange look in her eye like she was worried about what we might be talking about.

"Mom, did you know he grew up in West Stockholm?"

"Yeah, I knew that."

"And that he got caught in the Whirlpool, too?"

"No, I didn't know that," she said and looked at me.

"A shared experience apparently," I said with a smile.

"Okay," she replied. "Well, Michael, go on out to the car. We need to get home to get Grandpa's supper. I've got something to give to…Mr. King."

Mr. King? I really didn't like that reference, but I guess she was trying to teach her son about respecting your elders, so I let it go.

"Okay," he said. "See ya!" he said to me before heading out the front door.

"He's a good kid," I said.

Mary smiled. "Have you got a pen?" she asked.

I handed her one from under the counter. She quickly scribbled something on the card she had bought. She handed the pen back to me before stuffing the card in the envelope and sealing it. Then she gave it to me.

As I took the card, she put her other hand over mine. I looked up to see her look directly into my eyes. She really was a beautiful woman. I wished there was something more I could do for her.

"Tell Karen to call me," she said. "I wrote my number in the card."

"I will," I said.

She gave my hand a little squeeze before releasing it. Then, without another word and without looking back, she walked out the front door. We had so much more that we needed to talk about or at least so much more I wanted to talk about. But it probably wasn't going to happen. Not now. Not ever.

12

Revelations, 1979

I leapt onto the bus when it stopped in front of our house Monday morning. I was still flying about Saturday night. I wanted to scream to the world what had happened. But who could I tell? Kevin and Karen wouldn't have believed me. In fact, Karen probably would have called up Mary, except she couldn't because Mary's parents were really strict and didn't allow phone calls or anything on Sundays. I guess it was a religious thing. But, even if Karen had called, it's not like Mary could deny it. And even if she did, I knew what we had done. I was busting to tell someone. Jay was back from his mother's, so he'd be on the bus this morning. I could tell him. Unless Mary chose to sit with me instead of Karen. Wouldn't *that* be something? I wondered if that might happen. After we'd spent the night together, she just might decide to sit with me instead of my sister. We could even scooch down behind the seat and make out. I'd seen other couples do that, so maybe we could, too. Would we be a couple now and go out on dates like other couples? How could we not after what we had done? Maybe Mary would start spending time with me instead of Karen. I'd find out soon enough. We were getting closer to Mary's house. Jay might have to find somewhere else to sit this morning.

The bus pulled up and stopped in front of Mary's at the end of Livingston Road and I heard the doors open. I saw the top of her head as she came up the steps. Her dark hair was swept forward, so I couldn't see her face until she turned to walk down the bus aisle.

Then I could see her. She really was a pretty girl. She came up to my seat and I looked up at her and smiled.

She walked right past without even looking at me. I turned my head and watched her walk back to where my sister was sitting. She sat down next to Karen without ever looking up. I turned back around in my seat and stared forward. She hadn't even pretended to notice me. She used to at least give me a look before. Now she couldn't even look at me? I thought we had shared something special Saturday night. *I* thought it was special. Didn't she? And if it wasn't, then what did that mean? What was the point? I'd waited through all of Sunday just wanting to see her again and she blew me off. Completely. I turned around to see her and Karen sitting together in that seat three rows back and on the other side of the bus. They were talking. What were they talking about? Was she making fun of me? Calling me "little"? Was she even telling Karen what had happened? I turned back around. So what? What did I care? She was stupid and Karen was stupid and sex was stupid.

"Shove over," Jay said. I'd been so distracted that I hadn't even noticed we'd reached Jay's house. I moved over to let him sit down. No one else was going to sit with me.

"How's it going?" he asked.

I shrugged my shoulders.

"How was your weekend?"

"Alright, I guess," I replied.

"Mine was awesome!" He then started telling me about going on some weekend trip with his mother and her new boyfriend. I tried to listen and look happy for him even though I'm not sure what it was he had done. I couldn't concentrate on what he was saying. All I could think about was how could she do that? How could we have spent a night together and it meant nothing to her? Maybe she was a slut after all. Is that what sluts do? Fuck you and then ignore you?

The rest of the day was more of the same. I went to my classes, but nothing seemed to make sense to me. None of it mattered. I listened to what the teachers said, missed most of the questions I was called on to answer. What difference did it make? The ride home was more of the same, too. Mary ignored me when she got on the bus, and Jay went on about what a great weekend he had had. Yeah, big whoop.

"You want to come up to my place?" he asked as we neared my house.

"Sure," I answered. "I'll get changed and ride up."

I was about to get up and walk to the front of the bus when I saw that not only did Kevin and Karen get up but Mary did, too. She sometimes got off at our house so she and Karen could hang out. Then she'd walk back to her house before dinner. The bus stopped and the four of us stepped off and crossed the road to our driveway. Kevin ran for the porch and the kitchen door. Mary and Karen walked ahead of me. I followed behind, but they were inside before I was even halfway up the driveway. I set my book bag down on the porch and sat on the steps. The last thing I wanted to do was go inside and listen to Karen and Mary gossiping about girls at school or guys they liked. I guess I wasn't one of them as far as Mary was concerned. But I had promised Jay I would head up to his place, so I dragged myself into the house just as Kevin was heading out. He pushed me into a kitchen chair as he bolted out the door. I got back up and wandered down the hall to the stairs and headed up to my room to change out of my school clothes. Karen's door was one down from the door to my and Kevin's room. The door was open, and I could hear them talking. I didn't care what they were talking about. Unless Mary was talking about me. Maybe she was. Maybe she was telling Karen what we had done. I snuck up to the door.

"So, you're sure?" I heard my sister ask.

"The test don't lie," Mary replied.

Then they were silent. Test? It was only the second week of school. What test could they be talking about? I leaned a little closer to the door. Either they weren't talking or they were whispering. Did they know I was outside the door?

"What are you going to do?" Karen finally asked.

"I don't know." I could tell from Mary's voice that she was starting to cry.

"Have you told your parents?"

"Are you kidding? Of course not! My father's going to flip if he finds out!"

I was really confused. Why would her father care if she flunked a test? I knew her family was religious and all, but to punish her for failing a test seemed a little extreme.

"You've got to tell them. What else can you do?"

Mary was quiet for a long time, though I heard her sniff back tears a few times.

"I could, you know, do something about it," she finally said.

"Where?"

"Watertown," she said.

Watertown? Nothing they were saying made any sense. What could you do in Watertown, a city some seventy miles away, to take care of a failed test?

"Or Syracuse," Mary said.

"Can you afford that?"

"I don't know." Mary's voice broke with her tears. As much as she had pissed me off today, I felt such a longing to burst into the room and give her a hug. It didn't matter what she was talking about. It didn't matter that she had ignored me. I hated the thought of her being so sad. No matter what, she had been so sweet to me that night. I wished I could make it all go away, take away whatever it was that was hurting her.

"Is he going to help pay for it? Well, if you decide to, you know, do it?" Karen asked.

"I don't know. I haven't even mentioned that idea to him."

"Well, he should. It's as much his problem as it is yours."

Ah, there was someone else involved in this, someone else who had made her this sad. Maybe it was someone who helped her cheat on the test or something.

"I know, but he doesn't have any money."

"Well, I've got some money stashed if you need it."

Mary sniffed back her tears again. "Thanks," she said. I heard the bedsprings squeak and figured they were hugging each other.

"How much is an abortion?" Karen asked.

My breath caught in my throat.

An abortion?

That meant that the test they were talking about wasn't a school test, it was a…. I couldn't even form the thought in my head. If they were talking an abortion, then that meant Mary was…. I still couldn't finish the thought. I mean, I hadn't had any rubbers with me Saturday night. I hadn't even considered the possibility of needing them when I went down there. Was she talking about what I think she was talking about? Did I get her…pregnant? My legs went weak, and I felt like I was going to fall to the floor in a heap. I crept backwards to my bedroom, slipped inside, and closed the door as quietly as I could. I sat down on Kevin's bunk.

Jesus Christ! My first time getting laid, and I'd gotten her pregnant? What was I going to do? That was the only thought running through my head: What was I going to do? I didn't have any money for an abortion. And what would Mom and Dad do when they found out? Would Mary have to move in with us so we could raise the baby? *My* baby? *Our* baby? No wonder Mary hadn't talked to me on the bus. As much as I was about to freak out, she must have been freaking out twice as much.

What do I do? I couldn't get that thought out of my head. What *do* I do? Nothing in my life had prepared me for this moment.

I could call Uncle Bruce. Where had that thought come from? Why would I call Uncle Bruce about this? I barely knew him. But he seemed like the kind of guy who could offer some advice. Or maybe even offer some money. After all, if Mary decided to have the abortion, we'd have to find a way to pay for it. Maybe Uncle Bruce could lend me the money. It might be better than having to talk to Mom and Dad about it.

What do I do?

I stripped down to my underpants and socks so I could change from my school clothes to something else. I pulled on a pair of dirty Wranglers and a t-shirt. I had told Jay I would meet him at his house. I could at least keep that promise for now. That's what I would do for now. When I finished changing, I stepped to the door and opened it slowly. I stood there silent until I heard their muffled voices. They were still in Karen's room. I snuck out of the room and quickly went down the stairs and out the door. I picked up my bike from where I'd left it by the porch and walked down to the road. I didn't need to get myself killed by some car speeding down the main drag. It would solve all my problems, though. When I saw there was no traffic, I climbed on and pedaled down toward the bridge, flew across it, and took the left turn up Livingston Road to Jay's house.

I dropped my bike on the front sidewalk and headed up the steps of the porch to the front door. Shoot! In my hurry, I forgot to grab my pot. I had originally been excited to let Jay know I had some. I wanted to impress him with my California Sense, though I didn't think I'd tell him how I'd gotten it. His stuff hadn't gotten me high like that stuff had. And I was thinking I really wanted to get stoned right now. I needed something to take my mind off the news I had heard. I wondered when Mary was going to tell me. I wondered if Mary would tell Karen who had done it. And how was I going to tell my parents? Oh, my God, I needed to get stoned.

I was just about to knock on the door when Jay opened it.

"What took you so long?" he asked.

"Uh, nothing. My brother was being a jerk."

"Well, come on. Let's go get high!"

Jay came out onto the porch and closed the door behind him. I followed him again down the driveway to the barn. Rather than go in through the side door, this time he opened the big garage door at the front. He didn't give me a reason, and I didn't figure it was worth asking. My mind was spinning with enough other things anyway. We headed up the stairs to the second floor. Jay took his seat on the couch and I sat down heavily in the arm chair. I suddenly had a vision of Uncle Bruce's own Fortress of Solitude in Grandma's barn. His had been smaller, darker, more comfortable, really. And Jay's didn't have the little cubby hole in the wall that held *Playboy* magazines and a bottle of Cutty Sark.

Jay pulled a rolled plastic bag from his pocket. "I took it inside just to be sure nothing got into it. Been waiting for this all day."

"Yeah," I said. "Me, too." That was a lie. I hadn't even thought about it until we had gotten on the bus after school. It was only after I'd overheard the news that I'd really thought about it.

"I got home too late from Mom's last night," Jay went on. "And with Dad in the house this morning, there was no chance before school."

Before school? Who would get high before school?

He pulled out one of the joints he had already rolled and took a Bic lighter from the pocket of his jeans. He lit it and took a deep drag, then handed it to me. I took it. I hesitated before I took a drag. Was this really the best thing to be doing? I mean, it seemed like every time I smoked, I got into some kind of trouble. In one way or another.

Yeah, but his stuff didn't even get me high the last time. It probably wouldn't do it this time, either. But I kinda hoped it would. I needed to get away from these thoughts running through my head. I put the joint to my lips and took a drag. Not a big one; I didn't want to have a coughing fit. It was big enough to feel it fill my lungs. I handed the joint back to Jay as he blew smoke out. He took it and laid back on the couch.

"Oh, yeah," he said. He took another drag.

After my second time with the joint, I did start feeling it. Maybe I just needed to smoke a little more in order to start getting high. I didn't know. I was glad to start feeling the buzz in my brain.

"We need some tunes," Jay said. He pulled a small portable radio from next to the couch. "My Mom let me have her old radio."

"Cool. We can probably pick up the Potsdam station. They usually have some good music."

"Nah," he said. "I heard about this station out of Canada that has good stuff."

He handed the joint back to me before he started twisting the dial. I took another drag and listened to the static as he tried to tune in the station.

"We've only got one or two stations you can get out here," I said.

But, as he turned the dial, the music started to come through clear. Boston's "Peace of Mind" picked up somewhere in the middle of the song.

"Yeah!" Jay exclaimed as he set the radio down and took the joint from between my fingers. I continued to stare at my fingers where the joint had been. Even though I'd watched him take it from my hand, my mind still seemed to be surprised that it was no longer there.

I sat back in the armchair and looked up at the open rafters of the roof. It was so far away, such a high ceiling. I wanted to float right up there. Then I closed my eyes and let the music wash over me. Yeah, echoing Jay's exclamation in my mind. This was good. No worries, no thoughts, no troubles. Just…the music. I smiled at the thought even as the song came to an end. Another song, one I didn't recognize, started almost immediately.

"So, you never told me," Jay said. "How was your weekend?"

I burst out laughing. Jay laughed along with me, but when I sat up and glanced over at him, he looked confused. How on Earth could I tell him about my weekend? Any part of it? How it had started? How it had ended! Good God!

"What?" Jay asked.

"Nothing," I replied when I was able to stop laughing. At least I could laugh about it for the moment. "It's just that, well, it was a fucked-up weekend." I couldn't help but smile for using a bad word.

"What happened?"

I realized that even high, I couldn't tell him. Well, not everything. I could start with the funeral that we weren't allowed to attend and the family dinner. But not what happened after.

"They had my Grandpa's funeral Friday," I finally said.

"Oh, man, that sucks. How was it?"

"I don't know! We had to go to school!"

"Are you shittin' me? You couldn't even get out early to go?"

I had been mad, not because I wasn't able to miss a day of school but because for some reason, I was not allowed to attend my own grandfather's funeral. Did Grandma think we'd embarrass her somehow? Was she ashamed of us? I'd never been to a funeral, so I didn't know if it would have been something I even wanted to attend. But I did want to. I was curious. What was a funeral like? Thinking about it started to piss me off again. And anger was not something I wanted to feel.

"Whatever," I said and leaned back in the chair again. I tried to recapture the mellow feeling I had listening to the music, but it seemed to be gone.

"What about the rest of the weekend?"

"We had a family dinner at my grandmother's," I replied without sitting up. I let my mind wander back to that evening. "That was actually pretty cool. I finally got to meet my Uncle Bruce."

"Who's he?" Jay asked.

"He's…." It took me a moment to remember exactly how he was related to me. Yeah, Jay's pot had definitely gotten me stoned this time. I smiled at the thought and let my mind drift with the music. Surrender, surrender, but don't give yourself away….

"He's what?" Jay asked, waking me from my daydream.

"Oh! He's my uncle."

"You said that."

"Right. He's my mother's brother," I finally said. "He was in Vietnam."

"Wow," Jay said. He sounded impressed. I had been able to impress him about something. I smiled again over that. I'd gotten the feeling that Jay was not all that impressed with our town or our school or anything about me. He was, after all, from the city. What did we have here in West Stockholm to impress him? Cows and horses and trees, oh my!

"He ever kill anyone?" Jay asked.

That question made me sit up because the thought had not actually crossed my mind until Jay had asked. Had he killed anyone? Did that have something to do with him moving to Utica? Was that why he never came back? Was that what made it dangerous for him to be around?

"I don't know," I replied. "I never asked."

"Are you kidding? That would have been the first thing I would have asked. I bet he has. Probably blew some guy's head off. Or blew him apart with a grenade. Or maybe with a tank! Ran over an entire village or something."

I glanced over at Jay. He seemed a little too excited over the thought that my uncle might have taken a life. Honestly, I wasn't sure how I felt about it. Maybe it was the pot, but I suddenly felt really bad for Uncle Bruce. Had he done that stuff? Had he killed anyone? Was that why he avoided all of us?

"Was he drafted or did he volunteer?" Jay asked.

"I think he was drafted." I recalled Uncle Bruce telling me about being drafted and how he hadn't wanted to be there at all. Did it really matter how he ended up in Vietnam?

"Wow, to be in the shit."

Jay was beginning to scare me. Or maybe it was the pot. He seemed way too into the idea of someone being in a war. It's like he enjoyed the thought of being in battle or killing someone. I didn't like this side of him.

"I think I gotta go," I said.

"Already? It can't be that late."

"I know, but I gotta get home." That idea alone caused me some troubled thoughts. I hadn't tried to ride home high since, well, that Friday night. And I'd been pretty straight by the time I headed home on Saturday night. Or would that have been Sunday morning? Either way, the thought of riding my bike home in my current condition didn't thrill me. But I needed to get away from Jay for now. His obsession with war and death scared me. "It might take me some time to get there," I finally said.

"Yeah," Jay said. "You're pretty stoned, I think."

He laughed and I couldn't help but laugh, too. Yeah, I was pretty stoned.

"Yeah," I said, "I am pretty stoned." I laughed even harder when I realized that I had said my very thought out loud. I guess I hadn't needed my pot after all. Still, I figured I needed to bring it next time just because we had only smoked his pot so far. It was only right to share what I had since he had shared his.

We made our way down the stairs and out to the front of the barn. Jay reached up for the handle on the garage door and yanked it. The door came down hard, shattering one of the little windows. We both burst out in another round of laughter as shards of glass flew everywhere.

"Oh, my God!" I said. "Are you going to get in trouble for that?"

"Probably," he said. "Nah, I'll lie and tell him I broke it playing basketball."

It seemed logical as there was the basketball hoop above the door. But it seemed to me that he might still get in trouble. But what did I care? I had my own troubles to worry about. Bigger troubles than a broken window! We walked back to the front of the house, and I picked up my bike from where I'd left it on the sidewalk.

"I think I'll walk for a while," I said.

We both laughed again. I'm not sure if what I said was funny, but we both seemed to think it was.

"I'll see you on the bus tomorrow," Jay said as he headed up the porch and into the house. I gave him a wave as I started to walk back down Livingston Road. It felt like I'd been walking for a while when I looked up and saw that I'd only gone about two hundred feet or so. Was I walking too slow or was time just passing a lot slower for some reason? Either way, I was never going to get home at this rate. I laughed to myself at the thought. I threw my leg over the bike, braced myself in case my balance was bad, then pushed off down the hill toward the bridge. I surprised myself by staying upright. But the further I went down the hill, the faster the bike was going. It felt like I was flying faster than I'd ever gone before. I touched the brakes as I neared the corner thinking if I slowed down enough, I'd be able to see any cars coming. No, I was going too fast. Too fast! I wasn't even sure I'd be able to make the turn onto the bridge at this speed. If I didn't make the turn, I'd go crashing through the brush and trees and into the river! The lyrics of Meat Loaf flashed through my head. Dyin' at the bottom of a pit in the blazin' sun. I had to slow down! I stepped down harder on the pedal to apply the brakes and I felt the back wheel lock up. The bike came to a stop just before the stop sign at the end of the road. I had to put my feet down fast to keep the bike from falling over.

I got off the bike and walked beside it as I crossed the intersection to the walkway of the bridge. The sweat was pouring down my face and I was breathing hard. But it wasn't from the effort. No more riding for me. At least not downhill. Too fast!

I was safe on the boards of the walkway. No cars could hit me here. But then I wondered how sturdy the wood was. After all, it was just a boardwalk. I could hear the water rushing over the falls below me, twenty or thirty feet down. It would really suck if any of the boards gave way. I'd fall right into the middle of the Whirlpool!

Stop thinking that way! I walked faster to get across the bridge. There was nothing wrong with the bridge or the boards on the walkway. How many times had I crossed the same way with no worries? Why was it worrying me so much this time? Why was just riding my bike such a scary idea? Was it the pot? Was I *too* stoned?

Danny's house was there across the road when I got to the other side of the bridge. The driveway was still empty. There wasn't even a For Sale sign or anything in the yard. Did his family own the place or had they just been renting? It's funny that in all the years I had known him, that question had never come up. I guess it never really mattered. A home was a home was a home. It didn't matter if they owned it or not. And now it didn't matter because Danny was no longer there. Dammit! I didn't want to think about him. I missed him so much it hurt sometimes. Times like right now. I realized that I had walked over to the end of the driveway, so I turned the bike back toward the main drag.

There was no one on the porch at Moe's place. I hadn't seen him out there on the way to Jay's, and I didn't want to see him there now. I didn't want to see him; I didn't want to know him. I didn't want to think about it. But there it was, back in my head. It was all there. Every second of it, every detail. It bothered me that I couldn't get it out of my head. What did it mean?

At least I knew I wasn't gay. Mary had proved that to me. Fucking Mary. Was it really too much to ask that she be nice to me after that? She hadn't even looked at me on the bus or when she got off at our house. And what had she told Karen? Anything about it? Especially now that she was pregnant! What did that mean for her and me? For us? Anything?

I looked up and realized I had made it to the top of the hill by the Methodist Church. My mind had been so distracted that I hadn't realized I'd climbed all the way up. That meant the only obstacle between me and my driveway was the cemetery. I really hated that place. It's not that I believed in ghosts. I'm just not sure that I *didn't* believe in ghosts. But it was the middle of the day, well, late afternoon. Ghosts only came out at night, right? Still, I decided to risk riding the bike again so I could get past it as fast as I could. And while riding was easier this time, I didn't pedal too fast.

I wondered if Mary was still at the house. Was she going to stay for supper? How awkward would that be? Maybe she'd changed her mind about me. Maybe she'd be coming out of the house as I got there. I'd drop my bike on the other side of the driveway as she came out. She'd see me there and look up and our eyes would meet. Then she'd walk down the steps and cross over to me. I'd play it cool, show her I was mad because of the way she had treated me. She'd cross the driveway to where I stood. I'd look away to make sure she knew I was mad, show her that I didn't care. Then I'd feel her hand on my chin, and she'd turn my head, force me to look at her. Our eyes would meet again. And then she'd kiss me. It wouldn't be the same as when we had kissed in the White House. This would be softer, more…tender? I don't know. It would be a sweeter kiss than any kiss I'd ever had. I could feel the softness of her lips on mine and hear her voice in my head.

"No matter what happens," she said. "No matter how I act, just know that you are special to me."

Then she'd let go of my chin and walk away down the driveway. I'd watch her as she reached the end and turned down the main drag to go back to her house. She wouldn't look back before she disappeared from sight. That would be it.

I turned my bike into the driveway and struggled to get to the top. Just as I got to a point where I could drop the bike to the ground, I heard the door close. I looked up to see Mary was on the porch. She did look up to see me and our eyes did meet for a split second before she turned away. I watched her go as she hurried down the porch steps and quickly walked down the driveway and was gone. It had been nothing like the fantasy I'd just had, the fantasy I'd hoped for. I decided that I didn't want to know her, either. She had ignored me, pretended that I didn't exist. My own family did that. I didn't need her doing that, too. But then, why should I expect anything different from her?

We had macaroni and cheese for dinner that night. I was still feeling the pot I had smoked with Jay. It was like the buzz wasn't going away. It had mellowed a little bit, but it was very much me stoned while sitting at the dinner table with my family. Just like in that TV special. It was a weird thing. And I didn't realize how hungry I was until dinner was served. I ate through two plates of mac and cheese before Karen ruined the mood for the evening. My mother was at the sink, her back to us, and my father had already left the table when Karen spoke up.

"Mary's pregnant," she said.

Oh, my God! How could she just blurt it out like that? What was I supposed to do now? Now my mother was going to know, and I hadn't even had a chance to get myself together for revealing the news to her. Well, it was out now. And it was time for me to take responsibility. I cleared my throat with no idea what I was going to say.

"Really?" my mother said, never turning around from the sink. "Does she know who the father is?"

What a rude question! Of course she knew who the father was. It's not like Mary was some kind of slut. And now everyone would know who the father was. And my mother would know. And she would have to tell my father. It would all come out now even though I'd hoped I would have more time to deal with it myself. But, thanks to Karen, it was all coming out a lot sooner than I had planned.

"Her boyfriend, Brad," Karen said.

For the second time that day, I was knocked for a loop. Brad? Brad was the father? Who the hell was Brad?

"She did one of those at-home pregnancy tests," Karen continued. "That's why she and I didn't hang out Saturday night. She was a little freaked out."

It all became clear to me then. That's why she was at the White House. That's why she had been there all by herself. That's why she had been drinking alone. Trying to escape the truth. Kind of like what I had done that very afternoon going up to Jay's. I was trying to escape the truth. Or at least what I thought was the truth. Wow. So, I wasn't the father and wasn't going to be a father. I couldn't help myself when I leaned back in my chair and loudly breathed a sigh of relief. I don't think anyone noticed. I hadn't been the one that had gotten her pregnant. Still, that was no reason for Mary to treat me like she had. We had still had sex.

It didn't matter, I decided. Sex or girls or any of it. What was the point if all they were going to do was treat you like shit? Karen and my mother were still talking when I got up from the table and headed upstairs to do my homework. I had a worksheet due in the morning.

Fucking Mary....

13

Oh, Brother, 1994

The envelope was sealed, and Karen's name was printed on the front in crisp, neat block letters. I placed it on the shelf under the counter right next to my time sheet with the hope that putting it there might help remind me to take it with me at the end of the night. I hadn't noticed the newspaper sitting on the shelf and took it out to catch up on the latest local news. Gary and I had fun with the public records section: we looked to see how many of the arcade kids got in trouble with the local constabulary. It was usually something petty like shoplifting or truancy but every now and then, there was something more substantial like burglary or drug possession. When we found a notice on one of them, we'd cut it out and pin it to the bulletin board in the storeroom between the pool hall and the arcade. We had quite a collection of names and notices. Joe didn't think it was appropriate that we made sport of our young customers, but he also wasn't around to deal with the little criminals day after day. So, after perusing the public records and finding nothing worthy of the board, I skimmed through the rest of the paper. Near the last page were the obituaries.

There was no picture, but the small headline included his name, Bruce Wright. It took a moment for me to make the connection between Uncle Bruce and the man named in the obit. He'd always been Uncle Bruce. I knew my mother's maiden name, but it still didn't look right when I first read it. No one said they had placed an obituary. But I suppose it was just a matter of course for my grandmother right along with cooking the family dinner: it was what you did. And with the funeral the next day, it made sense. I was just about to read it when I heard the front door open. I turned to see Kevin walk in with a guy I didn't recognize.

"Hey," he said as he approached the counter.

"Hey. Aren't you supposed to be at work?"

"Nah, I got time off for bereavement!" he exclaimed. "Uncle Bruce got me a week's vacation!"

I could smell the beer on his breath. It wasn't even five o'clock and he was already drunk.

"This here's Tim," he said, indicating the light-haired guy in jeans standing behind him. Tim wore a green jacket that indicated he played rugby for the tech school. "Met him over at Backstreets. Told him I could get a deal on pool 'cause I knew the guy who worked there."

"Whatever," I said and handed him a tray of balls.

"We're only going to stay for a couple of games."

"Then home for dinner?"

Kevin laughed. "Back to Backstreets for a liquid dinner!" He held up an open hand to his new friend and they high-fived.

"What about Patty?" I asked.

"What about her? She can't drink."

"Isn't she expecting you for dinner?"

"She knows where I am."

Did she? I wondered what she really knew. Everyone else knew about Kevin cheating on Patty. She must have had some idea. Maybe she chose to ignore it, thinking he'd change. Or that she could change him. He and Tim walked over to the table to the left and I flipped on the lights. I set the number of players at two. Give him a break? Yeah, right. I watched Tim rack the balls and then Kevin broke them without sinking anything. As Tim leaned in to make a shot, Kevin wandered back to the counter.

"You didn't get any time off?" he asked.

"Not if I want to make a paycheck."

"Sucks." He looked back at the table to watch Tim drop the seven ball in a side pocket.

No, what sucked was that my brother got paid time off for an uncle he didn't even know.

"You going to the funeral tomorrow?" he asked.

"Yeah. You?"

"Didn't want to but Patty said I should. She even took my suit in to get it dry-cleaned. I hope she remembered to pick it up today."

"You couldn't pick it up?" I asked.

"Why? She was already coming into town to go shopping."

I couldn't suppress a sad chuckle and shook my head.

"What?" Kevin asked as he walked over to the table to take a shot.

"Nothing." I wasn't going to say any more about it. How fucking blind could one guy be? If he couldn't see the problem, I wasn't going to try to explain it to him. Besides, he was carrying on a civil conversation, something he could only seem to do when we were alone. He could only be civil with me when he was drunk and no one we knew was around. He didn't need to impress this guy, Tim, because Tim didn't know me from Adam. It would be a different story if someone else were there. As if to prove that point, the back door opened, and Jay entered with three of his friends.

"Hey, King!" he said as they approached me.

I took out a tray of balls and set it on the counter without saying a word. I made sure it was a tray that had brand-new chalk.

"Jay!" my brother called out.

Jay hadn't seen Kevin at first but walked over to greet him now.

"Kevin, my man!" They shook hands. "How goes it?"

"Like the Energizer bunny. It keeps going and going."

"Cool-cool," Jay said. "We should play sometime."

"We're heading back to Backstreets after this game if you want to come find us."

"Sounds like a plan, man. I might just look you up. Gonna grab some game ourselves first."

"Just be careful grabbing Kelly's balls," Kevin said. "You know how he can be."

They both laughed at their little inside joke. Fucking assholes. If it was just Kevin and I, he was fine. Throw another person like

Karen or Jay into the mix and I became the third wheel and the butt of whatever stupid thing he could think to say. Jay came up to the counter.

"How's life in the kingdom?" he asked as he took up the tray.

"It's been better," I answered as I sat back down.

"We'll take the front table today."

"Just to let you know that table costs more per hour than the others."

"Yeah, I know," he said. "But, it's payday, so why not splurge?"

"Whatever." He and his friends walked toward the table, and I switched on the lights to start the timer. I set the computer for five players. If he wanted to splurge, I'd make sure he paid his share. I did that on occasion with certain customers if I didn't like them or they pissed me off. I'd switch their rate up and down throughout their play. None of them knew any better and it increased our receipts ever so slightly. Besides, by Jay's own account, he was doing well. His father had gotten him in at the phone company in some kind of training program that allowed him to work toward an associate degree in electrical engineering while he earned a paycheck from the company. Not a bad deal, really. If I'd been offered something like that, I would have jumped at it, too. Unfortunately, my father's work at Ames didn't offer any such incentives. Hell, my father wouldn't even use his connections with friends in town to help me get a job, not even at his own store. I remembered applying for a job striping parking lots with a local company owned by a friend of my father's. It wouldn't have been a glamorous job, but it paid a decent wage. As a bonus, in the winter, when you couldn't stripe parking lots in New York, the owner took the whole crew down to Florida where he had various contracts that kept the business going all winter long. It was after I had applied that I found out my father knew the owner. They'd gone to school together. And having mentioned the man's name, my father decided to go visit him to catch up. "I didn't say anything about the job," he had said after returning home. I was dumbfounded! I wanted to scream at him, "Why not, you fool?" Nepotism seemed to be the only way to get ahead in this town. Even Kevin had gotten his job as a grounds and maintenance man at the tech college because he knew someone. But it wouldn't have made any difference at that point. I never did hear from the guy, not even a call for an interview. Don't believe anyone who tells you a small town is like an extended family. Well, then again, maybe it is. It's certainly as dysfunctional as any family I was a part of.

Kevin and Tim finished their game and brought the balls back to me.

"Done already?" I asked.

"Gotta save the money for beer."

I cashed them out and watched them head back out the front door. Kevin gave Jay another handshake before they left.

I took up the paper again and found the obituary once more, curious to see what someone might have written about Uncle Bruce. I was a bit disappointed that there was nothing in the brief article that I didn't already know.

Mr. Bruce Wright of Utica, and formerly of Potsdam, died unexpectedly on Tuesday, September 6th, at the age of 42. A 1970 graduate of Potsdam Central High School, Mr. Wright served two tours of duty in Vietnam from 1971-1973. Upon returning, he used the G.I. Bill to earn his associate degree in Business from the state college in Canton before moving to and opening a small business in Utica. Mr. Wright never married but is survived by his mother, Mrs. Ruth Wright, of Hopkinton; a sister, Mrs. James (Elizabeth) King, of West Stockholm; and a niece and two nephews. He was predeceased by his father, John Wright, who died in 1979.

Jesus, that's all a man's life was worth after forty-two years? Five sentences? It angered me that no one could have come up with something more to say about him.

"Hey, Moe, whaddaya know?" I heard Jay say in a sing-song voice.

I'd been so involved with the paper that I hadn't heard the front door open. But, when I looked up, there was Moe once again. The same young kid was with him as was with him before. Maybe it was the fact that it was still daylight or maybe it was because I'd gotten a good night's sleep or had a good breakfast. Whatever the reason, I found myself standing tall as Moe came in. I didn't want another encounter, but I was ready for him this time.

14

Takin' a Ride, 1979

Nothing seemed worthwhile anymore. Sure, I got up and went to school, went to my classes, did my homework. It wasn't like it mattered. But I knew if I didn't at least do my homework, I'd get in trouble at school and they'd contact my parents and I'd get in trouble at home, and I just didn't want to deal with any of that shit. So, the only point to any of it, I guess, was to keep everyone off my back and leave me alone. They never paid me much attention anyway. At least this way they would continue to not notice me.

Maybe being noticed is what I had been hoping for. If I had been the one who got Mary pregnant, they'd finally have to notice me. They would have to pay attention to me. But even Mary didn't pay me any attention. I didn't even care about that anymore. She was just like the rest. I was nothing to her, nothing to them. Easy to ignore, easy to forget. It was like that time at Ames. We had stopped by when my father was getting off work so we could pick him up and go out to Grandma and Grandpa's for Karen's birthday dinner. I think I was about eight. Yeah, I must have been because we were still living in Potsdam and we had been going to celebrate Karen's eleventh birthday. My mother wanted to get some last-minute thing Grandma needed, so we all went in. Karen and Kevin hung out by the service counter, and I wandered over to the books and magazines to find the latest issue of *Starlog*. I must have gotten distracted by it because when I finally looked up to see if my mother was back up front, Karen and Kevin were gone. They weren't standing by the service counter. I figured maybe they had gone back out to the car to wait for everyone. So, I put the magazine back in the rack and headed outside. But, when I got to the parking lot, the car was gone. I thought maybe I'd forgotten where we'd parked, so I wandered around the lot a little bit. But the car wasn't there anywhere. My first thought then was not that they had left me behind. I actually wondered if the car had been stolen. And that led to thoughts of my father having a fit if he found out my mother had left the keys in it or something. But this was Potsdam. No one stole cars in Potsdam. Maybe they were playing a trick on me and had pulled the car into another row in the parking lot, and they were about to pull back up front and surprise me. But that didn't make any sense because that wasn't the kind of joke anyone in my family would play. And my mother had been too upset at running late to get to Grandma's that she wouldn't have allowed something like that anyway. And that's when it hit me.

They'd forgotten me.

They had all climbed into the car and not noticed I wasn't there in the back seat with Kevin and Karen. Now, granted, with the station wagon we had at the time, I did like to ride in the far back so I could have the extra room, but didn't anyone double-check to see if I was there? So, there I was standing in the middle of the Ames parking lot with no idea what to do. And that's when the tears started coming. I wasn't crying because they had left me. Or maybe I was. Either way, I was crying because I was scared. I had no idea what to do. Should I start walking home? Should I go back inside and have them call my grandmother so someone could come back into town and pick me up? Just as I was about to sit down on the curb of the sidewalk in front of the store, the station wagon pulled back into the parking lot and drove up to where I was.

"What is wrong with you?" my mother said without even looking out the window at me. "You can't just stay with your brother and sister in the store? Get in this car!"

I was wiping the tears from my eyes as the back door of the wagon opened and my sister got out. Even in all this, I got stuck sitting in the middle. And it was all my fault.

"Now we'll be even later for dinner," my mother grumbled as Karen got in and closed the door.

They had ignored me then and they ignored me now. So, why did it bother me so much this time? I suppose it *was* because I thought this might have been the time that they couldn't have ignored me. They would *have* to notice me. That had turned out to be wrong. Just like every other thought I ever had.

Jay was about the only one who seemed to notice me now. He'd asked me to stop by his house after school every afternoon since Monday. And when Mary got off the bus at our house on Wednesday, I seriously considered it. But I just didn't feel like being around anybody. Instead, as soon as I changed into my old clothes, I grabbed my bike and headed up the road to the corner store. I had a couple of dollars and I figured I could get some candy or a soda. Really, I just wanted to get out of the house, and it was the only other place I could think to go.

The store was on the opposite corner across the state highway. It sounds more dangerous than it was. You could see the traffic coming from both directions and it was a pretty quiet road. Still, I took my time and had to wait for a big tractor trailer to go by before I ran across the road with my bike. I rolled it over to the bike rack at the side of the store. This was the only place in West Stockholm where I worried about my bike getting stolen. Too many strangers came by. I had just finished locking it up when I heard him say my name.

"Hey, Kelly."

I froze where I was. It was Moe. I hadn't seen him since…that night. Another reason I hadn't ridden up to Jay's place was so that I didn't have to worry about running into him. I hadn't given it much thought that he might be here at the store. Didn't he work during the day like everyone else?

"You too good to talk to a friend?" he asked, his voice closer now, right behind me.

I stood up slowly but still didn't turn around. Friend? How could I face him after what had happened, after what he had done? After what *I* had done? Not only that other stuff, but I had stolen his pipe and his lighter. He must have known it was me when he found them missing. What would he do? What would *I* do? What *could* I do? My bike was locked up and there was no running away from him. He was bigger than me, probably faster. I was stuck. I turned around to find him standing right by the bike rack.

"How you doin'?" he asked.

How was I doing? That's what he had to say? Nothing about anything else?

"I'm okay," I replied. Okay? What the hell was I saying that for?

You're being polite, I heard my grandmother say. That would have been her response. You be polite no matter what. Manners mattered. What else were you going to say?

I looked up at his face and then quickly looked away. His eyes bugged me.

"Yeah, I'm okay, too," he said as he sat down on the bike rack. "Thanks for asking." And then he laughed.

Did I imagine it? Had it all been some weird dream or vision that I had while I was high? I wondered. Maybe what I thought had happened that night hadn't actually happened. Was that even possible? Moe was acting like it didn't, like nothing happened. No, how could that be? Even if that other stuff didn't happen, I still had his pot. Did I maybe steal both the pot and the pipe that night? Maybe I had imagined it or made it up in my head or something.

"How was school?" he asked.

"Alright, I guess." Yeah, it must have been some kind of dream. Moe was acting way too normal for it to be anything else.

"How's that friend of yours? What was his name?"

"Jay?" I asked.

"Yeah, the guy that you were hangin' out with on Labor Day. How's he doin'?"

"Good, I guess." I was feeling calmer about the whole thing. There's no way that other stuff could have happened if Moe was being so cool.

"He's new in town, isn't he?"

"Yeah," I said. "He and his dad moved up from Utica."

"That's cool. Utica is a nice place to be from. Not sure I'd want to live there myself, but it's a cool place to be from."

"I guess," I said, shrugging my shoulders. I'd never been there myself. It must have been alright if Uncle Bruce lived there.

"You guys go to school together, then?"

"Yeah, we're in the same grade and have a couple of classes together. And lunch."

He leaned down toward me, and I couldn't help but pull away from him a little as he did.

"Is he cool like you?" He gave me a wink.

"Yeah, he parties," I replied, hoping I was using the right word.

"Awesome! So, he's like your best friend?"

I shrugged my shoulders again. Was he? Sometimes I wasn't sure.

Moe didn't say anything, and I looked up to see him smiling. He took out a cigarette and lit it, and then he chuckled.

"What?" I asked, not able to keep from smiling.

"Nothing," he replied, shaking his head. "You're just a man of few words, I guess."

A man of few words? Wasn't that what Uncle Bruce had said, too?

"Maybe I'm just stoic," I said, remembering the word Uncle Bruce had used.

Moe looked at me, then, and raised an eyebrow. Had I impressed him with the word? Had I even used it right? I still didn't really know what it meant, but Moe seemed to think it was a good word.

"Yeah," he said, slowly nodding his head. "Maybe you are, my friend."

He took another drag from his cigarette and tilted his head back to blow smoke toward the sky.

"You wanna take a ride?" he asked.

"What?"

"A ride," he repeated. "You wanna go for a ride? I know you like my car. I've seen you admire it when I'm cruisin' through town."

"It's alright," I said.

"Alright? It's a chick magnet," he said. "The girls in town see you riding around in that machine, and you'll have them eating out of your hand."

I didn't know what to say. I was always told not to accept rides from strangers. But Moe was hardly a stranger. And it was a cool car, no matter what Jay said.

"What do you say?" he asked as he crushed out his cigarette with the heel of his boot.

I still didn't answer him. I probably shouldn't. But what was the worst that could happen? This was Moe, not some no-name killer or drifter or something. And what I thought had happened the other night? It was probably nothing anyway. What harm could there be in taking a ride?

"Tell you what," he said. "I'm going to go jump in the car and bring it around here. If you wanna go for a ride, you can get in when I stop. If not, well, that'll be that."

He got up from his seat on the bike rack and disappeared behind the building. I heard the roar of the car when he started it up. Before I had time to think about it, Moe was pulling up next to me in the parking lot. The passenger door opened in front of me.

"Hop in, buddy," he said, leaning over toward the door.

I again heard my grandmother's voice in my head at that moment. It would be impolite to turn down his generous offer, was what she was saying. Yes, the polite thing to do would be to accept the ride. I stepped over to the car and sat down, pulling the big heavy door closed.

"There you go," he said. He reached down to the shifter, pushed the stick forward, and we were off toward the road. He crossed over the state highway and headed down the main drag toward the bridge.

The inside was as cool as the outside except that it smelled like cigarettes. Almost everything was black, from the dashboard to the seats to the carpet. The rumble of the engine vibrated my butt in the seat. A song by Bad Company was playing on the radio and that's when I saw that it was a Pioneer stereo. That was the best car stereo to have.

"Hey," he said. "Open the glove box."

I pushed the silver button and the door dropped open. The only things inside were an envelope, a lighter, and a couple of joints.

"Grab one of those numbers and fire it up," he said.

I pulled out one of the joints and the lighter.

"Had to roll some joints since I didn't have a pipe," he said.

Oh, shit! This was it. He knew about the pipe. Of course, he did. He knew I had stolen it because I was the only other person in the house that night. My heart started pounding in my chest. What was he going to do now?

Moe slapped me on the shoulder. "I'm kidding!" he said. "Joints are easier to get rid of if the cops pull me over. Go ahead. Fire it up."

I found myself looking at him a little longer this time since his eyes were on the road and he wasn't looking at me. He shot me a glance every couple of seconds. Those memories of the other night had to be some trick of my mind. This was the Moe I knew. Just a guy with a Firebird and some pot. Why not just go with it? What did it matter anyway? I put the joint to my lips and lit it as we flew across the bridge. I took a drag and then held it out for Moe. He took it with one hand while keeping his other on the steering wheel.

"My man," he said and then took a hit before passing the joint back to me.

"Where are we going?" I asked before I took another hit.

"You got somewhere to be?" he asked, smiling.

"No," I said, my voice squeaky as I tried to hold my hit.

"I know a place," he said as he blew smoke at the windshield.

I nodded and handed the joint back to him. I had nowhere to be. I had no one waiting for me, nobody that would miss me if I didn't come back. Fuck it. Let's go.

The joint went back and forth a couple more times and I was starting to feel the buzz by the time we reached the Sand Hill Road. This was the road that connected to another state highway, the one that led to Hopkinton and Lake Ozonia. This was the way we went to get to camp. This was one of my favorite roads. I didn't know why they called it the Sand Hill Road, but there were some sandy backroads that led off of it. And it was hilly. Was that why it was called the Sand Hill Road? Sandy hills off the road? Or was I just feeling a little stoned?

About halfway down, Moe made a right turn onto one of those sandy roads and we headed into the woods. They weren't thick woods, so the light streamed down through the trees turning my everything into a colored blur as we went. I'd never been down any of the backroads before. Looks like that was changing today. I smiled at the idea of some new adventure. My buzz was definitely settling into my stoic head.

Moe sped down the sandy hill road like an expert. I figured he had driven it before. He had to know where he was going, especially if he was feeling the same buzz I was. Then we came to a clearing, and he swung the car around to face out again before coming to a stop in the middle of the woods.

"I love this car," he said. "What do you think?"

"Yeah," I said. "I like it."

"Yeah?"

"Yeah." I giggled. "My friend, Jay, doesn't think Firebirds are cool. But I think they are."

"Your friend, Jay, sounds like an asshole." He took another hit from the joint before stubbing it out in the ashtray. I laughed out loud at his talk of Jay. Yeah, he could be an asshole sometimes.

Moe leaned back in his seat and looked out his window for a bit before he spoke again.

"I love it out here in the woods."

"Me, too," I said. I stared out my own window and the woods reminded me of camp. The trees were just starting to change colors for the fall. But they were mostly still green, like the woods at Lake Ozonia in the summer. It reminded me of the last walk I took in the woods before the end of the season. Karen and I had gotten into a big fight over me using her beach towel, so I just headed into the woods to get away from her. I'd gone farther than usual and had gotten a little scared when I turned around to head back. There wasn't a trail, so I wasn't exactly sure of the path. And I couldn't see our cabin anymore. It took me a lot longer to get back and I ended up coming out on the road a ways up from the camp. The idea that I had almost gotten lost was stuck in my head and scared me a little. Where were we now?

"It's so quiet," Moe said. "No one to disturb you."

"Yeah, right."

I looked up at Moe and he looked down on me. He had blue eyes. It was quite the contrast to my Uncle Bruce's green eyes. The color of good guys. Why was I thinking of Uncle Bruce at this moment?

"Got a good buzz?" he asked.

I smiled. "Yeah, I think I do."

He smiled back at me. God, why did I even think about Moe as being some kind of bad guy? He was the nicest guy I knew. Nicer than my brother. Nicer than Jay. Maybe even nicer than Uncle Bruce. Uncle Bruce was dangerous! Not Moe. Not only had he let me ride in his Firebird (such a cool car!), but he had gotten me stoned. A second time! He was such an awesome guy!

"Yeah," he said. "Good. But listen…."

I was ready to listen, but he stopped talking. What was it he wanted to say?

"About that pipe," he said.

Oh, shit! I stole his pipe! This was my…what did they call it? My reckoning? I was guilty. I couldn't deny it. I had taken his pot and I had taken his pipe and his lighter. I was guilty. I knew that. He knew that. Fuck. I bet he was going to leave me out here on this back road, make me walk home from here. Wherever here was. Where the fuck were we, anyway? I was lost in the woods again! He wasn't going to kill me over some pot and a pipe, right?

"I really liked that pipe," he said and looked at me. I turned away from his gaze.

"I'll give it back," I said. "We can go back to my house and get it. And I can give you the pot, too. I only smoked a little of it with my friend, Mary."

"Whoa, slow down," he said. "I'm not mad about the pipe. I don't really care about it that much. It's just a pipe."

I leaned back in my seat. Thank God. He wasn't mad. I knew he was a good guy.

"But," he said. "You know, you really broke my trust when you took it. And it wasn't a cheap pipe. I got it in Rochester. It's going to cost me something to replace it."

"I'm sorry," I whispered. Fuck! He wants me to pay for it. I didn't have much money. I took the couple of dollars I had on me out of my pocket. Better to just give it back.

"I don't have much," I said, holding the crumpled dollar bills out to him. "But I can give it back to you. We just need to stop by my house."

He looked down on me then and put his hand on my thigh. "Maybe we can work something out."

My hands were shaking so bad that I almost couldn't undo the lock on my bike. But once I got it unlocked, I just draped the chain over my neck, got on, and headed toward the intersection. I wanted to get away from the store as quick as I could. No, I *wanted* to go inside and buy some gum or some mints, but he had gone into the store right after he parked the car and let me out. I just wanted to get away from him.

I walked across the highway and got onto my bike. I felt so unsteady. I couldn't tell if it was the pot buzz or something else.

Jesus-fucking-Christ! What was wrong with me? Why did I get into his car? What was I thinking? Did I actually believe nothing would happen?

I was halfway back to my house when the Firebird passed. He honked the horn as he went by and waved at me out the window.

"Stop by the house anytime," he had said as I was getting out of the car.

No way, man. Not again.

I turned my bike into the driveway and laid it down by the porch. I expected Karen and Mary to still be there, but the house was empty. At least I didn't have to see anyone yet. No one in the kitchen, no one in the living room. I didn't call out to see if anyone was home.

My mind kept going back to it no matter how much I tried to stop thinking about it. The more I tried not to think about it, the more it kept coming back again. Both times! Stop it!

It was my own fault.

How did I know what would happen?

I knew. How could I not have known? What did that say about me?

At least he paid attention to me.

Maybe that was it. He noticed me. He saw me. He touched me. Who else was willing to do that?

No, screw that! I'd rather be alone than have anything like that happen again!

Right?

Of course.

I ran upstairs to my bedroom and took the pipe from its hiding place under my mattress. I should just throw it out. Get rid of the evidence. But I wouldn't having anything to smoke the pot if I did that. I put the pipe back under the mattress. I would throw it out as soon as the pot was gone. I didn't want it as a constant reminder.

Well, then, throw out the pot, too. Then you won't need the pipe.

But I liked getting high. It was an escape, the only escape I had. No, I'd keep the pipe until the pot was gone. Then I'd get rid of it.

I sat down on the floor and took off my shoes and socks. I don't know why, but I sniffed the inside of one of my sneakers before I set it down. Was it weird that I kind of liked the smell of my own feet? Except that it didn't smell good this time. I didn't smell good. I was sure I was covered in the stench of what I'd done. I was dirty from it. God, I could taste it.

I stripped down to my underpants. I wanted to remove those, too, but I needed to have something on to go back downstairs to the bathroom. Even if no one was home, someone could come in at any time. I nearly tripped as I ran down the stairs, slammed the bathroom door behind me, and turned on the water in the shower. I needed a shower. I needed to get clean. I knew it wouldn't do any good. It hadn't the last time. But as soon as the water was warm enough, I pulled off my underpants and stepped into the stream, pulling the shower curtain to conceal me. I wiped my already wet cheeks before I stuck my head into the spray. Then it was like my legs just gave out. I crumpled and sat down in the bathtub. As warm as the water was, I couldn't stop shaking. I pulled my knees up to my chest and let the water run over me, wishing it would wash everything away. It wouldn't get me clean, but it would hide my tears.

15

No Escape, 1994

Moe walked over to Jay, his young friend trailing close behind, and they shook hands. Somehow it didn't surprise me that the two of them had become friends. I knew that Moe was still dealing and that Jay was still buying. Hell, if I'd had the money, I would have been buying, too, just not from Moe. With no one else in the place, they felt comfortable enough to discuss it right there in the front room.

"I'm looking to buy," Jay said.

"I just got some good stuff," Moe replied.

They talked prices and amounts, but I wasn't interested enough to pay attention to the details. I was too surprised that Moe had not simply turned around and left. I'd seen Moe plenty of times over the years, but since that car ride, he'd never approached me again. Even more than that, if he was out and about, like playing Frisbee with the kids at the corner by the bridge, he would disappear when I showed up. If I saw him in the aisle at the grocery store, he would turn around and go the other way. And here in the pool hall, he always left if he saw I was working. Can't say that it bothered me; I wanted as little to do with him as it seemed he wanted to do with me. Today was different. He chatted a little longer with Jay.

"Stop by the house anytime," he said before he turned and walked up to the counter.

"I'd like a table, please," he said. The voice grated on my ears and made my skin crawl. It was harsh and cutting, but I did my best to let it go by me.

"Can I see some I.D.?" I asked.

Moe reached into his back pocket and took out his wallet.

"Not from you," I said. "From him." I nodded my head toward his companion without ever letting my eyes leave Moe.

"What for?" Moe asked.

"I need to verify that he's old enough to be in here. State law requires a person to be sixteen years of age or older to be in a pool hall unless accompanied by a parent or legal guardian."

"Bullshit," Moe spat.

I pointed to a sign we had posted above the counter. It included the exact wording of the law as well as the section numbers from the penal code. We'd had enough complaints from parents and visits from the cops to warrant making the signs very visible.

"He's sixteen," Moe said.

Of that, I was sure he was not. He could have been fifteen, but I thought that might have been pushing it as well.

"I need proof in the form of identification," I said.

"Well," Moe said, "he's with me. I'm his guardian."

"His *legal* guardian?" I asked. "I'll need proof of that, then."

"You think I carry papers like that around with me?"

"It doesn't matter what I think," I said. "What I know is that I can get in legal trouble if I allow a minor to remain in the pool hall over which I am charged."

I smiled then, my eyes never leaving his.

"If you can't prove his age or your legal guardianship, I'm going to have to ask you to leave."

"And if I choose not to?"

"Then I'll have you charged with trespassing. At the very least."

It became a staring contest after that. I'd always heard of such a standoff, but I had never been part of one before. He stared at me and I stared right back, the smile never leaving my lips. Then he said something that made no sense.

"You know, your uncle's gone," he said. "He's not here to stand up for you anymore."

My smile faltered a bit. What did he mean by that? How did he even know about my uncle? And Uncle Bruce had never been there to stand up for me. I was doing just fine standing up for myself at the moment anyway.

"You can either leave," I said, "or we can get the police involved. But something tells me you wouldn't want that."

Moe's eyes narrowed. I knew I could stand there all day if necessary, and I had no problem calling the cops on the bastard. I wasn't bluffing. It was his move next. A part of me really hoped he would decide to challenge me. Instead, Moe turned without saying another word and headed toward the front door, his young companion close behind.

"Hey, kid!" I yelled after them.

The boy turned around.

"You should find better people to hang out with."

The boy stopped in his tracks for just a moment before Moe pulled on his arm and the two of them were out the front door. As I watched them leave, I saw Jay whispering to his friends at which point they all looked at me and laughed. I knew what he had told them, and I knew what they were laughing about. I walked away and through the door into the arcade, the noise of the games drowning them out. I used to let it bother me, which is not to say that it didn't still bother me. It just bothered me less now. The old anger still swelled up, particularly in these last few days. It was like I was reliving that whole damn Fall of '79 all over again. Bits and pieces of it anyway. The worst bits and pieces. And death was a part of it all.

"Can I get a quarter?"

I looked up to see a little tow-headed kid maybe ten years old placing two dimes and a nickel on the counter. I gave him a smile.

"Sure."

I took his change back to the register and exchanged his three coins for one. Then I grabbed one of the quarters we had marked for giving refunds. I stepped back into the arcade and dropped the two quarters into his outstretched hand. His eyes widened when he saw the second quarter. I gave him a wink and a smile, put my finger against my lips.

"Shhhh," I said. "Our little secret."

He closed his fist over the coins and grinned like I had given him a million dollars.

"Thanks!" he said and ran off to spend his bounty.

I couldn't help but smile. Better to pass along some happiness where I could. No need to let my anger ruin an innocent kid's day.

No, it was more than anger. It was the shame that still lingered. No matter how far removed I might get from it, no matter how much time passed, it was still there like a fresh wound. They say that time heals all wounds, but as Uncle Bruce had said, the only thing time did was leave scar tissue. Worse, it left scabs. An ugly spot that covered the wound and was easily peeled away leaving that gaping injury to bleed all over again. It didn't matter what I called myself, victim, survivor, whatever. When the source of that pain was always right there in front of me, right in my face, that scab got ripped off again and again. Time could try to heal the wounds, but the lack of distance made it fucking impossible. There was simply no escaping it. The pain, the shame, the misery was going to stay with me as long as I stayed, as long as I was stuck here. There was no chance of getting away from it. A vicious cycle of hurt. A whirlpool of shame that let me up for one moment to catch my breath before pulling me back under again. Was it any wonder I drank so much?

"Hey!" I heard a voice call from the pool hall. Between being lost in thought and lost in the noise of the video games, I hadn't heard Jay come up to the counter. I walked back into the pool hall.

"We're done," he said.

I went to turn off the lights for their table and realized that I had never adjusted their rate down from five people to four. Oh, well, it's not like he could read the screen and we never gave out a receipt. I told him the amount and he handed me a one-hundred-dollar bill. If he thought that impressed me, he was wrong. Leon the Fish would gamble away that pittance in a single game of Nine-ball. I handed him his change.

"Thanks, friend," Jay said with a smile as he took the money. Then he and his companions left through the back door, still whispering and laughing.

Friend, my ass. I couldn't believe I had ever considered that asshole my friend. After what he had done to me, up to and including what he had obviously done just now, I would never count him as a friend ever again. Just one more pain I found impossible to escape while trapped in this fucking town. Trust was a hard thing to build but an easy thing to destroy.

16

Secrets Revealed, 1979

"Come on, man," Jay said as we sat down on the bus after school on Friday. "You haven't been up all week and I hate getting high alone."

"I don't know," I said. It's not that I didn't want to go to Jay's place but doing so meant I had to ride past *his* house. I didn't want to do that.

"It's Friday!" he said. "And it's one of the only weekends I'm not going to my mother's. We gotta do something this time."

As we neared my house, I saw that both Karen and Mary got up from their seat. That meant she was getting off at our house again. The two of them were spending a lot of time together since the news came out about Mary's pregnancy. The last thing I wanted to do was spend the afternoon with her in the house.

"Yeah, okay," I said. "I'll ride up in a bit. I got something to show you anyway."

"Cool!" Jay said.

I followed Mary and Karen and Kevin to the front of the bus. All I wanted to do was get changed, get my pot, and get the hell out but Kevin beat me up the stairs to our room. I didn't bother giving Mary a second look as she and Karen went into the living room. If she was going to ignore me, I could do the same to her.

It took forever for Kevin to finish up in the bedroom before I was able to go in to change. I had moved my pot from my sock drawer to between the mattress and box spring of my bed. I didn't trust people to not go through my drawers. Whether it was my mother looking for dirty clothes or my brother or sister looking for…whatever, just snooping. I figured it was safer under the mattress. So, once Kevin was out, I quickly threw on my old Wranglers and a t-shirt before feeling under the mattress for the bag, the pipe, and the lighter. I knew Jay would have a lighter, but I felt like I needed to take everything with me if I was going to surprise him. As I stuffed everything in my pockets, I wondered if I would have to show Jay how to use the carb on the pipe.

I walked my bike down to the end of the driveway, checked for traffic, and then pedaled off to Jay's place. I felt the knot in my stomach even before I got to the bridge. I knew it had to do with passing...*his* house. I tried to put it all out of my mind as I flew past and crossed the bridge, but it was like a thing I couldn't get away from. I couldn't ride my bike fast enough to escape it. It probably didn't help that I was carrying the pot and the pipe I had gotten from him, all the stuff he said I had earned. Earned? No, I paid for them. I just didn't want to think about the price.

I didn't even bother stopping by the front door when I got to Jay's place. I knew that if he were home, he'd already be up in the barn waiting for me. If he wasn't there yet, I could wait for him upstairs. So, I dropped my bike by the barn's side door and went inside.

"You in here?" I called out.

"You know it!" came a muffled reply from upstairs.

I bounded up the steps to join him on the second floor. As I approached the couch, I saw he was messing with the radio once again.

"I keep losing that Canadian station I like," he said as he twisted the dial until the music came through clearly.

I flopped down in my usual spot.

"Alright," Jay said. "Now that we've got some music, let's party!" He pulled his bag of pot from his pocket, but before he could take out a joint, I tossed my own bag onto the coffee table. Jay picked it up. "What's this?"

"My pot," I said.

"Your pot? What is it? Some of the homegrown stuff they're dealing around the high school?"

"No, it's California Sense," I said, trying to sound like I knew what I was talking about.

"No way!" He opened the bag and put his nose into the opening. He took a sniff, and his eyes grew wide. "Holy crap!" Then he held it up and looked it over. "This is all bud, no seeds. Where did you get sinsemilla around here?"

Sinsemilla? That must be what "Sense" was short for. It was another one of those words I stuck in the back of my head so I'd know what to call it. Jay seemed genuinely impressed.

"I got it…around," I said.

"You gotta tell me where so I can get some of this." Jay took his papers out of his pocket, but before he could think about rolling a joint, I set the pipe down on the table.

"Jesus, King, you're full of surprises!"

"Don't…don't call me that," I said. I was self-conscious about my last name, and I hated it when someone called me by that name alone, like the gym teacher. I especially didn't like being called Mr. King, which some of the teachers did. I don't think Jay even heard me. He was too busy examining the pipe. "It's got a carb right there," I said and pointed to it.

"Yeah, I know what a carb is," Jay said, annoyed. "Did you get this from the same place you got the Sense? You must have. There aren't any head shops in Potsdam." He set it back down on the coffee table. "It's nice."

For a moment, we both just sat there looking at the bag of pot and the pipe. I also took the lighter out of my pocket and set it down on the table. It was starting to feel a little awkward when Jay finally spoke up.

"Well? It's your pot and your pipe. You gonna load up a bowl or what?"

"Sure," I said and took up the pipe and the bag. I guess the proper etiquette was for me to make the start since it was my stuff. The only other time I'd loaded the pipe was with Mary at the White House, and it had been dark and she had been drunk. But now, in the light of day in front of Jay, I was uncomfortable about how I was loading it. It was awkward to try to hold the pipe and the bag and still get a pinch or two of pot out without spilling it on the floor. I finally held my legs together, set the pipe between my knees and that freed up both hands, one to hold the bag and one to put the pinch in the bowl. Then I set the pipe on the table again so I could roll up the bag. I held the pipe and lighter out to Jay.

"No," he said, "it's your pot. You get to do the honors."

I imagine he wanted to see how I would handle the pipe and the carb, but I was practiced now and lit the pipe with no problem. I was still careful to not take too big a hit before I handed it over to Jay. He took a hit as I was blowing smoke out. I felt a little twinge of pride when he coughed out a little of his first hit. I didn't cough; he did. Jay recovered quickly and handed the pipe back to me. I took another small hit and then set the pipe and lighter down on the table since Jay was still holding his breath.

"Wow," he rasped as he slowly exhaled. He picked up the pipe to take another hit and leaned back on the couch. "You gotta tell me where you got this." He held the flame to the bowl and lit it again.

I didn't want to tell him. But then, I could tell him who I got it from. I didn't have to tell him any more than that, right? No need for him to know. As I exhaled, I could feel the buzz of the pot creeping up on me.

"Remember the guy on the corner? Moe?"

Jay thought a moment, blew smoke out into the space.

"Oh, yeah, that creepy dude drinking beer on his porch. He deals?"

Deals? What did that mean? I hated that I didn't know all the lingo. I took the pipe and lighter from Jay to take another hit. I just nodded as I lit the pipe again. I held it out to Jay when I was done, but he ignored it and laid down on the couch.

"Good to know there's someone in this town who can get good pot. How much was it?"

I froze then and let the smoke escape. What had it cost me? It hadn't cost me anything, right? No, not really. Not money, anyway. But, dammit, I didn't want to think about that! And I wasn't about to tell Jay the whole story. God, why had I even brought the pot with me? We could have just smoked Jay's.

Jay turned his head on the arm of the couch. "How much was it?" he asked again.

"I…I don't remember," I replied, then put my head back to try to listen to the music. What was it that was playing on the radio? I think it was Styx, but I couldn't remember the name of the song.

"Oh, come on," he said. "For this kind of quality, it ain't cheap. When did you get it?"

"Last Friday. While you were in Utica."

"So, it's only been a week. You couldn't have already forgotten how much it was."

"I don't know," I said. The conversation was making me uncomfortable. I didn't want to remember what it cost me. My head was starting to get dizzy from the pot. What difference did it make to him how I got it?

"What difference does it make?" I asked.

"'Cause I might want to buy some from him! This is giving me a really nice buzz."

"I don't think he's selling it anymore."

"What? So, he was only in business long enough to sell it to you?"

Jay sat up on the couch suddenly. He made enough noise to make me lift my head from the back of my chair.

"Oh, my God," he said. "Did you break into his house? Did you steal it?"

I couldn't help but smile at that before replying, "No, just the pipe."

"You stole the pipe?"

I laid my head back on the chair again. "Sure, I had to have something to smoke it with."

"Are you kidding me? You stole the pipe but not the pot? Come on, you broke into his house, didn't you?" He laid back down on the couch. "It's no big deal. Me and my friends used to do it all the time back home. We'd steal stuff like records and food and booze. Sometimes we'd take something bigger. My friend, Tony, took this guy's portable television once."

"I didn't steal the pot," I said.

"But you stole the pipe."

"Yeah."

"That doesn't even make sense," Jay said. "What were you doing in his house so you could steal the pipe?"

I realized that every time I opened my mouth, I just dug a deeper hole. What difference did it make anyway? Maybe I should just say I stole it. Except now he probably wouldn't believe me since I said I didn't steal it. Or maybe I should just tell him. No, that probably wasn't a good idea. But who was he going to tell if I did tell him? Man, the music was sounding really good. I wished I knew the name of the song that was playing.

"Well?" Jay said.

"What?" I lifted my head to see Jay looking over at me from his reclined position on the couch.

"What were you doing in his house if you didn't break in?"

"He invited me in for a beer," I said.

"Now I know you're lying. No guy just invites some kid in for a beer."

"He did."

"And what were you drinking?"

"Michelob!" I blurted out. I remembered what beer it was. That would be the clincher.

Jay was quiet for a while before he said, "Okay, maybe he did. No one would lie about drinking that crap. Still doesn't explain how you got such good pot and don't remember how much you paid for it."

"He gave it to me," I said.

"Bullshit!" Jay sat up on the couch again and picked up the Baggie from the table. "This is close to a dime bag. And some really good Sense. Nobody just gives this shit away. What'd you do, blow him for it?"

"No!" I replied quickly.

Jay laid back down on the couch. "Then you must have let him blow you."

I didn't say a word. I didn't know how to answer that. And as soon as the silence fell, I knew I should have said something —

anything — to fill the silence of that moment. I lifted my head and saw Jay looking at me.

"Oh, my God! I was just kidding, but you did, didn't you?"

"No!" I protested, but it was too late. I knew it was too late. My silence had given away the secret. My silence had said more than I could have.

Jay sat back up on the couch, his eyes wide, and then he started to laugh.

"You let him suck your dick!" he said and laughed louder.

"No," I repeated. "That's not it."

Jay continued to laugh, and he rocked back and forth on the couch. Every so often, he would try to say something and then would lose the words in a fit of laughter. I could feel the heat rising in my face, knew I was turning beet red.

"Queerbait!" he said and laughed some more. I didn't know what he meant by that, but I'd heard the word before and knew it wasn't good. His laughter started to calm down and he said, "Since I smoked your pot, do I have to blow you, too?" And then he was off on another fit of laughter. When he started to calm down again, he picked up the pipe and took another hit. Apparently, the pot was still good enough for him to smoke. "Guess I never expected you were gay, King" he said.

I picked up the bag of weed, rolled it back up, and stuck it in my pocket along with my lighter. I was going to wait for the pipe to cool down a bit before I tried to stick that in my pocket. But there was no way I was going to stay any longer.

"I'm not gay!" I said.

"You sure about that?" Jay asked.

"Ask Mary Chase."

"Mary? Your sister's friend? What would she know about it?"

"Nothing, except I fucked her last Saturday!"

Jay laughed again. "Oh, you gotta be kidding!"

"I did! I rode down to the White House on Water Street that night. She was there and drunk. We smoked some of my weed and then we had sex."

"Bullshit!" Jay said. "You're lying! There's no way you went down into that house by yourself. And Mary's, like, eighteen or something."

"Fifteen," I said. "Same age as Karen."

"Yeah, okay, fifteen. So why would she do you?"

"I don't know. She was lonely. And drunk."

"Yeah," Jay said and laughed again. "She'd have to be, wouldn't she?"

"Screw you," I said and picked up the pipe. I stood up and stuffed it into my pocket.

"Why not? You seem to think everyone else has!" He laughed again.

"I'm going home," I said and made my way to the stairs.

"Careful you don't get laid on the way!" he called after me.

What an asshole. I picked up my bike and rode away. Whatever buzz I had was mostly gone now, so riding wasn't too bad. Even if I had to walk, there was no way I was going to stay and listen to that jerk make fun of me. If I wanted that, I would've stayed home.

There was no sign of Moe as I pedaled past his house on my way back. I did my best to get past the cemetery as fast as I could as well. Maybe it was the pot, but a part of me wondered what it would be like to lie forever in the ground.

Only Kevin was home when I got back to the house. He had a strange look on his face, like he was hiding something. I didn't think too much on it since he was always hiding something. Or keeping secrets. Karen arrived just before Mom and Dad got home. She had walked Mary back to her place. As soon as she got back, she and Kevin went off to talk about something, which also didn't surprise me much. They were always excluding me from their plans and activities. Mom made dinner and we all sat down to eat. And even though I was used to Karen and Kevin excluding me, it seemed like they had some secret they were sharing. Every so often, they would glance at each other across the table and smile, even stifle a laugh. It was weird.

After dinner, the three of us sat around the living room watching television. I couldn't understand why. Both Karen and Kevin usually went out as soon as they could on a Friday night. But this time, they were still sitting around the living room with me after our parents went out. Kevin even sat down next to me on the couch and Karen sat in the armchair against the far wall.

"Gee, Karen," Kevin said. "Any plans for tonight?"

"No, not really," she replied.

"What about you, Kelly?" he asked. "Any plans?"

I looked at my brother, confused. He had never asked about my plans, never cared what I was going to do.

"No," I said.

"You sure?" he asked.

"Yeah," Karen said. "You're such a stud, you must have plans for tonight."

I looked from Kevin to Karen and back again, unsure of what was going on.

"Maybe you can suck Moe's dick tonight," Kevin said. "You know, pay him back."

I couldn't move. I'd heard the phrase about someone's blood running cold, but I had never really understood it. I did now. That's exactly what it felt like. Every ounce of heat in my body just faded away. The two of them just kept looking at me, smiling. I looked from one to the other, my breaths coming fast and shallow. What the hell was going on?

"Or maybe I'll call up Mary," Karen said, "and she can come down and fuck you again!"

Oh, God, how had they found out about any of this? The only other person who knew was....

There was only one other person. That fucking bastard!

"She did fuck me," I tried to say, but my voice was almost nonexistent. My throat was too dry for me to speak.

"Right," Karen said. "I'd sooner believe Kevin fucked her than you."

"Your dick's probably too small to do anything anyway," Kevin added.

That son of a bitch! How could Jay betray me like that? I mean, it was one thing for him to know and laugh at me, but it was something else for him to tell my brother and sister. Or just my brother. I realized then that Jay must have called Kevin after I left and then Kevin told Karen when she got home. That's what they had been whispering about all afternoon.

"She did," I said. And then I felt them. The tears were welling up in my eyes. I couldn't stop them. I tried to hold them back, but I felt the tickle of the first one roll down my cheek.

"Oh, no!" Kevin exclaimed. "We made the baby cry! Oh, are you gonna cry for us, little baby?" He leaned toward me making crying noises, and that's when I pushed him away and got up from the couch. I wasn't going to stay here and put up with this. I ran to the door, went out to the porch, and grabbed my bike.

17

A Wake, 1994

It was official. He was gone. The funeral had been the dark and somber event that I'm sure my grandmother required and one I felt Uncle Bruce would have hated. Still, it gave me a chance to see him one last time. I'd never been to a funeral before, so seeing him lying there in the casket really took me by surprise. I knew that was how a funeral worked, but it still freaked me out a bit. He looked so…alive, like he was sleeping. I half-expected him to sit up right there in the front of the room.

Still, he hadn't looked quite like I had expected, but fifteen years does that to a person, I suppose. His hair was short and graying and he'd trimmed the beard down to a goatee from the full beard he'd had back in '79. Whoever had done the makeup had done a good job. It wasn't too much so that he looked made up, and the bullet wound was hardly noticeable. He was dressed in a dark blue suit with a white shirt and matching tie. I wondered if he would have preferred his denim and leather instead.

The service had been pleasant enough with the minister from my grandmother's church officiating. He spoke so generically about "the deceased" that I wondered if he had even known Uncle Bruce. I wondered the same about the small congregation of people who had come. Had they really known him? And for that matter, as much as I felt close to him back in '79, I had to ask myself if I had known him that well. But I still probably knew him better than most of my family. I thought the wake might give me a chance to meet some of his friends.

It made sense to hold the reception at the VFW on Market Street since Uncle Bruce had been in Vietnam. They had gone all out with a buffet and an open bar. I knew the open bar could be dangerous. Not because I was driving; the VFW was just about a half-mile from the Arlington. Plus, I did have to work later, so I couldn't really get too drunk. No, I was more worried that I might say the wrong thing to the wrong people if I got loaded. I was surprised, really, that anyone in the family had sprung for such a reception.

I made my rounds through the room to meet the people I didn't know. A three-sided bar took up a good deal of space in the back, and tables lined the walls, so it was easy to move from one table to another. I did my best to avoid family. I had no desire to talk to any of them. I had gotten to the funeral after everyone had been seated, so I'd found a seat near the back of the room rather than make my way up front to sit with the family. I'd only gone up to the casket after everyone else had made their way out, so most everyone had left by the time I paid my respects. This reception would give me a chance to meet a few of Uncle Bruce's friends from his high school days. They had all known him pretty well back then and were happy to talk about him. They related stories of smoking cigarettes out behind the school, getting caught drinking underage at a party, the usual high school hijinks. But they all admitted to having lost touch with him over the years.

"After he went to Vietnam, we just kinda went our separate ways," his old girlfriend, Rhonda, had said. "It was like he didn't really want to be around people after that."

A few other friends related the same thing. They had been tight in high school, but when he returned from Vietnam, he had been different and distant. Some of them had tried to connect with him over the years, even traveling down to Utica to see him. But they said he had never been the same after the war. As near as I could figure, he'd lived a very solitary existence. Even as everyone apologized to me for not being able to offer more, I actually felt better for having talked with them. It told me that Uncle Bruce hadn't chosen to ignore me specifically after he went back to Utica. It was just who he was. For whatever reason, he couldn't or didn't want to relate to other people. He lived his life alone by choice. I always wondered if he'd been lonely, but the more I learned, the more I realized that there was a difference between being lonely and being alone. I also began to realize how much my life mirrored his in some of those ways. I'd just been in a different kind of war and fought different battles in my life. I was, for the most part, alone but not lonely.

I finished the beer I was drinking and decided I needed a little something to honor Uncle Bruce. I don't know if Cutty Sark was his favorite, but it was the one Scotch I always saw him drinking. It was the bottle that had been in his secret hiding hole in the barn and that he had had at the lake that night. So, I asked the bartender for a Cutty Sark, neat.

"You're not driving, are you?" I heard my sister ask from behind me. Was she trying to be funny? She knew I didn't have a car.

"No," I replied as I picked up the glass the bartender set down in front of me. He'd poured a double. I took a sip and let the warmth flow down my throat. "It's just a hop, skip, and a jump back to my place from here."

She was decked out in your basic black dress with low-heeled shoes.

"Peter couldn't make it?" I asked.

"He was able to pick up a shift at the plant."

Peter's trademark once again: find an excuse to miss a get-together. This time it was an extra shift at work to avoid having to deal with the family. I guess I couldn't blame him for that. Karen asked the bartender for a raspberry wine cooler.

"I didn't see you at the service."

"I was there," I said. "I got there after everyone was seated and found a spot in the back. Where's Zachary?"

"Mom has him." She pointed toward a table near the wall. I saw the back of my mother's head and my nephew's seven-month-old head bobbing back and forth from her lap.

"It was a nice service," she said.

"I guess." I took another sip of the Scotch.

"Really?" she sneered. "You can't say anything nice even at a time like this?"

"What do you want me to say?" I asked. "The minister really had a lot to say for a man he hardly knew? I seriously doubt Uncle Bruce would have even wanted a service like that."

"Oh, please, you barely knew him, either."

The anger that rose in me then almost spilled over, but I took a drink from my glass and let the Cutty Sark take that anger down with it. She'd never have any idea how much better I'd known him. Even if it had only been that one single night. And I'd never give her the satisfaction of knowing about it. Part of me wanted to tell her, was dying to tell her. It took every particle of my being to keep silent. It wasn't for her to hear. It was mine and mine alone.

"You couldn't even be bothered to dress properly for it," she said.

"What do you mean?" I asked as I tweaked my tie. I was wearing my best slacks, a white shirt, long-sleeved, and the only tie I owned. I had even done the laundry the night before to make sure everything was as clean as possible.

"What's with the flannel shirt?"

I tugged at the shirt tails and wrapped it around me. I'd hung onto the shirt, cherished it, for the last fifteen years. I wasn't about to explain that to my sister either. This was one of the only times I had ever worn it out in public since Uncle Bruce had essentially given it to me.

"It matches the tie," I replied. Which was true. The red and black of the flannel went well with the brown of the necktie. Or maybe it didn't. What did I know about fashion? "And it's supposed to be chilly later tonight."

"Gotta love an open bar," my brother said as he came up behind my sister. "Coors Light," he said to the bartender. Then to me, he said, "Nice shirt," before grabbing his can of beer and walking away. I watched him go. He didn't appear to have a destination in mind even though his pregnant girlfriend was sitting alone at a table on the other side of the room; he just wandered among the other guests.

"Who's paying for all of this?" I finally asked. Karen pointed to a man in a dark blue suit standing near the hall to the restrooms. "Who's that?"

"Not sure," she said, "but Grandma said he was footing the bill."

I left my sister at the bar and walked over to meet the man who was paying to get me loaded. Yeah, yeah, getting loaded was not a bright idea and I should have more respect for such a solemn occasion, but I figured my brother would beat me to it anyway and be blasted and embarrassing long before I was. It was when he started doing shots that I would decide to leave.

"Excuse me," I said as I approached the man. He was a little taller than me, thinner, clean-cut. "I hear you're the man we have to thank for this reception."

"Not exactly," he said. He held out his hand to me and I took it. "Jonathan Bridges," he said.

"Kelly King," I replied. He had a firm handshake, which I liked.

"Oh, you're Kelly?"

"Yeah," I answered, a little wary that he seemed to have some idea who I was.

"Well, then, you have your uncle to thank for this reception," he said.

"Really? You do know he's the reason *for* this reception, right?"

"Of course," he said, looking a little embarrassed. "I'm sorry, let me explain. Your uncle requested that this reception take place in the event of his death."

"Who are you, exactly?"

"Sorry," he said again. "I'm Jonathan Bridges."

"Yeah, we've established that."

"Yes, I'm the executor of his will. And his lawyer. Bruce stipulated a certain amount of his estate for the funeral and reception."

"That funeral was his idea?"

"No, no, the details were left up to his family, specifically his mother, if she were still living, and his sister, if she was not."

"That makes sense," I said. "I can't imagine he would have wanted that kind of service."

"No," Mr. Bridges said with a smile. "I don't believe so, either. But this reception was definitely his idea."

"Did you know him well?" I asked.

"That's a difficult question to answer," he said.

"Yeah, I get that a lot."

"How about you? Did you know him well?"

"Not as well as I would have liked to," I said. "We shared a certain history, but he was a distant relative, if you know what I mean."

"I understand," he replied. "He was a very…solitary person."

I nodded. I took a sip of my Scotch, and Mr. Bridges stared uncomfortably around the room.

"He did speak of you, though," he finally said.

"Really?" I was more than surprised hearing this. My uncle who had never answered a single letter from me had spoken of me to his lawyer. It made me wonder — and worry — what Uncle Bruce might have said. Had he broken his promise to me?

"He did, but this isn't the appropriate time or place," he said. He took a business card from his pocket and wrote something on the back before handing it to me. "I'm staying at the Clarkson Inn until tomorrow afternoon. You should stop by before I leave so we can talk."

"Sure," I said, looking at the room number written on the card. The Clarkson Inn was one of the only hotels in town and, from what I'd heard, it was pretty fancy. "I live in the Arlington right across the street."

"Well, then, why don't we meet in the dining room for breakfast. Say, nine o' clock?"

"Yeah, sure."

"Excellent. We'll talk more then. Excuse me," he said and walked over to talk with the bartender.

I stared at the card for a moment, then flipped it over to read the front. It did, indeed, show him as Jonathan Bridges, Esquire, with an address in Utica. What the hell would a lawyer have to discuss with me? I wanted to follow up with him, but when I wandered back to the bar to get a refill on my Cutty Sark, he was already gone. My mother was there holding Zachary, getting his sippy cup filled with apple juice. My sister and brother were there as well. I set my glass down and asked the bartender for another. I didn't really need another. It would be my second on top of the beer I'd had when I first arrived, and I hadn't eaten anything all day. So, to say I was feeling the buzz was an understatement. As the bartender was returning my glass with another double of Cutty Sark, I remembered Mary's card. I had stuck it in my back pocket.

"Before I forget," I said as I pulled it out. I held the sealed envelope out to her. "Mary Chase asked me to give this to you."

"Oh," my brother said. "Your old girlfriend!"

I ignored his comment. He was drunk, and I was feeling the alcohol myself. I didn't need to let my anger get the better of me.

"When did you see her?" my sister asked as she took the card.

"She stopped by the pool hall looking for her son."

"She wasn't looking for you?" my brother asked.

Patty was sitting next to him on a barstool and tugged on his sleeve. I don't think she understood the full history involved in his comment. Or maybe she did. It would not have surprised me if he had told her everything as well. Of course, even Kevin and Karen didn't know the whole story, only what that prick Jay had told them, and I had never divulged everything to him. Even still, I didn't trust anyone in the family to show any respect or decorum when it came to things like that. If it was good gossip, it spread like a wildfire and burned every acre I might have.

"Give it a rest," I said to no one in particular.

My brother laughed and took a swig of his beer. My sister opened the card.

"Mary said you should give her a call," I said. "She said she wrote her number on the card."

"You better get her number, too," my brother said.

I continued to do my best to ignore him, but I wasn't sure how much longer I could hold it all back. Maybe it was time for me to leave. I wanted to find Mr. Bridges again before I did.

"Anyone see the man in the suit who was just here? I need to speak with him."

"Speak with him?" my brother asked. "Or get his number? Maybe have a good time with him, too?"

That was it. Fuck decorum, fuck solemnity, fuck them all.

"Really?" I said, turning to him. "I get molested by the neighborhood pervert when I was a kid and you're still going to throw that back in my face?"

My mother turned to look at me then. I saw her blue eyes, her sad and old blue eyes. It was like she finally saw me for the first time. "What?"

"Yeah, that's right," I said. "I was molested as a child. Sexually abused! Maybe if you'd been paying a little more attention to your family rather than your next fling, you might have noticed."

"What?" my brother said. "You're the one with no girlfriend."

"Yeah," I said. "Imagine that. After the way I was treated by all the women in my life, including Mary Chase." I looked directly at my sister. "Yeah, I did fuck her back then. Ask her sometime and she might even be willing to tell you about it now. Between you, this mother of ours, and our grandmother, it is any wonder I don't have a girlfriend? Just because you've all left me unable to trust any woman ever doesn't make me gay."

I didn't keep my voice down and people were beginning to stare. I didn't care. Maybe it was the alcohol or maybe it was the twenty-seven years of their bullshit, but I was on a roll and saw no reason to stop or turn it back now.

"And it's not like either one of you have anything to crow about in the area of relationships." I looked directly at Karen. "Peter spends more time at work than he does at home. Why is that? Maybe he doesn't really want to be there. And what about you?" I asked, turning to my brother. "You ever going to marry Patty or just continue to have more babies? You gonna sleep around on her after you get married, too? Yeah, that's right, we all know about your little flings. So, really, you're all shining examples of perfect relationships. Top that off with the train wreck of a marriage our parents had and I want nothing to do with relationships."

"Hey," Patty said, "take it easy. We're all family here."

"And what exactly does that even mean?" I asked. "Treat each other like shit? Or maybe just me. Name-call and ridicule and make fun? And then abandon to sleep on the streets when family becomes inconvenient? You know, Uncle Bruce had the right idea all along. Better to stay the hell away from anything called family."

I picked up my glass of Cutty Sark.

"Cheers," I said and drained the glass in two swallows. "And now, if you'll all excuse me, I have to go to work, and you can all go to hell."

I dropped my glass down on the bar and walked out the front door without a look back.

18

Runaway, 1979

I slammed the door behind me. It might have been hard enough to break the window, but I didn't care. I picked up my bike from where it lay next to the porch and jumped onto it, pushed off, and soared as fast as I could down the driveway. I swung out onto the main drag and heard the screech of tires and the blare of a car horn. I just pressed down on the pedals as hard as I could.

"What the fuck?" I heard someone yell from behind me.

"Fuck you," I said, though probably not loud enough for anyone to hear.

The cemetery was a blur on my left. The ghosts didn't scare me anymore. Then I was flying down the hill toward the bridge. Moe's house was there on the corner of Water Street and the White House further down. I tried to ignore both, tried to focus on the road and the bridge ahead of me. I didn't even want to look. But I couldn't help it. I tried to see if he was sitting on the porch. He wasn't and the front door was closed. I could see a light through the front window. Was he in there by himself? Or had he talked someone else into hanging out with him? Or was it just me that he chose? And why was it me? What did I do to make him do that? Was I the slut? And now everyone would know it. They would know what I did, know what he did to me.

I heard the car before I saw it coming across the one-lane bridge. Its horn cut through the air like a siren. The setting sun glared off the chrome grille right into my eyes. I swerved out of the lane and onto the sidewalk of the bridge, my bike still flying as fast as I could make it go. Luckily, there was no one on the sidewalk and I got to the other side of the river and headed up the hill that led to the back way out of town. The Sand Hill Road. I would never see it the same again. Not anymore. But a few miles up this road and I found myself on the highway to Hopkinton. After that, it was only seven or eight miles to the lake. I didn't know how far it was to Hopkinton. I didn't care about that either. I just needed to get out of town and the lake was the only place I could think to go. I hoped Uncle Bruce would still be there. I don't know why. It's not like he even liked me or anything. If he wasn't there, I'd just break in. The screen door on the back porch would be easy enough to pry open. Or I'd break a window. It didn't matter. They wouldn't know where I'd gone. Probably wouldn't even come looking for me. I could get water from the spring and fish from the lake and stay there for a while. We'd see if anyone even missed me. The road was getting blurry. I let go of the handlebars just long enough to wipe tears from my eyes.

The ride to Hopkinton was longer than I thought it would be. A bike goes a lot slower than a car. The sky was already getting dark when I turned right and then took the left turn onto the Lake Ozonia Road. I finally stopped there. I'd been pedaling almost all the way from West Stockholm, just resting when I could coast down the hills. But, as I looked up the road ahead of me, I wondered if it was such a good idea to continue. I didn't know what time it was, but it was nearly dark. And there weren't any streetlights on the camp road. Once I was into the woods, it would be dark as dark could be. I wasn't worried about any other traffic; the lake was always pretty quiet when summer was over. Just about everybody was gone by Labor Day. It was the thought of keeping to the road that worried me. I didn't have a headlight on my bike. Would I be able to see the road if it got much darker? And the woods would be black all around me. What was in those woods between here and camp? My only options were to go down to my grandmother's house and have her yell at me for running away from home or to turn around and ride back to West Stockholm, and neither of those things was going to happen. Even I didn't care if I never saw any of them again. I stepped down on the pedals and headed off down the road.

I knew it was seven or eight miles from Hopkinton to the camp, but what I hadn't realized was that it was mostly uphill. Sure, there were some hills I could coast down once in a while, but the lake was at a higher elevation. It was the start of the Adirondacks. So, even as I coasted down one hill, I had to work that much harder to get up the next. And the darkness only got deeper the further I went. It was a clear night, and the moon was out somewhere, though I couldn't see it above the trees. Enough light filtered through the woods that I was able to keep to the road and when I looked up, I could see the stars framed by trees on both sides. But it was still dark, and the moonlight through the trees cast strange shadows onto the road. It was so quiet, the only sound being my own breathing and the creaking of my bike. I could hear things scurrying in the forest. I heard them but I couldn't see them. I told myself that they sounded small, like a chipmunk or maybe a raccoon. There were bears and bobcats in the woods, though. But nothing sounded as big as a bear and bobcats were supposed to have a scream that sounded like a woman shrieking. I didn't want to hear anything like that.

I thought about what it would be like getting to the cabin, pictured it in my mind. Uncle Bruce would be there. Not waiting for me exactly, but still standing on the porch when I pulled up on my bike. He'd welcome me in with a smile, then sit down and listen to me tell him how I wanted to go back to Utica with him. He might tell me he couldn't do it, but I'd convince him what a great idea it would be. I could do his dishes, clean his house, wash his motorcycle. I'd be there to help him out in his store. I'd have one of those white aprons on as I swept the sidewalk out front and then mopped the floor inside. I'd even teach myself to cook so he wouldn't have to do it himself. He'd want me to come along because I wouldn't ask for anything but room and board. All I needed was for him to give me a chance to prove myself. He'd agree and we'd get on his bike in the morning and ride out of town together. I could leave the whole family behind, be free of all of them including Jay and Moe and Mary.

It seemed to take even longer to get to the lake than it had taken to get to Hopkinton, both because of the elevation and also because the dark hid most of the landmarks I was used to seeing. Even riding in a car at night, you could see things in the headlights. I was too busy keeping myself on the road, thinking about my future with Uncle Bruce, and worrying about the sounds in the forest to think about landmarks even if I could have seen them. So, I was really surprised when I found myself coming up to the turn for Mud Pond Tote Road, which went right and ran around the other side of the lake. It meant I was less than half a mile from the camp. Then the water came into view and I could see the lake itself, the still surface like glass in the quiet night. It was so calm compared to the roiling river back in West Stockholm. I could also see the moon better. It must have been rising because it seemed to be pretty high in the sky now. It wasn't full, but it was still bright. As the trees thinned out on the lakeside, more moonlight came through, and that light helped guide me up the final hill and down around the curve to the camp.

Our cabin was one of the few that was built across the road from the lake. It wasn't anything grand, just a two-story shack, really, but it was the only place in the world where I'd ever felt safe. Lights were on inside and I could see the motorcycle parked next to the big rock out front. Uncle Bruce was still there.

I coasted down that final hill and pulled up to the rock, parked my bike next to Uncle Bruce's, then headed up the steps to the porch. Light from the living room painted the boards of the porch in a dim white light. The screen door was closed, but the inside door was open.

"Uncle Bruce?" I called.

There was no answer.

I opened the screen door and stepped inside. I made sure not to slam the door as it closed behind me. I looked back out the screen door, held my hands up to block the light, and tried to see across the road to the boathouse. It didn't look like there was any light down there, but I couldn't be sure. The lake was calm, so maybe he had gone for a canoe ride.

The camp had a different feel coming into it alone, knowing everyone was gone. And knowing the trees outside would not be green when the light of day finally came back. It was fall — well, almost fall — and everything was different. I walked into the kitchen to see if there was anything to drink. I was dying for just a sip of water. I found beer in the fridge and thought about opening one of the bottles of Budweiser, but a beer wasn't what I wanted. The jug of water looked much more inviting, so I pulled it out and set it on the dining table. That's when I found what Uncle Bruce had left.

Sitting on the table was a spiral notebook, a pen laying on its cover. I resisted the urge to open it up and see what he had written inside. Beside it was an empty glass tumbler. I recognized it as one of the ones my father would use to drink his gin. Next to the glass was an almost empty bottle of Cutty Sark. Was there a stash of liquor at the camp or did Uncle Bruce bring it with him? Or was it the bottle from the hiding place in his Fortress of Solitude? The most intriguing item of all, though, was the gun lying next to the bottle of Cutty Sark.

I'd never seen a gun in real life. I didn't know much about them besides what I saw on television and in the movies. It was a pistol, a handgun. And it wasn't a revolver. It didn't have that round cylinder for the bullets like the ones in the Westerns. Was this the kind of gun they called a .45? Was it loaded? How did it work?

That's what I really wanted to know. How did it work? How did you fire it? *Was* it loaded? I picked it up. It was heavy. And cold. I walked with it to the living room, turning it over in my hands as I sat down on the couch. There was something on the back of the gun that moved when I pressed my finger against it. Was this how you cocked it? I pushed it back, heard a click, and felt the trigger move under my other hand. That must be how it got cocked.

How did you un-cock it? I didn't know that part of it any more than I knew if it was loaded. Would it fire if I pulled the trigger? What if I pulled it? I looked down the barrel, put the barrel up to the side of my head. What would happen now if I pulled the trigger?

I wouldn't ever have to go home. I wouldn't have to listen to my brother and sister laughing at me. I wouldn't have to face Jay, who had told my deepest darkest secret to them. I wouldn't have to wonder what Mary really thought of me. I wouldn't have to see Moe ever again. I wouldn't have to do anything. They could put me in the ground next to Grandpa.

I wondered if it would hurt.

"Kelly?"

I looked up at the sound of my name, not recognizing the voice, and saw Uncle Bruce standing on the porch looking at me through the screen door. He opened the door slowly and came inside. "What…what are you doing here?" he asked.

I quickly lowered the gun to my lap. I didn't have a good answer for him. In all the time it took me to get here from home, I fantasized about getting here and finding him. I had worked it all out in my head. But now that I was here – now that *he* was here – I couldn't find anything to say.

"I just…." My voice trailed off. I just what?

Uncle Bruce stepped over to the couch. He sat down next to me.

"It's okay," he said in his gruff voice. "I'm not mad. You just surprised me is all."

Without another word, he slowly and gently took the gun from my hands. He did something with it, let the thing on the back go to its original position. He then pressed another button and a big black something slipped from the handle of the gun. Before setting the gun on the other side of him on the couch, he slid the barrel back and a bullet popped out. He caught it in midair and put it in the pocket of the red and black flannel shirt he wore.

"I was out in the canoe," he finally said. "The lake is like a mirror if you want to go for a ride."

I shook my head.

"So, what's going on?"

I shrugged my shoulders.

"You rode a long way," he said. He got up from the couch and walked into the kitchen. I heard glasses clinking and looked around the corner to see him filling a large glass with water from the jug I had taken out of the fridge. Then he emptied the Cutty Sark bottle into the smaller glass before stepping back over to the couch.

"All out of Scotch. You'll have to suffice with water."

He held out the glass of water. I took it and took a long swig. The cold felt good on my dry throat. I emptied the glass in another big gulp.

He stood over me. I couldn't bring myself to look up at him. I saw that he was barefoot, his motorcycle boots standing near the chair across the room. Everything from the last days was just starting to fill my head again, all at once. One thing piled on top of another. It was like a pot being heated on the stove. I felt like it was all going to boil over on me. This wasn't like my fantasy at all.

"It's a long ride from West Stockholm," he said.

I didn't know what was going on inside of me. My face was hot, my stomach was tied in a tight knot. I wasn't sure that I wouldn't throw up. I clenched my jaw against it, my whole body tensed.

"Did you want something? Do you need something?"

A single tear. That's how it started. I felt the tickle as it rolled down my cheek. I tried my best to hold it back. I didn't want to look weak in front of Uncle Bruce. He was too cool to see me like this. That's when the pot boiled over. Once it started, there was no stopping. I wasn't cool. I looked down at the floor so that Uncle Bruce wouldn't see that first tear. But there was no hiding the flood of everything that came after it. I didn't just cry. I sobbed. My whole body shook with the emotion released from that single tear. I dropped the glass and it rolled away as I bent over and put my face between my legs. I didn't want Uncle Bruce to see me like this. But I couldn't stop it.

"Hey," he said.

I put my face into the arm of the couch. I felt the couch move as he sat down next to me, and I felt his hand on my back. He just set it there. He didn't rub my back or anything, just held his hand there near my shoulder.

"Kelly," he said. His voice was softer now, not the deep gruff voice. I couldn't answer him. The tears wouldn't stop, wouldn't allow me to say a word. Then I felt him pull on my shoulder. He sat me up on the couch. I still couldn't look up at him, but when his hand was on my chin and he lifted my face, I couldn't help but look up into his eyes. His face was softer this time. It was the same face, the same beard, the same long hair, the same green eyes – good guy eyes! – but something in those eyes was different. He saw me. He looked right back at me, those green eyes soft and seeing me.

"Talk to me, man," he said.

I wrapped my arms around him, squeezed him as tight as I could, and buried my face in his chest. I couldn't tell him. I couldn't make him understand. How could I? I didn't understand what I was feeling. It was hot and painful and awful and the worst I'd ever felt. The things that had happened. The trust that had been broken. Everything that had added up to my ride from West Stockholm.

"Hey," he said again. He wrapped his own arms around me. "Whatever it is, you don't have to be ashamed."

That was it! That's what I was feeling! That was the thing I couldn't name, the word I couldn't find. It was shame. I was ashamed, a deep and penetrating shame. Oh, my God, would Uncle Bruce really understand? Would he? My fingers dug into his arms as I tried to hug him even closer to me. I wanted to be so close to him. I wanted to not feel what I was feeling. I wanted to be featureless and separate from everything. No, I wanted to be him. I wanted to ride out with him tomorrow and disappear from this life and never speak to my family again. Like him, I wanted to be gone.

I felt his arms tighten around me then, his chin resting on my head. "You're okay," he said. "Whatever it is, you're safe now. You're okay."

I don't know if it was what he said or how he said it, but I felt like he was telling me the truth. But after all the betrayal I'd faced in the last few days, I really wasn't sure. Still, he had found the word I was missing to describe what I was feeling. He was here. He didn't yell; he didn't blame me. He let me hold him. More than that, he held onto me. He touched me. And who would he tell that didn't already know everything? My sobs calmed a bit and I sniffed back a few more tears.

I never let go of him and he never let go of me. I told him everything, from Danny leaving to all that had happened with Moe and Mary and Jay right up through Karen and Kevin making fun of me just a few hours earlier before I had ridden away. Maybe I left out a few details, but it didn't take away from what I did tell him. I told him everything. And as I spoke, it felt like he held me even tighter. He never let up the grip he had with his arms around me. When I finally stopped talking, we just sat on the couch for what seemed like forever, me never letting go of him and him never letting go of me. By the time he finally spoke, my eyes were dry. I don't think I had any tears left.

"You have to go back home," he finally said.

That's when I let go of him. I sat back up on the couch. "What? No!" I said, feeling the tears wanting to start again.

"Tomorrow," Uncle Bruce said. "I'm leaving in the morning. You're going to have to go home."

"Can't I come with you to Utica?"

"Oh, Kelly, I can't do that. You know I can't."

"But I don't want to go back home. I can't…."

"I know. I know you don't want to. But you have to," he said. "There's nothing I can do about that."

I got up from the couch, picked up the glass that I had dropped, and walked into the kitchen.

"I'm going to have to call your mother in the morning and let her know where you are."

I set the glass in the sink. Of course, he would. Just one more person who was going to betray me. One more person to break my trust.

"I won't tell her what you told me," he said.

I turned around and saw him still on the couch but looking around the corner at me. "Really?"

"Really," he replied. "If you don't want me to, it'll be our secret."

I looked out the windows above the dining room table. All I could see was blackness. It wasn't just dark; it was black with my own face reflected back at me in the window glass. Then I saw Uncle Bruce appear behind me in that reflection like he was coming out of the blackness. He put his hands on my shoulders.

"I can keep a secret," he said. "I've got lots of my own, lots of my own shame."

I caught his eyes looking at mine in our reflection. I wanted to ask him about his shame, but I couldn't. If he was willing to keep my secret, I'd let him keep his. I tried to smile, but I couldn't. I wasn't sure if I'd ever be able to smile again.

"It's late," he said. "Come on."

I let him lead me to the open door that led to the stairs. It was dark up those stairs. There was usually a nightlight on at the very top, but that was only in the summer. The darkness was a little scary even though I knew what was up there. Then I was surrounded by darkness as Uncle Bruce turned off the light in the living room. A small gasp escaped me, but a beam of light played across the doorway. I turned to see that Uncle Bruce had a flashlight to guide us.

"Up you go," he said, and I started up the stairs. The light played on the steep risers ahead of me.

"What time is it?" I asked.

"Not sure. Past eleven at least."

The second floor was mostly an open space divided by some thick cardboard walls. In all, there were enough beds to sleep eleven or twelve people. The beds were nothing but bare mattresses now; all the sheets and blankets had been put away for the winter. Only the bed at the top of the stairs had anything on it. And that was just a sleeping bag that had been tossed onto it.

"Hop in," Uncle Bruce said and indicated the sleeping bag.

"Where are you going to sleep?" I asked.

"I'll be okay."

I kicked off my shoes and was about to take my pants off, but I saw Uncle Bruce looking at me. He saw me looking at him and he turned around. I slipped out of my Wranglers and then slipped into the sleeping bag with my t-shirt still on. Uncle Bruce came up to the bed, took off his red and black flannel shirt, and tucked it under my head for a pillow. When I inhaled, it smelled just like him.

"You good?" he asked.

"Yeah," I said as I snuggled into the bag and hugged the shirt.

The light went out and darkness surrounded me again. It didn't bother me because I knew Uncle Bruce was there. I heard the springs of the other bed squeak as Uncle Bruce laid down on it. I was tired, but I didn't feel like I would fall asleep anytime soon.

"Uncle Bruce?" I asked.

"Yeah?"

I'd wanted to ask the question since I had seen it on the dining table. There weren't any wild animals to be worried about and no criminals coming to break into the camp.

"Why do you have that gun?" I asked.

The darkness was filled with silence for the longest time.

"Go to sleep," he finally said.

He didn't want to talk about it. I guess I understood that. I didn't want to talk about the stuff I had talked about, either. They were secrets I hadn't planned on sharing. If he didn't want to talk about the gun, I wasn't going to push it.

"Uncle Bruce?" I asked.

"What is it?"

"Why do you stay away?"

I heard him exhale a long breath. I was upsetting him. I didn't need to know.

"Never mind," I said.

"No, it's alright," he said. "It's a fair question when you only see me, well, once in a long while."

And then he was silent again. Maybe he was waiting to see if I would fall asleep or maybe he had fallen asleep. Or maybe he didn't want to answer my question. It didn't matter. Not really. He would be gone in the morning and I wouldn't see him again until maybe someone else died. Maybe my grandmother next time, like she had said. Then he would come back, and we'd meet up like strangers again just like that day he had first pulled into the driveway back in West Stockholm. All of this would be forgotten, and we'd start over again. Except I wouldn't forget.

"Let's just say you're not the only one feeling some shame," he said.

"What do you mean?"

"You remember I was in Vietnam, right?"

"Yeah," I replied.

"Let's just leave it at that."

Jay's question came to my mind then. Now I kinda wanted to know. But should I ask? Was it wrong if I asked him? Probably. It was his secret and if he didn't want to tell me, I shouldn't bring it up. Sure, he had asked me if anything was wrong, but I was the one who chose to tell him everything. I had asked him what I needed to know. There was no reason to ask him anything else. Still, he had cared enough to listen to me. I wanted him to know I would listen, too, and keep his secrets if he wanted me to.

"I won't tell anybody your secrets," I finally said.

"I know that," he replied. "I know I can trust you. But I've got some pretty awful secrets."

The question came out before I could stop it. "Did you kill anybody?"

I heard the springs of his bed squeak and thought maybe Uncle Bruce was sitting up.

"That's really none of your business!" he said, the anger apparent in his voice.

I'd done it again, said the wrong thing. Why couldn't I just keep my stupid mouth shut? I felt the tears from my mistake coming back up to my eyes. I couldn't keep the sob out of my voice when I spoke.

"I'm sorry," I cried.

The bedsprings squeaked again and then I felt his hand on my shoulder.

"Dammit," he said, his voice calmer than it had been. "No, I'm sorry. I didn't mean to yell at you."

I felt him lay his head against my own, and I could smell the whisky on his breath.

"This is why I stay away," he said. "I sometimes have a problem with my anger."

I remembered the anger he had shown in Grandma's barn. It had scared me.

"Are you…dangerous?"

Everything was still and silent, but he never lifted his head from mine. Then I felt the bed shaking just a little. I didn't understand why until I heard the sound. He sniffled first before I heard him weeping.

I reached my hand up and put it on the hand that was on my shoulder.

"I don't want to be," he whispered. "But it might be that I am."

He lifted his head from mine and tried to pull his hand from my shoulder, but I gripped it a little tighter. I needed him to know that I was here for him like he had been there for me, but I didn't know how to tell him that.

"Just know that it's not you, Kelly. I'm not mad at you."

He tried to pull his hand away again, but I just gripped it tighter. He put his other hand over mine. It was too dark for me to see him, but I felt his breath on my neck.

"Shove over," he said.

I scooched over in the sleeping bag. He climbed onto the bed, slipped one arm under my neck and wrapped the other around me and the sleeping bag. I wrapped my arm around his.

"You don't need to hear my stories," he said. "You've got enough of your own pain."

We laid there together for a long time before he spoke again.

"I watched men fall in my rifle sight," he finally said.

I hugged his arm tighter. I didn't know what else to do.

"I counted at least six men."

I felt his breath on my neck, hot and slow.

"I hope you never have to know what that's like."

A light seemed to come on for me in the darkness. He was ashamed of what he had done just like I was ashamed. He had done things he had not wanted to do, too. And he didn't want to go home, either.

"You were drafted, right?" I asked.

"Yeah, I was."

"Then it wasn't your fault," I said. I closed my eyes then. I had nothing more that I wanted to know, and I was sure that Uncle Bruce didn't want to talk anymore.

He hugged me a little tighter then.

"You're a good kid, Kelly," he said, his breath warm on my neck. "You've got nothing to be ashamed of. You're okay."

"You, too," I said.

His arms were tight around me, and I held onto him as best I could and we must have fallen asleep like that because the next thing I knew, the sun was filtering in through the branches of the trees outside the window. I was no longer in the sleeping bag, but the red and black flannel shirt that had been my pillow was now laid over me like a small blanket. I was about to call out his name when I heard his voice downstairs.

"I told you, he's fine."

No one answered him before he spoke again. That's when I realized he was on the phone. I only got his side of the conversation.

"I don't know. I don't know."

His boots clunked on the wood floor as he paced.

"He just showed up saying something about Karen and Kevin being mean to him."

There was certainly more to it than that. I waited to see if Uncle Bruce would break his promise to me.

"I don't know. You know how kids can be."

I'd never thought about Uncle Bruce and my mother being brother and sister. I wondered if they fought like we did since they were so different in age.

"No, he's just a little more sensitive, I think. Listen, I'm about to head back to Utica. He can either ride back home himself or someone is going to have to come pick him up. No, he's still asleep. Well, it was a late night. Yeah. No, I've got a quick stop to make before I get out of town. Okay, I'll leave him a note saying someone is coming up for him. But listen, don't be a bitch about this. You know exactly what I mean. This isn't his fault. Don't take it out on him."

Then there was a long silence on his end of the phone call. I was beginning to think he had hung up when he finally spoke again.

"Just go easy on him, will ya? As a favor to me if nothing else. I'll even leave you the money to cover the gas if that's what Charles needs. Yeah, I will. Maybe for Christmas. I'll give you a call when I get home. Okay, sounds good."

I heard the click of the phone going back in its cradle. I almost got up then to go downstairs to say goodbye. But, somehow, I knew that wasn't what Uncle Bruce wanted. I think he wanted to sneak out with no goodbyes. I'd probably cry again anyway. So, I curled up under his flannel shirt, taking in the smell of it, sure he would take it with him. I listened to him walk around downstairs, putting away dishes and whatever else might have been taken out and used. I heard him go out to his motorcycle a couple of times and figured he was loading up his stuff. Then I heard him coming up the stairs. I laid as still as I could on the bed, my eyes closed. I heard his footsteps across the floor, felt his hand on my head, then felt his kiss on my forehead.

"Take it easy, little brother," he said softly. "You're gonna be okay."

The next thing I heard were his footsteps down the stairs, across the living room floor, and out onto the porch. Only a few seconds later, I heard his bike roar to life. I took the flannel shirt with me as I ran to the window at the front of the cabin. I was just in time to see him pull out of the driveway and head up the hill. He disappeared quickly behind the trees, but I listened to the drone of the engine as it faded into the morning.

And with that, he was gone.

I hugged the shirt, then slipped my small arms into the long sleeves before I got dressed and went downstairs.

I found the note he'd left for me on the dining table along with a couple of dollars that I assumed was for gas. The note explained that someone was coming to pick me up. He had also put his address at the bottom with a brief note saying I could write to him if I needed to. He might not answer, but he'd be okay with getting letters. I folded it up and stuck it in my back pocket.

I went down to the boathouse, opened the combination lock to get in, and walked out onto the dock. The water was still pretty quiet, the autumn trees reflecting back with a kaleidoscope of color. I just sat staring at the water until I heard a car coming up the road. I knew it would be my mother and I knew she would be mad, so I locked up the boathouse and got back to the cabin just as she was pulling into the driveway.

The ride back to West Stockholm was silent and awkward. She never looked at me and barely said two words during the entire drive. I was okay with that. At least she wasn't yelling at me. The only real excitement came after we got back to West Stockholm. As we were crossing the bridge, I saw a state trooper's car and an ambulance parked in front of Moe's house. My mother slowed as we passed by, and I saw Moe sitting on the front porch covered in blood. I don't know what might have happened to him, but I couldn't help but smile as we headed up the hill and back to the house.

19

The Will to Escape, 1994

"Here we are," Mr. Bridges said as he stopped the car in front of a small, three-story house. It was covered with red vinyl brick face and had fading gray trim. But the lawn was tidy, and the sidewalk was clean. "It may not look like much," he said, "but it generates enough income to pay the bills and leave you a little something."

He reached into the back seat and brought his briefcase to the front, set it between us on the seat, and opened it. He took out a manila envelope and handed it to me.

"The electrical and plumbing were updated about ten years ago, so everything is up to code or better. Four of the five apartments have long-term tenants. It's all there in the paperwork."

"What about the fifth one?" I asked.

"That was your uncle's," he replied.

Of course. Stupid question.

"And here are the keys to the kingdom," he said as he held out a ring of keys.

I laughed out loud at that. I'd always hated that phrase before, but here it was. The Kingdom. I finally had one.

"Sorry," I said. "Inside joke." I took the keys from him. "You know, because my last name is King."

"Oh, right. Well, that's it. The liquor store is right there at the end of the street. It's been cleaned up since the, uh, the incident, so it's ready to open whenever you want to do so."

"What about the liquor license and all that?"

"It's been taken care of," he said. "You can run it on your uncle's license until the new one is issued by the state in your name. Of course, that assumes everything goes well and there are no problems that I should be aware of?"

It was definitely a question and not a statement.

"No, no problems that I'm aware of."

"Very well." Mr. Bridges closed his briefcase and set it back on the back seat. "Then, you're all set."

I looked out at the house again. "I guess I am." I couldn't believe it was actually mine.

"And if you need anything or have any questions, you have my number."

"Okay," I said. A driveway led behind the house to a small garage and parking lot.

"I'm in the office almost every day."

"Sure."

"Is there anything else I can do for you?"

"What?" I felt like I was caught in a weird dream, expecting to wake up at any moment. But his question made me look to the lawyer sitting next to me behind the wheel of the car. He seemed a little impatient. "Oh, Christ," I said. "I'm sorry. You're probably waiting for me to get out."

"Everyone handles their grief differently," he said. "But I do have to get back to the office, so…."

"Of course." I held out my hand to him, and he took it. "I really want to thank you for everything you've done, both for me and for my uncle."

"You're very welcome. Your uncle was a client for a lot of years. It's the least I can do."

"I've probably asked you this already, but were you two friends?"

Mr. Bridges let go of my hand and looked uncomfortable with the question.

"I'm sorry," I said. "I don't mean to intrude on your own grief."

"It's not that," he said. "I'm just trying to reconcile the relationship I had with him. Bruce was a client for about twenty years. We shared a meal now and then or a drink. And while I want to say he was my friend, I'm not sure our relationship ever went much beyond lawyer and client." He smiled then and was quiet for a moment. "There was a time, about fifteen years ago, when I thought we might become friends. He had just returned from a trip to northern New York. I think someone in the family had died. Anyway, that was around the same time that he made out his will. He'd retained me for other services related to the store and the rental property, but this was a much more personal thing than we'd ever discussed before."

Fifteen years. I knew the time he was talking about.

"He made an appointment and we met for lunch." Bridges smiled, held both hands up in front of him. "I remember it because of his hands."

"His hands?" I asked.

"Yes. They were swollen and red with fresh wounds on his knuckles. It looked like he had been in a fight or maybe punched a wall a few too many times."

Bloody knuckles. No shit.

"I asked him what had happened, and he brushed it off. I asked if he had seen a doctor and he just said, no. He assured me that it was no problem but that he might need to retain my services for an assault charge. But, from the way he laughed, I assumed he wasn't serious."

I smiled and couldn't help but laugh a little myself. So, that was why Moe had been bloodied up that morning when my mother and I got back from the lake. And it was probably why he turned the other way every time he saw me. He hadn't been scared of me. He had been scared of Uncle Bruce. That had been the one stop he had needed to make on the way out of town when he had left.

"What's funny?" Mr. Bridges asked.

"Nothing," I said. "I just know what incident he would have been talking about."

"Would you like to fill me in?"

"Maybe someday."

He looked at me as if he really wanted me to tell him all about it, like his important evening had become less important but, if anything, it was a story for when we knew each other better.

"Well, whatever it was, he became very somber about the whole thing, and he told me that getting his affairs in order had suddenly become very important to him and that he wanted to leave most everything he had to one nephew. And, as you know, that nephew was, or rather is, you. He was adamant about getting it all in order as soon as possible."

He fell silent for a moment as if he were trying to gauge what he wanted to say next.

"He told me he wanted to be sure his nephew was taken care of. It was the most intimate conversation he and I had ever had, and I thought perhaps our relationship had become one that was more than professional. But it turned out not to be. I'd really kind of hoped…."

His voice trailed off and he was lost in thought for another moment. Then he took a deep breath and looked at me again.

"I just want you to know that I really liked your uncle. He was more than just another client to me. He was a good man and I wished he and I had had a more personal relationship like I have with so many of my other clients. But he was very much a loner. I'll just never understand how a nice guy like him could have been so lonely."

"No," I said. "He wasn't lonely. He might have been alone, but I don't believe he was ever lonely. There's a difference." I knew that difference. It was possible to spend all your time by yourself and not be the least bit lonely.

"So, you two were close, then?" Mr. Bridges asked.

"Yeah," I said. "We were close." Even when we were far away from each other, not having spoken in fifteen years, I was closest to a man I had technically only ever met once. I pulled the door handle and opened the door. "I'd like to retain your services if I can."

"You're certainly welcome to do so," he replied. "It would be good to know that Bruce's business is well in hand."

"Well, that remains to be seen," I said with a laugh. "But I would like to have someone in my corner who knows what's come before and who can help guide me toward what's coming next. And it sounds like Uncle Bruce had that kind of faith in you."

"Well, thank you. I hope that's true."

"I'll get settled in and give you a call." I closed the car door and returned the wave he gave me. I watched his Cadillac drive off down the street before I turned my attention to my place.

My place. What a weird concept. Before I went inside, there was one thing I wanted to check in the garage. I followed the driveway that led down the right side of the house. Rather than a backyard, there was a small parking lot for the tenants. That made sense since parking overnight on the street was illegal. And there was a space for every tenant, each space designated with the apartment number on a sign. The spot for apartment number five, the one on the third floor, had a surprising sight: a dark bronze Subaru Outback wagon. It was my uncle's parking spot, so it was his car. I guess I had expected something more sporty, like a Mustang. Maybe he'd found his inner hippie. I walked past it to the small garage. The building was only big enough to hold maybe one car, but I wasn't expecting to find a car in there. I searched through the ring of keys I'd been given until I found one marked with a tag that read, "Garage." I unlocked the door and pulled it open.

I found what I thought I would.

The surrounding walls were covered with tools and such, and a bench against the left wall told me this was where Uncle Bruce had done whatever repairs he might have needed to do on the house. A small lawnmower and red gas can were in the far left corner. But, right in the middle of the floor was his motorcycle.

It wasn't the same motorcycle he'd been riding in '79, but it was just as nice. This one was a Honda Shadow. A big bike. I guessed it was the 1100cc model. And it wasn't the silver black phantom bike he'd had before. Uncle Bruce's latest bike was a deep red.

Uncle Bruce's bike? No, this was my bike. And the pain of the dagger that rammed into my heart then sent shivers through my entire frame. Yeah, it was mine, but at what cost? Sure, you could argue that I didn't even know the man who had left it to me. And that might be true. But he knew me, and I knew him as best as he would let me know him.

"Can I help you?"

I turned to see a tall, thin, and auburn-haired middle-aged man with a neatly trimmed moustache standing by the open garage door. "I'm sorry?" I asked absently.

"This is private property," he said. "Is there something I can help you with?"

"That depends. Who are you?"

"Who am I?" he returned angrily. "I live here! Who the hell are you?"

"The name's Kelly King." I stepped toward him with my hand out.

"Is that supposed to mean something to me?"

I stopped where I was. "Oh, um, I thought maybe Mr. Bridges would have informed everyone. I'm the new owner."

"Oh, shit!" he said and walked over to where I stood. He held out his hand and I offered mine again. He took it lightly in his. "I feel like a damn fool, but the name didn't register. Yeah, we all got letters from the lawyer that there would be a new landlord."

"It's okay, I understand. Nothing like an intruder invading your space."

"I'm the one intruding," he said. "But I can kind of show you around if you like."

I returned his smile. "That would be great."

"My name's Steve. My wife, Gayle, and I are here on the first floor."

I locked up the garage and we walked up the steps to the back porch and stepped through the back door into a hallway that ran the length of the house. It was a spacious hallway and there was a bicycle parked by the door on the other side. Steve pointed out the door on the right as his.

"I was sorry to hear about Bruce's, um, passing," he said.

"Were you a friend?" I asked, already sure what the answer would be.

"No, not really. But…." His voice trailed off.

We stopped at the bottom of the stairs that led from the front door up to the second floor. Steve shook his head, then. I'd gotten so used to these kinds of responses that I couldn't help but smile. My uncle had affected a lot of people. I wondered if he had been aware of that.

"Can't really be friends with the landlord, I guess," I said.

"It's not that. He was more than a landlord. But less than a friend. It's hard to explain. I don't know if I can make you understand."

Steve looked up then and caught me smile. "Something funny?" he asked.

"No," I said. "It's just that I might be one of the few people who would understand."

"You knew Mr. Wright?"

"He was my uncle," I said.

"Oh! I didn't realize! I'm sorry for your loss."

"Thank you."

"So, you're taking over the whole thing? The liquor store, too?"

"That's the plan," I said. "I'm a little new at all of this, so please be patient while I try to work out the kinks."

"No problem there," Steve said. "I'll be as patient with you as Mr. Wright was with me. Let me show you the second floor."

We started up the stairs. From what Mr. Bridges had told me, the two first-floor apartments were three bedroom and the two on the second floor were two bedrooms.

"Patient?" I asked. "How so?"

Steve stopped at the top of the stairs. I was a step down from him. He looked down at the floor before looking over to me.

"I had a problem a couple of years ago. Got laid off from my trucking job. And I had a hard time finding another one. The recession and all that. Anyway, I went to Mr. Wright to let him know that we'd probably be moving out since I couldn't make the rent anymore."

He leaned against the wall, crossed his arms.

"I was worried. Had a wife and a daughter to take care of and I wasn't sure where we were going to go. I got a brother over near Syracuse and thought he might let us stay there until I got back on my feet. Wasn't looking forward to asking him but didn't have much of a choice."

Steve was silent, then. He seemed ashamed to continue. I wasn't sure what to say. I could understand his feelings. I knew the shame in admitting that you couldn't make it on your own, and I hadn't had a wife and kid to support. Then I saw him wipe his finger across his eye.

"So, I don't know if I told him all of this. Doesn't matter. Anyway, you know what he told me?"

I shook my head.

"He told me to stay where I was, to not move out. I told him I didn't have the money for rent. He says he doesn't care. I told him I didn't know when I'd be able to pay the rent. And again, he says he doesn't care."

He chuckled then. I think it was more to hide the choke in his voice.

"So, we stayed. For six months. For six months, I couldn't pay the rent and he let us stay. Never asked for a dime. Of course, I did finally get another job. Still got it today. The day I was finally able to take him a month's rent, I told him I'd pay him all the back rent when I could. And you know what he told me?"

I again shook my head, a smile playing across my lips because I had a feeling I knew what he was going to say.

"He said don't worry about it. Don't worry about it! Six months of back rent! Who does that?"

I smiled. "I guess my Uncle Bruce does that."

Steve smiled, then. "Yeah, he did. I couldn't ever thank him enough. But I tried. I started mowing the lawn, shoveling the sidewalk, stuff like that. I'll keep it up for you, too."

"We'll see," I said. "I'm actually looking forward to doing a little yardwork myself. Been a long time since I had a lawn to mow."

Steve pointed out the apartments on the second floor and then pointed me up the stairs to the door on the third floor.

"That's the penthouse suite," he said.

"Thanks for the tour," I said. "And the story. I always like to hear stories about my uncle."

"I tried my best to be a friend to him. He never accepted my invites to dinner. Gayle always wanted to repay him for his generosity. Never could get him to accept."

"He was a pretty solitary guy," I said.

"Well, there's a standing open invitation if you need a good home-cooked meal."

"Thanks," I said. "I might take you up on that sometime."

"I hope so. Well, I'll leave you to it. Let me know if I can help you settle in."

"Will do. Thanks again."

Steve gave me a wave as he headed down the stairs to his apartment. I liked him. I decided I might have to get to know my tenants a little better than Uncle Bruce had. But, for now, it was time to see where I would be staying. I found the key that was tagged "#5, Third Floor" and put it into the deadbolt keyhole. It turned easily and I pushed the door open.

This was it. This was Uncle Bruce's place, his latter-day Fortress of Solitude.

Solitude. That's what he liked, that's what he wanted. It wasn't my fault that I couldn't be closer to him. I tried, but it was his choice, not mine. He had left that day and had not come back. There was nothing more I could have done. I sent him birthday cards after I found out when his birthday was — October 28th. I sent him Christmas cards. I wrote him letters when I was feeling particularly… unloved or just when I needed to talk, knowing it would be a one-sided conversation. I told him how much he meant to me. Well, maybe not. I mean, when I was younger, I did my best, but I never knew what to say to get my point across. Sometimes I didn't even have much to say and would draw a picture to fill the page before I mailed off my letter to him. At first, I had waited for a reply. After all, it was only polite to answer a letter when you got one, right? But no answer ever came, and after a while, I stopped expecting one. I still wrote him, though, and let him know how my life was going.

Even if he didn't respond, I felt like he was the only person I could talk to. So, I kept sending my letters and cards. At least for a while. Then other things came up and I started to forget his birthday, or I didn't get a card sent out until long after Christmas. And the letters were fewer and fewer until I finally stopped writing altogether. I found other people to talk to, other people who saw me, other people who would listen. Gary had been one of those people. I wondered if I'd ever be able to tell Gary how much his friendship had meant to me. That might be even harder now as I expected to be living in Utica for the foreseeable future. I guess I'd have to write him a letter. I smiled at the thought.

The house itself had been built sometime in the '30s and had been converted to apartments, so the kitchen off the entryway was a little odd. It hadn't originally been a kitchen, so it was small and awkwardly designed, but it had everything it needed. A stove, a refrigerator, a sink, and some counter space. There was also a small dining table under the window at the back wall. Two steps led up to a door. I walked through the kitchen to see where the door went. That's when I saw the door on the left that opened to the bathroom. Okay, so I knew where I could take a piss. The bathroom was also a relatively new renovation but with only a bathtub and no shower. I thought I might need to change that. I was, after all, quite fond of showers.

The other door led onto the roof of the second floor. It looked like it might be a nice place to sit and look out over the city on a cool night. For now, though, there was the rest of the apartment to explore.

Walking back to the entryway, the living room was right off the entrance. It was sparse, about what I expected from Uncle Bruce. Hardwood floors covered with a rug, a threadbare couch and matching chair, a couple of end tables, a television on a stand. Nothing fancy, but it was certainly livable. Two windows at the far end looked down on the street in front of the house. Two doors led off the living room. One was open and I could see the bedroom with a full-size bed, a bedside table, and a dresser. The walls had a couple of pictures that I would have to inspect closer at some point. The other door off the living room was closed. I assumed this was the other bedroom. Being that Uncle Bruce lived alone, I wondered what that room might contain. It was probably just storage. When I opened the door, I realized how wrong I was.

Against the far wall was a small desk with a typewriter. On one side of the typewriter was a stack of white paper, and on the left side was another stack of paper that had been typed on. But this wasn't what surprised me the most. It was the pictures on the walls. A window to the right let a little light in through the yellowed curtain, but when I hit the light switch next to the door, I was suddenly surrounded. Every wall was covered with pictures, and what surprised me the most were the pictures of me. They were very prominent. And they were from my entire life, all my school pictures from grade school right up through high school. One frame even contained my graduation picture. I knew my mother had sent our school pictures to all the relatives, but I'd never thought she bothered to send them to Uncle Bruce. Yet here was the proof, hanging on the walls. Sure, there were pictures of my brother and sister in there, too, but it seemed like he had dedicated almost an entire wall just to me. Honestly, I didn't know whether to be flattered or creeped out by it.

Just next to the window was a small filing cabinet, the top drawer open about an inch. I pulled the drawer open and saw that it was filled with cards and envelopes. I immediately recognized my own handwriting. I took out the first few envelopes and leafed through them. They were my cards and letters. The entire drawer looked like it was filled with everything I had sent him over the years, every one of them opened, every one of them showing that they had been read at least once before being put back in their envelope. Well, that answered one of my burning questions. Uncle Bruce had, indeed, read every one of my letters.

I stepped to the desk and picked up a few sheets from the pile of paper on the left. I saw a lot of typos and X's and misspelled words. It looked like some kind of story or memoir. Was Uncle Bruce a writer? Was this a book he was working on? I set the pages back on the pile determined to read through all that he had written. No matter what it was, it would probably give me more insight into who he was. Maybe it would be something I could organize and finish for him.

I turned to go back into the living room and sat down on the couch. I opened the manila envelope the lawyer had given me and dumped the contents onto the cushion next to me. There were several folders that I figured I'd have to go through eventually. It was all legal crap that I knew would be a real joy to wade through. It was amazing to think that almost overnight, I had gone from a free spirit to a businessman. Definitely not what I had expected. But there would be time enough for all of that later. I picked up my duffle bag from the floor and set it on top of the files and folders. I unzipped it and took out the bottle of Cutty Sark that was buried in my clothes. I knew stuffing it in there would protect it from breakage. The thought crossed my mind to just take a swig straight from the bottle, but I thought a toast to Uncle Bruce deserved at least a glass. I set the bottle on the end table and went back to the kitchen.

The cupboards were old, probably part of the original renovation. At least, it didn't look like they had ever been upgraded or remodeled. When you don't entertain, you don't need to worry too much about appearances. I could dig that. As long as it was functional and clean, what did it really matter? You don't like my place? You don't have to come back. The first cupboard had some plates and dishes. As I expected, they were nothing fancy. They were functional. I opened the second cupboard door and found one shelf of regular drinking glasses and another with the kind of glasses you'd expect to find in a good bar. I think the big ones were highball glasses and the small ones were considered Old Fashioned glasses. I never did learn the names of the various cocktail finery because I almost always stuck with beer. And shots, which naturally came in shot glasses. I took down one of the shorter glasses and took it into the living room. I poured some Cutty Sark into the glass and swirled it a little.

"I feel like I should say something," I said, even though there was no one there. "It's hard to say I'm going to miss you, Uncle Bruce, because I never really got to know you. You never let me. I really wish you'd made more of an effort to keep in touch. But I know you had your issues and Christ knows I have mine. You'd probably have ended up hating me for being too clingy. And seeing all those pictures in the other room at least lets me know that you were thinking of us. And of me."

I looked up toward the ceiling. It's not that I believed he was up there somewhere looking down at me. I just needed a place to look as I held up my glass.

"So, here's to you, Uncle Bruce. Thanks for everything, and you know I'm not talking about the stuff here."

I took a sip of the Cutty Sark. Scotch had never really been my thing, but I was starting to get a taste for it. It was smooth and went down easy. Easy enough that I took another sip before setting the glass down and picking up some of the papers from the lawyer.

It was getting dark; I was finding it hard to focus on the papers. Or maybe it was the Cutty Sark. I wondered what time it was. I'd gotten up early to catch the bus from Potsdam that morning and had been with the lawyer for most of the day. I knew he dropped me off close to seven p.m. I looked around and realized there wasn't a clock in the living room. I got up from the couch and headed back to the kitchen. Yup, there was a clock on the wall just above the stove. Nine-thirty already. Between the long day and the Scotch, I didn't figure I'd last much longer. And I was cool with that. Too many late nights in Potsdam. Maybe it was time to turn things around, especially now that I had a business to run. I felt the buzz coming on in my head. It felt good, but I knew I'd never stay up long enough to truly enjoy it. I drained the last of the Cutty Sark from my glass, rinsed it, and set it down next to the sink. For a moment, I wondered if there was any food in the house so I could have breakfast in the morning. But there was a grocery store right across the street on the corner, so I could always get something there if in the morning I found the cupboards were bare. Yeah, it was bedtime. Before I made my way to the bedroom, I took the bottle of Cutty Sark into the kitchen.

I hit the light switch by the bedroom door, and the room lit up with a soft pale light from a small lamp on the nightstand. Like every other room in the apartment, it was sparse with nothing more than the bed, nightstand, a five-drawer dresser, and a bookshelf filled with books of various sizes and descriptions. I remembered the books he had had back in the barn in Hopkinton. There were more titles here that I didn't recognize. I guess it wasn't only my letters that he read. I thought I might have to work my way through his library. What surprised me the most was that the bed was made. No one had been in the apartment since his death as far as I knew, and even if someone had been, would they have taken the time to make his bed? I flipped back the covers and sat down. My bag of clothes was in the living room still, but it didn't matter. It's not like I wore pajamas to bed. So, I stripped down to my underwear and climbed in. As I lay my head down on the pillow, I was reminded of the smell of Uncle Bruce's shirt and sleeping bag that night at the cabin. I hugged the pillow close to my face and breathed deep. I would worry about tomorrow in the morning. Tonight, I wanted to simply sleep wrapped in Uncle Bruce's smell and remember the man I barely knew who had had such an effect on my life back in the Fall of '79.

About the author

Lee Lewis was born in the '60s on an Air Force base in Texas. He's lived here and there, studied stuff that he found interesting, earned a college degree, and worked at a variety of jobs from taxi driver and pool hall attendant to technical writer and college instructor. He's currently living the dream somewhere in Florida. And he still hasn't figured out why.

The Fall of '79 is his first novel.